D1393973

GEORGE SQUARE 1919

# GEORGE SQUARE
# 1919

## A NOVEL BY
## RUSSELL GALBRAITH

MAINSTREAM
PUBLISHING

Copyright © Russell Galbraith, 1988

All rights reserved

First published in Great Britain in 1988 by
MAINSTREAM PUBLISHING COMPANY (EDINBURGH) LTD
7 Albany Street, Edinburgh EH1 3UG

ISBN 1 85158 173 1 (cloth)

No part of this book may be reproduced or transmitted in any
form or by any other means without the permission in writing
from the publisher, except by a reviewer who wishes to quote
brief passages in connection with a review written for insertion in
a magazine, newspaper or broadcast.

**British Library Cataloguing in Publication Data**
Galbraith, Russell
    George Square 1919.
    I. Title
    823'.914[F]

ISBN 1-85158-173-1


Typeset in 11 on 12pt Imprint by Bookworm Typesetting, Edinburgh
Printed in Great Britain by St Edmundsbury Press, Bury St Edmunds, Suffolk

# CONTENTS

This book is for my mother
Jean Chapman Galbraith
and to the memory of my father
John Russell Galbraith,
Citizens of Glasgow

This book is a work of fiction. However, some of the names belonged to real people and most of it did happen.

"The barricades were up in the streets of Europe's cities. Revolt with all its bloody terror was abroad in the world." — Emmanuel Shinwell, *Conflict without Malice*.

"We were carrying on a strike when we ought to have been making a revolution." — William Gallacher, *Revolt on the Clyde*.

"Mr Churchill said that before taking any action in dealing with the strikers we should wait until some glaring excess had been committed. The moment the revolt advanced over the line of a pure wage dispute, and the strikers were guilty of serious breach of the law, then was the moment to act." — British Cabinet Minutes.

"The organised workers of Scotland put forward an orderly and legitimate demand for the Forty Hours. The Government's reply is bludgeons, machine-guns, bayonets and tanks. In one word, the institution of a Reign of Terror." — Manifesto of the Joint Strike Committee.

# PROLOGUE

Recognising his own bad mood, Churchill scowled. Black dog he called it. A mean-tempered old cur with lots of fleas, black dog had been skulking at his heels for weeks.

It was a cold, raw day, typical of London in mid-January, with the wind rising from the Thames and more rain forecast as the Secretary of State for War and Air crossed Parliament Square on his way to the House of Commons. Dressed formally, in striped trousers and morning coat with a white silk scarf to protect his throat against the worst of the ice-cold wind, a large cigar protruded from the left-hand side of his mouth and in his right hand he carried a stick.

A policeman on duty at the entrance to the House of Commons reserved for Members of Parliament watched with interest as Churchill approached the gate. His pace was brisk and pigeons hunting for food darted about his feet. Passers-by muttered some interest and a young officer, wearing the insignia and uniform of a lieutenant in the Flintshire Fusiliers, saluted. Puddles covered the pavement outside the Palace of Westminster and Churchill skipped the worst of them with a scowl.

The policeman greeted him warily. "Good morning, Secretary of State," he said.

Churchill removed the cigar from his mouth and nodded absently. "Good morning, officer," he growled. "Have you been on duty all night?"

The policeman saluted briskly. "Yes, Secretary of State. An unpleasant morning ahead of us by the look of things, wouldn't you say so, sir?" he inquired.

Churchill shrugged. "We'll see," he replied.

The policeman smiled. He expected the Secretary of State for War and Air to enter the gate he was guarding and cross New Palace Yard to a side door, beneath a canopy of wood and glass, favoured by MPs and officials. To his surprise, however, Churchill chose to remain

11

outside the railings which surrounded the Palace of Westminster and head instead towards an entrance maintained primarily for the use of visitors.

Another policeman, younger than the first, emerged from the little black-painted guardbox which stood inside the Palace gate. "What's wrong with him today?" he inquired, indicating the stooped, retreating figure of the Secretary of State.

His colleague shrugged. "Who knows?" he replied. "But he's got something on his mind sure enough."

A large crowd had gathered outside St Stephen's Gate in the hope of gaining admission to the public galleries of the House of Commons some time during the day. As Churchill approached, people moved out of the way to let him through. "God bless you, sir!" a woman cried.

Churchill paused and smiled. "Thank you, madam," he replied, removing his cigar and treating the woman to a courteous little bow. The gratitude of the people, he thought, his spirits brightening; that's what made politics worthwhile!

From the rear of the crowd, a man's voice, heavy with hatred, struck him like a blow. "What about the Dardanelles?"

The smile froze on Churchill's lips. He looked round the crowd, eyes narrowing, trying to find the man who had shouted.

Those nearest to Churchill shifted uneasily. The woman who first attracted his attention tried to reassure him. "Don't mind them, sir," she said.

For a moment Churchill thought she was going to cry. "It wasn't your fault," the woman added gently.

Churchill turned away.

"Murderer!" It was the same voice hurling venom.

Churchill climbed the worn stone steps to St Stephen's Gate without looking round. Behind him he could hear men cursing, women screaming, voices raised in pain, as the beginnings of a fight broke out.

Two policemen emerged from inside St Stephen's Gate and approached Churchill anxiously. "Are you all right, Secretary of State?" one of them inquired, reaching to help him.

Churchill glowered. "I've been heckled before!" he snarled.

The two policemen retreated hurriedly, leaving him to his anger.

Other policemen had appeared, and were trying to quell the uproar, which was spreading, and about to become a brawl.

Churchill ignored the commotion. He dropped the remains of his cigar into a sand-filled bucket inside the doorway of St Stephen's and headed for his room.

Sunlight scattered the shadows in Westminster Hall, where the ghosts of history brooded, silent and sullen. Churchill glanced at his watch which he carried on a chain across his stomach. An hour until prayers, he thought, reminding himself that he was due to answer questions from the despatch box on the floor of the House of Commons in the afternoon: it was a prospect which never ceased to excite him.

An attendant, dressed in House of Commons livery, wished him good morning as he entered the corridor which led to his room. Churchill nodded.

His room was empty when he arrived. He had indicated that he wanted to be left alone for an hour in the morning, to think, and his staff, sensing the likelihood of a bad mood left over from the night before, were happy to comply.

Churchill propped his stick in a corner and dropped his coat and hat into the middle of a large, leather armchair. Thinking it was cold in the room, he shivered slightly, and wound the white silk scarf once round his neck before settling at his desk.

His private secretary had cleared the desk of papers at the end of the previous night's business and some anonymous cleaner must have spent part of the early morning shift polishing the fine old mahogany top until it shone. Churchill, ruminating moodily, drummed his fingers on the gleaming surface, marking the wood.

A picture hanging on the farthest wall caught his eye. It was down on one side, he noticed. Why hadn't someone else seen it and fixed it, Churchill thought irritably.

He rose from his desk and crossed to the wall, straightening the frame with his finger. It was a picture painted long ago, of geese flying high in winter, above a frozen lake on which a solitary skater moved. Churchill stared at the scene which he had created, envying the birds their joyous flight; and choosing to ignore the dangers which would beset them on a journey just beginning.

That man in the crowd, he thought gloomily, black dog growling at his heels again. What did he know, taunting him about the Dardanelles? Didn't the fool realise that in war the final victory went to those who were imaginative, fearless and bold?

Churchill returned to his desk, scowling, and felt in his pocket for a cigar. He was forty-four years old, he reminded himself, in the prime of life, enjoying good health and at the peak of his powers, and the future looked empty. While he was sitting there, idle, Lloyd George was in Paris, arguing the peace. Churchill drew on his cigar and thought about the contents of the Prime Minister's note: his news was gloomy but hardly surprising.

According to Lloyd George the Germans still refused to accept that they had been defeated in the war; the French were being bloody-minded, as usual; while the Americans, flushed with a sense of their own importance, viewed themselves as the only real victors in the war, and the saviours of Europe. Wilson, the Prime Minister wrote, showed little sign that he understood the probable consequences of his demands.

True to his nature, Lloyd George remained optimistic, however, and confident that a lasting peace could be achieved in Paris.

Churchill smiled, despite his mood.

He would have loved being a fly on the wall when Lloyd George and the others slipped away from their officials to continue their talks, in private, in Wilson's study in the house he was occupying in the Place des États-Unis, not far from where Lloyd George was staying in the Rue Nitot. Even on their best form, he'd bet that Wilson and Clemenceau, never mind poor Orlando, would be no match for Lloyd George. That old Welsh wizard will outsmart the lot of them before he's finished, Churchill thought wryly, and still find time to enjoy himself.

Then what? Churchill grimaced. In the end, of course, whatever credit was going would go to Lloyd George.

He thought about the state of his own relations with the Prime Minister and shrugged, resignedly. Churchill was forced to admit, to himself at least, that after years of friendship it had been foolish for the two of them to quarrel so bitterly over his own role in the new coalition. There was never much chance of him being given the Treasury; and after the Admiralty, which he would have preferred, Churchill was forced to concede that the Ministry of War and Air wasn't a bad second best.

Anyway, short of leaving the government entirely, which was unthinkable in the present circumstances, there was nothing he could do to prevent the Prime Minister from having his own way. To resign would have been foolhardy, Churchill realised. Where would it have taken him, except into the wilderness?

No, he'd decided finally, burying his pride; although tempting for a while, throwing Lloyd George's offer of the War Office back in his face would have been a stupid gesture, useless and wasted, and of long-term benefit to neither of them.

For the moment at least, Churchill believed, both men needed one another, himself needing Lloyd George rather more than the Prime Minister needed him. Which meant that he would remain at the War Office until David decided otherwise, Churchill thought darkly, even if the long and bitter conflict which had sustained the place for so long was itself at an end.

Churchill sighed and studied the end of his cigar.

Even without the war, he supposed, there was enough going on to keep everyone in the government busy between now and the next election. For instance, he couldn't help thinking, the struggle in Ireland was beginning to look unwinnable. What a burden the place had become, Churchill thought.

A wicked idea produced an involuntary grin: perhaps they could give Ireland to the French.

Yes, thought Churchill with a malevolent chuckle, he would put the idea to the Prime Minister the next time he saw him. Lloyd George could make the offer just before everyone trooped off to the great Hall of Mirrors in Versailles where it was intended the final treaty should be signed. It was obvious that everyone wanted to leave with something belonging to somebody else. So let the French have Ireland. What would old Clemenceau say about that, Churchill wondered. Probably have a fit, he decided. But it would serve the lot of them right, Churchill grinned, puffing on his cigar in joyous mood.

The moment of humour passed and Churchill continued to brood.

Apart from Ireland, and of more immediate concern, was what they proposed to do about Scotland. The question had been raised, briefly, in Cabinet the previous day. Lloyd George was away, of course, and the meeting was chaired by Bonar Law.

The present trouble centred on a strike of shipyard workers in Glasgow who were seeking a forty-hour week, with no reduction in wages, and a guarantee of work for men returning from the war. The strike was spreading to industries in other parts of the country, including the mines, and threatening to disrupt the public services. The Secretary of State for Scotland, a dull and cautious man, had been forced to admit that talk of revolution was being expressed openly in the city. He had been most agitated, and quite serious on the subject when confronted privately by Churchill himself. Although Churchill wished the matter to be considered seriously, however, the Cabinet knew that the Prime Minister was of the opinion that the problem would quite simply go away; and the worst thing the government could do was over-respond. Those who agreed with him, and were against Churchill, were impatient to move on to other business, and scoffed at the rumours which they dismissed as just so much wild talk. It will come to nothing, you'll see, was the message reaching Churchill's ears.

Churchill remained dubious, however.

It seemed to him that if the Secretary of State for Scotland was able to confirm reports of seditious talk, openly expressed in the second largest city in the empire, then the matter required proper consideration and investigation.

Scotland, especially the industrial heartland around Clydeside, with its smoking factories and teeming tenements, was the kind of place where the seeds of public disorder, spread by communist discontent, Churchill assumed, could easily take root and flourish. Churchill didn't question his own assertion that it was communists, inspired, probably, by messages of support from Lenin, smuggled from Moscow, who were behind the trouble in Glasgow.

The belief made him cautious.

Although he abhorred the man and his politics, Churchill acknowledged the enormity of Lenin's achievement in seizing power in Russia. He wanted, more than any of his colleagues, to send an army to Russia to crush the infant state. He also recognised that despite Lenin's foolish talk, and his followers' murderous ways, the doctrine of communism was threatening to spread right across Europe. Hadn't the fleet mutinied in Germany, shortly before the war ended, for example, and workers' committees taken command of shipyards and factories, going so far as to proclaim a new republic? Then there was France, crippled by war, and teetering on the brink of revolution, as always. How, then, Churchill wanted to know, could anyone ignore the signs from Scotland?

Churchill drummed his fingers on the desk. Had the malignancy taken hold in Britain already, he asked himself. The thought made him shudder: images of the Czar and his family, exterminated by Lenin like rats in a sewer as symbols of the old order, were never far from his mind.

He consoled himself with another thought.

At least the Cabinet was united in the belief that it was the Bolsheviks, and not the Boches, who were the true enemy. Even the Prime Minister agreed with him on this.

Those who insisted that the dangers of an uprising in Scotland were overstated did so on the grounds that no-one in Britain had the means to organise a revolution. Who would have the money, the determination, the men and the guns, to challenge the authorities on the streets, they argued sneeringly. Plenty of guns and lots of ammunition, together with men trained to use them, as well as others willing to support them through the worst days of the fighting, those who opposed Churchill liked to add. It also seemed to them conclusive that a revolution would need to attract people, especially among its leaders, who were prepared to die in its cause, either during the fighting or later, at the hands of an executioner, once they had been defeated.

People who expressed this view, Churchill noted sourly, seemed to derive considerable satisfaction from it, being convinced that ordinary men and women would refuse to sacrifice themselves in this way. He believed that they were the ones, no matter how important, who least understood the danger which the country required to confront with all possible speed.

Hadn't the strike in Glasgow already attracted men among its leaders who were prepared to bring the entire country to its knees in order to achieve their own political ends? Who could tell how far they were prepared to go in pursuit of their monstrous ambition? For all anyone in the government knew they could have been in touch with like-minded groups in other parts of the country already. Perhaps their plan had been coordinated to explode within days. All the main centres of population could be affected, Churchill speculated, stretching the government's resources, and providing the revolutionaries with their chief hope of success.

Churchill didn't doubt for a moment that the authorities were being forced to deal with dangerous, unscrupulous men who wouldn't hesitate to take full advantage of the aftermath of war, with its attendant difficulties encouraging unrest, in whatever cause offered them best advantage. He imagined that a national strike was the very least they hoped to achieve. Then, with the country at a standstill, and men returning in thousands from the war, men who did know about guns and were used to fighting, anything was possible. Let the workers assume control of the means of production and the country would fall into the hands of the Bolsheviks for certain, Churchill told himself gloomily. After four years of the most catastrophic war, the people of Britain deserved a better fate. How, then, to frustrate the latest peril? Smoke from his cigar curled about the room. Churchill smiled. He had an idea.

17

# CHAPTER ONE

A huge crowd had gathered outside the main gate of the Fairfield shipyard, in the Govan district of Glasgow, to listen to the chairman of the Workers' Strike Committee, Emmanuel Shinwell. The workers respected Shinwell as a man who wasn't afraid to stand up to the bosses. They also agreed he was a good speaker and, in a city where political oratory was given the status of an art form, Shinwell was guaranteed an attentive audience wherever he went and, more often than not, a fair hearing. His style was simple and to the point.

"Fellow workers!" Shinwell roared across the heads of his tightly-packed audience. "What we are seeking is fair! We don't want anything which isn't our due. All we want is a forty-hour week with no reduction in wages."

The crowd cheered and stamped their feet appreciatively. Most of them were dressed in their working-clothes, and looked ready to start the day: without exception, however, those who had a job were already on strike, and none of the men would be working anywhere that day.

Frank Munro had found a place, on the edge of the crowd, a few feet from where Shinwell was standing, on top of an old pattern drum which someone had procured as a makeshift platform. Not for the first time, but with diminishing reluctance, Munro found himself admiring the power and passion of the man.

"The employers can afford to meet our demands," Shinwell was saying. "Why should the government stop them? Who asked the government to interfere?"

His eyes swept the crowd, searching for some imaginary traitor. Some of the men shifted uneasily.

"Did we ask them to come poking around in our affairs?" Shinwell demanded. "No! We don't want them!"

The men cheered again.

Although only thirty-five, Shinwell had been prominent in trade union circles in the city for years. Frank Munro didn't doubt for a minute that the chairman of the Workers' Strike Committee enjoyed being a celebrity.

"We stand or fall together, remember," Shinwell told the men. "And we are together, aren't we?" he cried.

He looked round the crowd, arms raised, a quizzical, challenging look on his face. No-one offered to contradict him: for there was also a darker side to Shinwell's reputation. People said he was a bit of a brawler, a hardman, and Shinwell didn't deny it. Indeed, he liked to boast that he kept a punchball hanging in the lobby of his home on which he practised every day; and on more than one occasion he had been known to use his fists to settle an argument which he might otherwise have lost.

Not surprisingly, the vigour of his methods attracted enemies. Years ago, it was rumoured, in the course of a dispute over who controlled the highly lucrative Glasgow dock traffic, the leader of a rival union went so far as to order his assassination. Shinwell was walking on the suspension bridge, between Clyde Street and Carlton Place, when the attack occurred: a shot was fired and a man walking beside him was killed by mistake.

It could have been his luck on this occasion, or in the belief that his enemies wouldn't try the same trick twice; at any rate, for whatever reason, the attempt on his life failed to discourage Shinwell's ambitions. He remained the kind of activist, set on winning, who liked to lead from the front.

"The employers want to reduce wages," Shinwell warned. "We won't let them! And not just for ourselves. Men returning from the front are entitled to a decent house with a fair rent, a decent job, and a decent wage. This is a fight which working people must win. We cannot afford to lose."

He spoke for nearly an hour and the crowd didn't budge, despite a cold, damp wind which gnawed at their bones, unhindered by their thin working-clothes. Then he took questions.

"What about the power workers?" a voice cried from somewhere in the middle of the crowd.

"They're with us!" Shinwell roared back, raising his fist in triumph.

"Will the watermen be with us as well?" someone else wanted to know

"We are all together!" Shinwell assured them in a powerful voice, his right hand slamming the air for emphasis.

Finally, when no more questions were forthcoming, Shinwell left them with one last, rousing challenge.

"Remember," he cried, looking round and fixing, or so it seemed, each man present with his stare, "what we are seeking through this dispute is a better life for all our people. And by that I mean not just the working people of Glasgow, but working people everywhere!"

His words ended in a roar: the crowd cheered lustily, some of them applauding until their hands ached. Smiling, and well pleased with that part of his day's work, Shinwell descended from the pattern drum on which he'd been standing. Some of the men crowded round him, shaking his hand, patting him on the back, while the rest began to disperse, heading for home or the nearest pub.

Frank Munro waited until the strike leader was more or less alone before presenting himself. He knew there was strong feeling amongst some of the workers that their case wasn't being presented fairly in the newspapers, including his own: only the other day, Shinwell himself had been excoriated in a leading article, written by Munro's editor personally, as the villain at the heart of the strike and the man who was trying to destroy the very fabric of British society.

Munro's opinion, which had been ignored when the leading article was being prepared, was that, far from being intractable on the question of what kind of terms the workers might finally accept, it was Shinwell who had contained the worst elements of the strike by imposing his authority on the wilder elements on the strike committee. Certainly, in Munro's experience, Shinwell always treated him courteously and usually tried to be helpful.

Now, as he emerged from the crowd, the strike leader nodded recognition. As always, there was a fierce gleam in his eye. All that work with the punchball at home, Munro thought mischievously: he suspected that the tough, two-fisted image which Shinwell liked to project wasn't the real man.

"Mr Shinwell," he began, "did you know that the government has issued a statement saying it won't intervene in the dispute?"

"I'm not surprised," Shinwell replied.

"They say it's entirely a matter to be settled by the employers and the workforce," Munro continued. "Would you care to comment?"

"What do you expect me to say?" Shinwell inquired.

"I wondered how you felt about it?" Munro explained.

"You must know what I feel about it," Shinwell told him. "I disagree."

Munro nodded. "But can I please quote you in that opinion, Mr Shinwell?" he asked.

Shinwell shrugged. "Suit yourself," he replied. "There's nothing surprising about it, is there? What did you expect me to say?"

Munro was aware of beginning to feel uncomfortable. Shinwell eyed him innocently. "Tell me something, Mr Munro," he began, and Munro steeled himself, expecting criticism.

"If you don't mind, that is," Shinwell continued slowly. Munro shook his head; Shinwell smiled.

"Then tell me," he pounced, "what do you think?"

Munro stared at him for a moment, considering his reply. "It hardly matters what I think, Mr Shinwell," he argued. "That's not the issue."

A puzzled frown replaced Shinwell's easy smile. "Isn't it?" he asked. "But why not, as a matter of interest?"

"I'm not one of the people on strike," Munro replied, immediately regretting the crassness of his response.

"Ah," said Shinwell, making great play of trying to understand. "I see. And, of course, not involved. Is that it?"

He was staring at Munro, demanding an answer. Munro wanted to avoid becoming engaged in a pointless quarrel: he had experienced the strike leader's change of moods before.

"Well?" Shinwell insisted.

Munro, unwilling to defend his position, shrugged. Shinwell, surprisingly, accepted his capitulation without demanding further humiliation. However, he hadn't finished.

"I want to tell you something, Mr Munro," he said. "It might help you when you are writing for your newspaper. If you wish to do me and them a favour, you can pass the message on to your friends who work on other newspapers. It is this: whether you believe it or not, it matters a great deal what you think about this dispute, Mr Munro. You, especially, with access to the columns of your newspaper, are a man of considerable influence. But there are other people whose views matter, ordinary people who might not be engaged in the strike either, but who are nonetheless involved, and whose opinions are important to us. Do you think we are doing all this just for ourselves? No, Mr Munro, like I tried to explain a few minutes ago, what we are doing is for the benefit of all working people. You work, don't you, Mr Munro? You aren't an employer, are you, a capitalist? Then, believe me, you do have an interest in what is going on. Whichever way it ends, the outcome of this dispute will decide the quality of life for working people in this country for a generation at least."

Munro put the question bluntly. "What happens if you lose?"

Shinwell shrugged. "We can't afford to lose," he replied sternly. "We won't lose."

Munro refused to be swept aside. "It remains a possibility," he retorted.

"Don't you agree we are fighting a just cause, Mr Munro?"

"When did that become a guarantee of victory?" Munro wanted to know, his instinct for caution deserting him for a moment.

The nature of his response this time wasn't lost on Shinwell. "At least you have an opinion now, I see," he remarked, smiling.

"That isn't the point," Munro told him, his anger in check.

"No," Shinwell agreed, "it isn't. The point remains employers who want to cut wages, landlords who want to raise rents, and a government which won't find jobs for thousands of men returning from the war. We don't intend to forget the point, Mr Munro."

"Or contemplate defeat?" Munro inquired, returning to his question.

Shinwell nodded agreeably. "Once we have the forty-hour week all sorts of problems can be solved," he maintained.

Munro had heard both sides of the argument before, and thought he knew them backwards. Put simply, the employers claimed they couldn't afford to concede on the forty-hour week; nor were they prepared to budge on anything else, it seemed: it was up to the government to decide what to do about the men returning from the war. On this question, at least, Munro was on the employers' side. By what possible stretch of Lloyd George's imagination, or political sleight-of-hand, could responsibility for the men who fought in the trenches be placed anywhere else, except at the government's door? he wondered.

Shinwell put his hand on his shoulder. "Today the government has said they won't intervene. It's got nothing to do with them, what's going on here. Is that right?"

"More or less," Munro replied. "The tapes are running a story from London which says you and the employers must sort things out between you."

Shinwell nodded. "Before you go, then, I will tell you something else," he declared.

Munro waited, hoping his mood wasn't about to change again.

"That's what they say today," Shinwell continued. "But before very long they will be forced to change their minds. You wait and see."

He was eyeing Munro closely.

"You see whether they like it or not, it's got everything to do with them," Shinwell added, finally. "I've already told you, the whole future of the country could be dependent upon what's happening here. Sooner or later, the government must take sides."

His eyes sparkled mischievously. "We live in interesting times, Mr Munro. Don't you agree?"

# CHAPTER TWO

Henry Wason had been astonished when Colonel Naismith first told him he would be going to the War Office to meet Mr Churchill. With a sense of shock, and an awful feeling of foreboding, Wason realised this was the first occasion his chief had bothered to visit him in his room, after more than seven years in the service. Now, in hushed and worried tones, Colonel Naismith was telling him that the Secretary of State for War and Air, no less, wished to discuss a matter of the utmost importance to the country. With him, Henry Wason.

Wason didn't believe it. He was used to his superiors telling him they had plans for using him which never materialised. Usually, he reminded himself sourly, all the best foreign jobs went to that dreadful man Reilly. The star of the service, Sidney Reilly had been to Russia and China; even, incredibly, at the height of the war, Germany, and it was impossible not to admire his courage. But Reilly's success meant Wason was always left with nothing.

Wason had been in the last act of settling down to coffee and biscuits, accompanied by a diligent examination of that day's *Morning Post*, a ritual timed to begin at precisely eleven o'clock each morning, when Colonel Naismith burst into the room and announced it was time for them to be going. The meeting, if indeed there was a meeting, had been scheduled for noon. At worst the War Office was a ten-minute walk away. Why the hurry? Wason wondered irritably.

He dropped his newspaper on the floor and tried hard to conceal his sense of annoyance at the brutal way in which his morning routine had been cruelly interrupted. From the impatient look accompanying the order, and the tone in which it was delivered, Wason realised his chief was in no mood to argue; or likely to reconsider the necessity for haste already indicated.

In his anxiety to remove himself from the room with all possible speed Wason almost collided with the little French table beside his chair on which his morning coffee waited, untouched, in a silver pot, with matching sugar bowl and tongs, and china given to him by his mother standing on a silver tray. He was aware, beyond the point of being simply nervous, of the disapproving manner with which Colonel Naismith surveyed the room. It also occurred to him that the Secretary of State for War and Air might want to see them earlier than planned: some change of mind, a new emphasis, a shift in his diary; with Churchill anything was possible. The response, if the great man asked for him on a sudden whim and he wasn't immediately available, Wason preferred not to consider. The fact that his own routine, established over many years, had been interrupted without an apology, wouldn't count for much; nor could he expect any sympathy from the worried-looking man fretting at the door.

Wason had been recruited to the Secret Service a year after leaving university, and in some desperation, when it became clear that no-one else appeared anxious to employ him; and this despite the intervention of various important family friends whom Wason always assumed would help him find something suitable when the time came to begin a career. His experience so far extended to filing reports which reached the office from agents who were actually out there, somewhere, operating in what his superiors always insisted on calling the field, in conditions of unimaginable danger.

Wason had seen reports from as far away as China and Japan; other agents, he soon learned, had infiltrated Russia and Turkey; several were scattered about the United States, although he couldn't think why, considering that the Americans and the British were supposed to be friends. While, most outrageous of all, he discovered, a number of brave souls had been despatched to Germany at the height of the war; an act of bold courage on the part of those involved the immensity of which Wason could barely comprehend.

They arrived at the War Office almost fifty minutes early for their meeting with Churchill. An aide greeted them thankfully, although without much warmth, Wason noted, pleased with his sense of observation.

"The Secretary of State will see you immediately."

At least they weren't going to be kept hanging about for an hour or more, fuelling their anxiety, Wason thought with immediate relief.

26

He felt glad, after his earlier misgivings, that his chief had the foresight to insist on being early; trust the old man to keep them out of trouble.

"Thank you," said Naismith. "I thought perhaps we should come early, just in case."

The aide nodded casually. Wason judged that he was only a year or two older than himself and the thought annoyed him for some reason which he couldn't identify. He knew that the man was studying him closely, assessing him, wondering why he was the one Churchill had chosen, perhaps. The thought that he looked perplexed pleased Wason and improved his spirits for a moment.

"He asked me to try and find you," the aide continued, leading them towards a huge double door.

The aide knocked once, lightly, and pushed the door open without waiting for a response. Wason followed his chief into the room.

The aide waited by the door. "Sir," he said, attracting Churchill's attention, "Colonel Naismith and Mr Wason whom you were expecting."

Churchill was seated at a large desk by the window. He made no attempt to rise. It seemed to Wason, as the door closed behind them and the aide disappeared, that the Secretary of State was watching them with a mixture of curiosity and belligerence, amounting almost to hostility.

Wason had been warned not to do anything, or say anything, which would antagonise Churchill: the idea that he might commit either heresy, or both of them together, in one single, terrible, thoughtless act, which would bring the entire edifice of the War Office in all its glory tumbling about their heads, terrified him. He determined to say nothing. Until, suddenly, Wason realised that his chief, who had entered the room ahead of him, was lingering to one side and quietly excising himself from the proceedings.

Surely he didn't mean to leave him alone with Churchill? The thought terrified him.

"You must be Mr Wason," Churchill grunted.

Wason nodded. "Yes, sir," he replied. "I mean, yes, Secretary of State."

Churchill was staring at him. "You know what is required of you?"

Wason hoped he looked and sounded confident. "I think so, sir," he replied, although his chief hadn't told him much about his orders; or what was expected of him.

Whatever it was they wanted him to do, Wason assumed his assignment was so secret even he couldn't be trusted with all the details.

Churchill peered at his desk. "We face an implacable foe, Mr Wason," he declared.

It seemed to Wason that Churchill was addressing himself and the room, its objects providing a familiar and favourite audience; his own presence, and that of his chief, forgotten.

Churchill raised his eyes from the desk and stared at him, without speaking, for what seemed to Wason an extremely long time. It was a hard look, Wason thought, a dreadful examination of his soul.

"Our enemies will not rest until we are defeated," Churchill said.

He looked again at the desk and shook his head. Wason didn't dare take his eyes from him. He was certain now, with a feeling of shame and disappointment amounting to pain, that he was about to suffer the greatest humiliation of his life: Churchill was going to turn him down. It was an awareness of failure that Wason knew he couldn't endure: he swayed slightly and tried hard not to cry.

"Your mission," Churchill went on in an unfriendly voice, "is of the utmost importance to the well-being of our country. The quality of life in England as we have known it could depend upon you in the years which lie ahead. I am not stating the seriousness of what you are being asked to do too highly. We need to know what is happening there. Tell me," he added, glowering at Wason and making him wish he could shrink from the desk; or, better still, vanish from the room. "What do you know about the place?"

Wason concentrated his mind to find an answer which would impress the Secretary of State. "I was at university there," he replied, unable to think of anything else to say.

"At Glasgow?" Churchill demanded, obviously puzzled.

"No, sir," Wason told him, fear tightening his stomach at the thought of contradicting such a man. "I was at St Andrews."

"That's what they told me," Churchill responded, without enthusiasm. "Turned down by Oxford, I suppose."

Wason nodded glumly, unable to stop the words. "Yes, sir," he admitted.

Churchill glanced behind Wason, searching for Naismith, a scowl beginning to dominate his jowly features. "You're all they could find, apparently," he said in a mournful voice. "But at least you know the country."

Wason waited.

"It's a start," Churchill concluded, without conviction.

Wason wondered if he should look away, thought better of it, and held the Secretary of State's gaze; although the man terrified him.

"My local knowledge is good, sir," Wason stammered, fearful that the nervousness of his response would force Churchill to change his mind.

Churchill stared at him for a moment; and Wason thought, with a wild sense of encouragement, that his features softened.

"Very well, then," Churchill growled, dismissing Wason and his chief with a wave of his hand, "you know what needs to be done. It is essential that we are given reliable information about what is going on up there. It will be your job to find out, Mr Wason, and report to me. By way of Colonel Naismith, of course. No-one else must know about this," he added seriously.

"Yes, sir," Wason replied, his spirits soaring.

Churchill was staring at him.

"Thank you, sir," Wason added.

Churchill nodded. "Shouldn't you be going about your duties, Mr Wason?" he inquired courteously.

"Immediately, sir!" Wason agreed, transfixed.

Churchill smiled. "Good luck, Mr Wason," he said, rising and offering his hand.

# CHAPTER THREE

Fog engulfed the city. It was like the far side of the moon, Frank
Munro imagined, black with its promise of terror. From the
river a ship's siren wailed its forlorn alarm.

Munro sat, alone and cold, in the upstairs section of a tram heading
for Springburn. Except for the trams all other traffic had been forced
from the road for the night. Munro had chosen a seat in the front
compartment, immediately above the driver. Sitting there meant it was
easier for the cold and fog to reach him from the street. But it also
allowed him to use the light from the destination board to help him find
his way. A faint, defiant glimmer, it provided a puny defence against
the fog.

Munro could hear the driver blowing into his hands, and stamping
his feet, to keep out the cold. He reckoned they were somewhere about
West Regent Street just short of Bath Street, which meant it had taken
about twenty minutes to travel a couple of hundred yards. It wasn't
spectacular progress, Munro thought wryly. But it was still the best way
home and, in this muck, reliable.

On the neighbouring track another tram trundled by, going south,
and faces, floating and unreal, like people drowning, peered at him
through the gloom. Everyone always wondered what everyone else was
doing, out on a night like this, Munro reflected.

Well, he had been working.

In more than twenty years, except for holidays, Munro couldn't
remember not working on a Sunday. What was there to do on Sundays,
anyway, he used to inquire of his wife whenever she complained. They
weren't church-goers, and the rest of the city closed down in deference
to those who took their religion seriously. It was a consideration for the
wishes of the over-godly which Frank Munro resented.

He was aware of the tram bumping gently across a junction, and set
of points, which he thought must be Sauchiehall Street; lights in the

city's most famous thoroughfare had been obliterated by the fog.
Munro lived at the top of Hope Street, opposite the Theatre Royal;
another two stops away. He pulled the collar of his coat across his face,
trying to protect his throat, and picked his way down the iron staircase
to the platform behind the driver.

"What a night," the driver grunted, blowing on his hands, and
stamping his feet against the cold.

"Aye," Munro agreed, holding on to the platform rail, and staring
ahead, trying to distinguish something, anything, which he could
recognise and acknowledge, through the fog. "It's a real pea-souper."

"It's that, all right," the driver replied.

He was wearing a short, green jacket, no coat, on which his
tramwayman's badge was pinned. A rough, woollen scarf, full of holes,
Munro noted, partially covered his face: mittens protected his hands
only as far as the middle knuckles of his fingers, leaving the rest
exposed.

"At least you're hame," the driver added, enviously. "That right?"

"Aye," Munro confirmed. "When do you finish?"

"Another four hours'll see me done," the driver told him. "It's been a
split shift. I started at four o'clock this morning. Still, the Springburn
run's no' too bad. You get a good crowd. Cheerful, you know? There's
usually a laugh o' some kind."

Munro nodded, and tried not to cough. The driver moved his scarf to
one side to suck on the fingers of his right hand, warming them.

"Why don't you wear the big gloves?" Munro inquired. "You know,
the leather kind? Don't your hands get awful cold in those things?"

"I had a pair," the driver told him, "and lost them. I didn't like them
very much, anyway. They're awfu' clumsy. These dae me fine. Besides,
you get used to it," he added, with a shrug.

He brought the tram, which had been moving slower than walking-
pace, anyway, to a sudden, juddering halt. "This'll be you about here,"
he said.

The pavement should have been about ten feet away: but Munro
couldn't see it. "I don't know how you manage in this muck," he said,
holding on to the rail, and taking the step of the tram with exaggerated
care.

"Easy!" the driver replied, chuckling into his scarf. "Ah jist follow the
rails. It's the caur that does the work."

He clanged confidently on the bell and, with a cheerful cheerio,
persuaded the awkward, lumbering beast at his command towards the

junction with Cowcaddens. As the tram crept past, Munro discerned the face of the conductor, sitting inside away from the platform, trying to keep warm, peering at him, eerily, through a window. Munro turned and inched towards the pavement, arms outstretched. He was trying to locate the pole at the pavement's edge; or the kerb itself.

From the Clyde, a mile or so away to his left, he heard once again the plaintive cry of some ship in distress, carried across the roofs of tenements unseen; and pictured a terrified coolie crew, lining the rails, and staring, bewildered, at the dark, dead city to which they had been brought from the other side of the world.

Whatever his own predicament, Munro decided grimly, he was at least better off than the poor bastard pulling on that chain. Fog reached into his throat and he began to cough, hands cupped in front of his mouth, and over his nose, to prevent more of the poison from reaching his lungs. Bugger them, he thought uncharitably, dismissing his concern, who moved that bloody pavement?

His mind raced. Having missed the pole, and overstepped the kerb, how come he hadn't made contact with the front of the building in which he lived? Perhaps the tram had stopped in the middle of the previous crossing. Was he standing, like an idiot, in the middle of Renfrew Street? At least there was no traffic about, and no chance of anything knocking him down. Damn it! he thought; what a bloody night. He resisted the temptation to call out, in the hope that someone else was about, to direct him to safety. He felt a big enough fool standing there on his own, utterly lost.

Munro rubbed at his eyes which had begun to stream: where the hell am I? he wondered.

More of the thick, vile vapour reached his lungs, and he began to cough again, making him stagger: without warning he found himself against a wall, cold and damp from the fog. His coughing spluttered to a halt. He ran his hands over the wall and touched a door. With his other hand he reached out and felt the opposite wall. Laughing silently to himself feeling foolish, in spite of his relief, Munro realised what had happened. Having missed the pole he was seeking, and failing to locate the pavement's edge, dafter still, he had walked right into an open closemouth: for all he knew, the one leading to his own first-floor flat.

The place was in total darkness. There must have been a gas failure, Munro thought, or, more likely, the lamplighter was behind on his rounds.

He reached for the door on his right-hand side and felt for the bell.

The little brass handle was loose in its frame. Munro pulled on it hard and heard the bell, which he knew would be hanging from a spring inside, come alive. He gave the handle another tug, just to make sure, and waited for an answer.

There was the sound of a door opening, a pause; then a man's and a woman's voice raised inquiringly.

"Who can it be?"

"How should I know?"

"Who would be out on a night like this?"

"What time is it?"

"I hope Sadie and the weans are a' right."

Munro pulled on the little handle, gently, not wishing to cause further alarm.

"You'd better see who it is."

The door opened slowly to reveal a small, bald-headed man, dressed in pyjamas, whom Munro recognised as a neighbour from two closes away. The little man, whose name was Steedman, was obviously surprised to see him. "Oh, it's you, Mr Munro," he said, trying hard to recover his composure.

"It's Mr Munro," he added over his shoulder, for the benefit of his wife, who was trying to conceal the fact that she was wearing a nightgown. "Is there something the matter?"

Munro smiled foolishly. "Would you believe I'm lost?" he inquired, trying to make a joke of his predicament.

Mr Steedman stared at him, uncomprehending.

"The fog," Munro added, feeling even more foolish having to explain it. "I came into your close by mistake. Missed the kerb, missed the pole, even missed the wall. I thought I'd finished in the middle of Renfrew Street."

Mr Steedman chuckled. "That's a good one," he said.

"Sorry to have bothered you," Munro apologised again.

"Nae bother," Mr Steedman assured him. "You been working?"

Munro nodded.

"Better get away hame then. You'll be ready for a cup o' tea. I'll keep the door open for a minute, just to let you out. But hurry up, it's damned cauld!"

"Thanks," Munro replied. "Good night, Mrs Steedman," he added. "Good night, Mr Steedman."

As he felt his way along the wall, the door behind him closed, killing the light, and leaving Munro still searching for the place where the street began. Finding it, he turned left, came upon the next closemouth, recognised the empty space, like a blind man feeling with his stick; and then, satisfied, moved on, slowly, a foot at a time, never absolutely sure of his position; until, thankfully, he located the entrance to the close where he lived. It was in darkness also; but Munro didn't care. His flat was one up on the left. There was a turn on the stair, where the steps narrowed dangerously: Munro hugged the wall, swearing quietly. He was expecting trouble, locating his key in the lock. Miraculously, they engaged first time, like himself walking right into that bloody close, Munro scolded himself ruefully, without even touching the walls, damned fool!

# CHAPTER FOUR

**M**unro busied himself about the flat, where he lived alone, putting a match to a fire which was already set, making tea, and generally settling down for the night.

His wife Agnes had been dead for almost seventeen months, a month for every year of their married life. Her photograph, taken soon after they were married, showed a smiling, happy young woman in a fur stole and wide-brimmed hat, stood in a silver frame on the mantelpiece above the fire. The certificate said she died of pulmonary tuberculosis; bleakly, and in private, the doctor called it the Glasgow disease. She was buried in the Necropolis, a tumble of tombs to the memory of lives largely forgotten, which overlooked the city not far from the cathedral. Munro always made a point of visiting her grave on a Saturday which was his regular day off. Yesterday, however, he'd met John Maclean in the street, the honorary Soviet Consul in Scotland, whom he had been trying to find for more than a week, for an interview; and spent most of the day following him around to meetings which had taken them as far as Lanarkshire. It was the first time he hadn't gone to the cemetery on a visit since his wife's death which somehow implied a sudden and undeserved neglect; a feeling which had troubled him all day. He'd promised himself that he would make up for it, by going in the morning, before he went to work. If he couldn't find flowers, he'd buy a small plant; something with red in it, he thought: Agnes always liked red.

Munro, who was forty-six, had lived in Glasgow for more than twenty years, and worked on the same newspaper, the Examiner, for the whole of that time. He had been born in Crail, a village in Fife, where his parents worked as domestic servants in the weekend home of an Edinburgh lawyer. He'd begun his career on the Fife Free Press, a paper with a solid reputation for accuracy and fairness. At first, Munro ran messages most of the time, and made tea for the senior men; but it was a good start for a boy of fourteen. Eventually, he was given an opportunity to write things for the paper, small paragraphs initially, important in themselves, which, to his great excitement, duly appeared; and then, with experience, stories which filled a column. By the time Munro thought himself ready for Glasgow, at the age of twenty-two, he had become the paper's chief reporter, and, if he'd stayed, might one day have been its editor: he was promised as much, the day he left, by the owner. But his mind was made up. He wanted to work in Glasgow. It was the second city of the empire and, for him, the true heart of the country.

Comfortable in cardigan and slippers, the complete outfit a present from his sister in Dundee, Munro settled into his favourite armchair, with his back to the window, facing the photograph of his wife in her silver frame. Agnes would have been delighted and amused to recognise the ritual which followed: the fact that Munro had been pursuing the same routine, without variation, for years, and without ever being totally aware of it, had been one of the small treasures of her life. First Munro bent forward and stared into the heart of the fire, blowing gently: with customary surprise, he discovered that the fire was drawing nicely. Next he glanced round at the curtains, which he'd pulled together on entering the flat, to make sure they wouldn't shift to reveal the tiniest bit of night, which he hated. Then, having satisfied himself that the night remained outside, Munro checked on the teapot, which he'd deposited on the small table beside his chair only a minute or two earlier, to make sure it was warm. Then, finally, having done all this, he moved his pipe and tobacco from the small table, where they rested within easy reach, to the left-hand side of his chair and back again. All of this accomplished, he felt ready to pour himself a cup of tea, which he had ascertained would be warm, and began reading the following day's newspaper, which was already spread across his knees, and waiting to be read.

The front of the Examiner carried no editorial material whatsoever and was reserved, instead, for advertisements and general notices: Munro kept these until last. He always preferred to begin his reading by turning inside in search of the day's main news stories. He had looked through his paper briefly before leaving the office and knew that the biggest space had been allocated to an agency report from France on how well the peace talks were proceeding at Versailles: the Prime Minister, Mr David Lloyd George, appeared confident that he could achieve a just end to the war and an enduring peace.

It occurred to Munro, not for the first time, that the war was far from finished: the victors were still squabbling over the spoils. So many things remained to be settled in Europe: how would it all end? If the old men at Versailles weren't careful, he thought bitterly, they could find themselves going through the whole thing again: not them, of course, other, younger men, perhaps unborn; who could tell without knowing the future?

Thoughts inspired by what was going on at Versailles made him feel uneasy. Would the country stand for it a second time? Would there be the same headlong rush to volunteer? To die for King and country? Munro didn't pretend to have an answer: he knew, of course, that in the end, whatever happened, responsibility would be handed to the young. And what would they do? Munro wondered. Would they perpetrate the same avoidable errors, or different ones, appropriate to their own times? Or would they discover the secret of lasting peace? Would they begin to understand that ambition and greed, selfishly pursued, were unworthy of nations? Viewed realistically, when he considered the nature of the world they seemed certain to inherit, without wanting to be unduly pessimistic, Munro thought it unlikely. For the moment, therefore, he contented himself with the knowledge, to which he warmed a little each day, that those who survived the carnage were coming home.

He turned the page in search of home news and his own contribution to the paper.

His story about the latest moves in the forty-hour strike occupied half a column in the centre of the page. The owner, who was rarely seen by the staff of the Examiner and seldom left his home at Rhu, with its large rose garden and splendid views of Holy Loch and the Firth of Clyde, to visit the office, had given instructions to the editor that he didn't want a lot of space devoted to the strike as a matter of course: something needed to happen, there required to be a major new development, preferably one which reflected badly on the strikers, before it reached the paper. For this reason, the editor, who was nearing retirement and wanted a quiet life, explained to his deputy, Alick Robertson, who made the decision known to Munro, that the Examiner wouldn't be publishing his piece about John Maclean, based on the time Munro spent with him on Saturday, touring various meetings in Glasgow and beyond.

The decision conveyed to him by the deputy editor, who happened to be his closest friend, annoyed Munro but didn't surprise him. Maclean's name was anathema to the editor: come to think of it, Munro reminded himself, the little consul was anathema to most people in the Scottish establishment; not to mention all those other people in government in London who thought he was the devil incarnate.

Maclean, a former school-teacher, and an intense and passionate man, had set his heart on overthrowing the monarchy and establishing a Bolshevik state in Britain. He had been appointed Bolshevik Consul for Scotland by Lenin following the successful Russian Revolution in November, 1917, an appointment which the British government refused to recognise, apart from instructing the post office not to deliver any mail to Maclean which was addressed in this fashion. Then, as further proof of the Russian leader's regard, Maclean was elected an honorary president of the First Congress of Soviets. Maclean made no secret of his desire for revolution on Russian lines in Britain and he was easily the best-known revolutionary in the country, as well as being the most feared among those people, not just the so-called ruling classes, who counted themselves among the establishment; and who were certainly the ones with most to lose if Maclean and the people who supported him ever found themselves in power.

Six months before the war ended Maclean had been found guilty of sedition and sent to prison, not for the first time, but on this occasion for a period of five years. The severity of the sentence stunned his supporters and caused widespread public outrage. Petitions seeking his release became so numerous, the threat of violence on the streets so real, with Maclean's supporters promising mayhem, and other people, less involved, saying John Maclean never made any secret of his views, anyway, and hadn't he been in prison already during the war, that the authorities were forced to recant; Maclean, having served only seven months of a five-year sentence, was released.

A huge crowd, several thousand strong, cheering and singing and waving banners, some of them greatly moved by the prospect of their hero's return, were waiting at Buchanan Street railway station in Glasgow to welcome him home from prison. They spilled into the ticket hall and onto the platform to mob the approaching train: Maclean, when he appeared, looking weak and tired after his ordeal in Peterhead, where it was known he had been force-fed, was in danger of being injured by the enthusiasm of his own supporters. None too gently he was carried from the station and placed in an open carriage which some of the strongest members of his welcoming party proceeded to haul through the streets of the city. Following closely behind Maclean, and his exuberant entourage, for the purpose of his story, and without wishing to exaggerate what he had seen, it occurred to Munro that he was witnessing an unprecedented event: how else could he describe an occasion in which the determined advocate of a system, set on destroying the British constitution, and dismantling the Crown itself, was himself enjoying a triumphant return to a place whose people liked to boast it was the second city of the empire?

With a story to write, Munro couldn't help speculating: where was John Maclean going, how far and at what cost?

The answer to these questions still eluded him.

John Maclean wasn't part of the official strike leadership, of course. Shinwell especially didn't want his extremist views distorting the simple logic of his own campaign. Shinwell was conducting an industrial dispute in which he was seeking from the employers more money and better conditions for his men. He didn't wish to bring down the monarchy or see an end to parliament, so far as Munro knew anything.

Munro didn't accept for a moment, as some of his more excitable colleagues maintained, that the strike was a prelude to revolution. It's happened in Russia, went the cry, so why not in Britain?

In his experience, the same question, employing exactly the same words, was invoked by those who wanted revolution, who somehow thought it might be fun, and those who were opposed: only the inflection, the manner in which the words were used, was different.

Similarly, hardly a day went by without Munro hearing someone say, it could actually begin right here on Clydeside! Again, the same words from both sides: elated or fearful, depending on the speaker's point of view.

Not that Munro took any of it very seriously; most of it, he was convinced, was pub talk, anyway.

He acknowledged that Shinwell and the other strike leaders, operating within the law, wouldn't hesitate to cause the maximum social and political disruption throughout the city, and the whole of the country, if they could arrange it, in order to achieve their objectives. But in Munro's opinion Shinwell and all the rest of the well-intentioned men who comprised the Workers' Strike Committee weren't revolutionaries: far from it, in some cases.

Of course, this didn't mean, Munro was forced to concede, recalling those scenes of John Maclean being carried in triumph through the city, that men couldn't be found who wouldn't support the idea of revolution.

What the government needed to do, and urgently, Munro reflected, was ensure that the people who followed Maclean, truly followed him, that is, knowing where he would take them, given a reasonable opportunity, and what this would mean in terms of bloodshed, ordinary citizens killed, families, in all probability, armed against each other, friends on opposite sides; it was up to the government to ensure that the committed revolutionaries who could be found in the nation's midst were denied any realistic hope of ever attracting sufficient numbers to their cause. Munro believed that if the government continued on its present course of secretly supporting the employers against the strikers, they would turn masses of ordinary people against them. At the very least, they were running the risk of provoking a national strike; about the last thing the country needed now, or ever, Munro thought grimly.

Viewed simply, it could be argued, the strike was a straightforward industrial confrontation in which the workforce were seeking to better their conditions and, therefore, of no immediate concern to the government. At its heart, however, was the need for each man to know that his employment prospects were secure.

Then there was the question of what to do about all the men returning from the front, Munro, busy with his pipe and tobacco, reminded himself.

It was this last consideration, more than anything else, which convinced hm that it was the government's duty to intervene. He was prepared to ignore the widespread cries of outrage against those landlords who had been unwise enough to increase rents at a time when their tenants could least afford to pay; he also felt sorry, extremely sorry, he would admit when pressed, for those men and women, previously unskilled, and known locally as dilutees, who had been hastily trained in the course of the war to meet the demands of industry at home: they now found that the men whose jobs they had taken were coming home and expecting to be given their old jobs back; a state of affairs which Munro, for one, would have accepted, regardless of the upheaval. Because Munro believed, without equivocation, that the men who fought in the war had earned the right to work.

Privately, Munro was committed in his support of Lloyd George. He was convinced, however, that the Welshman couldn't survive an election without first solving the whole employment problem which meant, yes, of course, he didn't mind adding, the displaced dilutees. The euphoria currently surrounding Lloyd George, as leader of the nation in a victorious war, was a fragile asset, in Munro's opinion, and of depreciating political value. Now that the war was over people expected him to deliver on his promise: all adult men, who were fit to work, had the right to work.

Munro believed that all other problems, no matter how grave, including the wretched housing conditions which existed in most of the large cities, and which could be improved by a programme of development, which by itself would create thousands of jobs, could be left to find their own level of priority, later. Uppermost in everyone's mind, what people were waiting to see, waiting to hear, he maintained, was how the Prime Minister proposed honouring the commitment he had given; or, at the very least, be given some clear indication that, given time, the government had found a way to provide jobs for all the people; a condition of their lives which everyone considered was their absolute right.

Munro puffed at his pipe. Things would be different if Lloyd George was in London, taking charge, instead of in France, haggling, at the peace negotiations, he thought.

Of course, he reminded himself rudely, shaking away his own complacency, his faith in Lloyd George could be misplaced.

# CHAPTER FIVE

H enry Wason was trying hard to concentrate his mind on the
astonishing events of the past twenty-four hours. He found it
difficult to believe that what was happening was happening to
him. Whenever he recalled the moment when Churchill shook his hand
and wished him luck the thought made him shiver. It was an excitement
heightened by the serious manner adopted by Colonel Naismith when
giving him his final orders: evidently his assignment was to remain a
secret known to no-one else apart from Wason, his chief and Churchill
himself. If he learned something of importance in Glasgow his
instructions were to communicate, in the first instance, only with the
head of the service; and should direct contact with his chief prove
impossible, for whatever reason, he was informed gravely, then the
Secretary of State himself would accept his call. He was given a number
through which Churchill could be contacted at any time: the only
occasion on which he wouldn't make himself immediately available
would be in the event of a Cabinet meeting or if he was speaking in the
House of Commons.

The idea of telephoning the War Office and asking for Winston
Churchill amused Wason at first. Then he thought about the nature of
the conversation which was likely to ensue. Questions would be hurled
across four hundred-odd miles of telephone wire in a voice designed to
make strong men tremble. His assignment, according to Churchill, was
of the utmost importance to national security. It followed, therefore,
that Churchill expected his worst fears to be confirmed. The sudden
notion that the Secretary of State for War and Air might be mistaken,
Wason dismissed with a helpless shrug, and a glance through the
window.

Travelling through England he could see the occupants of a million
terraced rows, spawned by factories spewing smoke, then packed together, staring out enviously at the speeding train; before jostling with
green fields and scattered white houses for a place in his consciousness.

What if the threat of revolution didn't exist in Glasgow? Or he couldn't find any evidence to support Churchill's assertion that the strike leaders wanted to deliver the country into the hands of the communists? Churchill was well known for his flights of fancy. Perhaps he was wrong about what was happening in Glasgow.

Wason sighed. Having confronted the idea he was left feeling miserable. The Secretary of State for War and Air was the most terrifying man in England, unpredictable in almost everything except the weight of his wrath whenever he was thwarted. The prospect of incurring his displeasure by telling him he was wrong about anything made Henry Wason tremble. He hoped his chief would make a point of standing between them when he made his report; on the questionable assumption he would learn something worth reporting during his stay in Glasgow.

Wason remembered his training and tried to think positively. There was always the possibility that Churchill was right to be alarmed. If he could produce clear evidence that something serious threatened in Glasgow, demonstrate a plot, then his future career would be assured.

He glanced at his watch and peered out into the darkness. Black hills against a thundery sky prevented him from ascertaining their exact location. Beattock was behind them, of that he was certain: the train, lurching and straining on the steep gradient, required the assistance of an extra engine to complete the climb. This had been followed by a long delay while they took on water and coal, with hard-pressed railwaymen scurrying about on the track outside, looking anxious, tapping wheels, and paying absolutely no attention to the faces of passengers pressed against the windows, wanting to know what was happening, and the reason for the delay; the enormous engine at the front all the time belching steam, quite clearly impatient to be away.

But once started they wasted no more time on the final stages of their journey to Glasgow. From the time on his watch, and the speed of the train for most of the journey, Wason guessed they would be about half an hour late arriving at their destination. He didn't mind the delay. There was nothing for him to do on the first night, anyway. In the morning following a good breakfast he would begin his inquiries by walking the city, looking and listening, trying to assess the mood of the place. Wason enjoyed a good breakfast. It was the most important meal of the day, he believed.

Another hour at the most and they would be in Glasgow. Then what? Wason closed his eyes and made himself comfortable against the corner of his window seat. He would worry about that in the morning.

"In England people have lost their way!"

Wason groaned silently. The man in the seat opposite was an aggress-ive Scots minister who, at the start of their journey, wasted no time introducing himself as the Reverend Ronald Simpson from Paisley.

"The war has sapped them of their strength and moral obligation to one another. Don't tell me you disagree?"

Good manners forced Wason to open his eyes. All the way from King's Cross the minister had been trying to engage him in conver-sation. His own lack of enthusiasm, and the man's failure to interest him in anything he said, made Wason hope he would be left alone and in peace to consider his own problems. He felt no obligation to give any special attention to the ravings of a complete stranger. Wason spent a large part of his time trying to avoid the attentions of churchmen representing his own faith, which was nominally Church of England, going back in the family several centuries, and he had no appetite for a forced encounter with anyone in another cloth.

Mr Simpson persisted, however. He had opinions about everything, or so it appeared; and nothing he said in the course of the journey suggested for a moment that he could be wrong in his conclusions. His wife was a small, bird-like creature with bright eyes and nimble fingers, who picked up crocheting a tablecloth even before the train had left the station, and remained silent throughout the journey. Wason studied her for a time, fascinated by the intricacies and detail of the work, without her once looking up to acknowledge his interest. Her husband, on the other hand, was determined to command his attention.

"The class system has been destroyed," Mr Simpson was saying with his usual conviction. "People no longer accept the old divisions of master and slave."

Wason gaped at him. Was the man serious?

"Don't you agree?" Mr Simpson inquired, sounding truculent.

Truly astonished, Wason was forced to respond. "Slave?" he almost shouted. "What do you mean?"

The minister appeared shocked by the force of Wason's answer. He was silent for a moment, looking at him. Then, in a low voice, Mr Simpson inquired: "Do you think the comparison too strong?"

"Don't you?" Wason demanded, controlling his anger.

"No," said Mr Simpson. "It seems to me to be entirely appropriate."

"You can't be serious!" Wason exploded.

Mr Simpson looked grave. "Young man," he replied, sharply, and

Wason had to stop himself from wincing, "one thing about me you should know – I'm always serious."

Wason didn't doubt it. "Of course," he replied, nodding glumly. "I'm sorry."

"Life is a serious business after all," Mr Simpson added, as if wishing to underline the point, or emphasise his own position.

"You sometimes find that, don't you?" Wason heard himself inquiring, in a voice which appeared to come at him from far away. Earlier he tried guessing the age of his tormentor. Apart from helping to conceal his boredom, and disguise his irritation, which he was anxious to hide, the exercise offered an opportunity for him to engage his powers of observation; on which his safety might depend in the dangerous days which lay ahead. Sixty, perhaps. The minister certainly behaved and talked like a man beyond middle age. What about the wife?

Wason glanced at the woman, busy with her little needle, turning and looping the silken thread, ignoring them, mesmerised by her own skill, it seemed; like a demented spider.

Her silence pleased Wason. He was against the fashionable view that it was time for women to be given a bigger say in things: Mrs Astor was a friend of his mother and Wason wished she was back in America, peddling her silly ideas to the Indians. Bossy was how she struck him the first time they met. Never particularly happy in the company of older women at any time, Wason became even more uncomfortable when they turned out bossy as well: his mother, his aunt, and a sister whom he rarely visited and tried to avoid, were always trying to order him about, scolding him into doing things their way; a fact of life from childhood which Wason resented deeply.

The minister's wife, he decided, had the heightened look of a woman, already old, who realised that the best years of her life were behind her, wasted on the altar of her husband's opinions. It was hardly surprising she spent her time crocheting away like mad, ignoring him.

"How old are you, Mr Wason?"

The question stunned Wason: could the man tell what he was thinking? Thought of all the horrors presented by such a possibility alarmed Wason. He had always discounted the action of telepathy as a rational science: now he decided quickly against the idea of asking the other man if he had an opinion on the subject.

"Twenty-nine," he replied, frowning. "Why do you ask?"

"I'm forty-two," Mr Simpson informed him, enthusiastically.

Wason stared at him, annoyed at being wrong. Could the wife be older than her husband? In his own circle no-one would dream of marrying an older woman. Wason risked a glance at Mrs Simpson. Silent and unconcerned, she was engrossed in her work.

"As you grow older," Mr Simpson continued, contemplating the burden of his years, "you view the world from a quite different perspective."

Tiny cinders rattled like hail against the window. Wason stared out at winter fields, heavy with snow. Black smoke from the huge locomotive streamed out behind them. Caught in the wind, it dispersed into the night.

"There is something I would like you to consider."

Wason turned from the window. The minister was eyeing him carefully, his face serious. Wason nodded. "Go on," he encouraged, bleakly.

"I am assuming you don't know much about the working class," Mr Simpson continued. "How they live, that sort of thing."

Wason stared at him, conscious of being patronised.

"Well," said Mr Simpson, his voice becoming hard, "my question to you is this. Before the war, how do you suppose a working man, dependent on wages, his family wholly dependent on him for their food and clothing, and a house in which to live, could afford to upset the man who employed him?"

Wason suspected a trap.

"And by that I mean not just the owner of the business, whom he probably never saw, but the foreman and managers who were responsible for handing out jobs in the first instance," Mr Simpson added. "Do you appreciate the power such men enjoyed? Can you believe that they alone could decide whether a man worked for a single day, or a week, or a month, or not at all?"

He reached forward and tapped Wason on the knee.

"It is wrong for one man, without reference to anyone else, to wield so much authority over the lives of other men. Don't you agree?"

Wason stared at him in disbelief. Did the man's collar conceal a communist?

"Happily, things will change," Mr Simpson added with great authority. "And soon! You can take my word for it. The war has opened people's eyes. There is no way the working class can be trammelled as before. The unions are on the march."

Wason gasped. The man was a communist, obviously.

However, it also occurred to Wason that if an educated man, a minister of the church, with so much to lose, was prepared to express such views openly, then the threat to the country was more serious than even Churchill imagined.

Mr Simpson indicated dark shapes growing up around them. "This is where much of it will start," he remarked, embracing an anonymous-looking sprawl which Wason assumed was Glasgow.

The lights of the river appeared in the distance.

"Glasgow has an inner strength," Mr Simpson sighed. "In Glasgow you can still find God. Which is why it will always prevail," he added, earnestly. "London has lost its soul, I'm afraid."

The train had crossed the river and entered a huge, glass-roofed station, milling with people. Faces, smiling, uncertain, expectant, peered through the windows, looking for friends. Porters, pushing bogeys, bustled about, hoping for customers. They felt the train settle against the buffers and come to a halt beside a platform. Wason stood and reached for his luggage. Simpson's luggage was on the rack opposite. Wason made no attempt to help him with it.

"I've enjoyed our talk,' the minister said.

Wason responded awkwardly, shaking the other man's hand with a sense of unease. "It was interesting," he replied.

Mrs Simpson, busy packing needles and thread into a small, velvet-lined sewing-basket, smiled nicely. The tablecloth had been folded carefully, and placed on the seat beside her.

"Thank you for entertaining my husband," she said, as Wason fumbled with the door.

"I think you'll like Glasgow," Mr Simpson said. "Just be careful."

Wason turned. "What do you mean?"

Mr Simpson shrugged. "You need to know a bit about the place before you go wandering off on your own," he said.

Wason was enjoying himself at last. "You mean it's dangerous?" he inquired, innocently.

Mr Simpson almost smiled. "There are some districts where it is advisable to exercise a degree of caution," he explained. "During the day as well as at night."

"Thanks for the warning," Wason replied. "But I think I can look after myself."

Mr Simpson nodded.

"Goodbye," said Wason, descending to the platform and leaving them to each other.

A porter rushed to meet him. "Your bag, sir," the porter offered, saluting on the run.

Wason waved the man away and headed along platform one at a brisk pace in search of his hotel. He knew it adjoined the station. The awful memory of the Reverend and Mrs Simpson was behind him. All he wanted now was a drink, a hot bath, and a good dinner.

# CHAPTER SIX

A cold wind, carrying rain, burned against his face as Frank Munro emerged from the underground in Byres Road and turned right for the Curlers where he had arranged to meet his friend, and deputy editor of the paper, Alick Robertson. Munro had begun the week furious with Robertson for not arguing strongly enough against the editor's decision to spike his story on John Maclean. The editor's reactionary views were well known to everyone on the paper, and his desire to discourage John Maclean in his various activities, by failing to report them, came as no surprise. However, it had been Munro's belief that the deputy editor was made of better stuff, a more adventurous spirit, and certainly not the kind of journalist who trembled when brought face to face with the truth, however much he disliked it; an opinion which Munro delivered loudly and angrily from his desk in the reporters' room. He and Robertson had been alone in the room at the time. But Munro realised afterwards that his voice must have carried along the corridor to those rooms where the subs and leader-writers worked. It was just as well he and Alick had been friends for years, he told himself wryly, looking forward now to dinner at Robertson's large and comfortable house. Everyone on the paper, including the editor himself, no doubt, would have heard about the row and much enjoyed gossiping about it. "Bugger it!" Munro thought angrily, still annoyed at his outburst, and grateful to his friend for keeping his temper and not provoking him to even greater excess.

Brushing the rain from his coat, Munro entered the downstairs rear saloon of the Curlers and spotted Alick Robertson standing alone at the bar, drink in hand. As he elbowed his way towards his friend, who hadn't seen him, someone Munro recognised, but couldn't name, said hello. Munro nodded acknowledgement. The Curlers was an ancient pub, going back hundreds of years, which attracted a mixed bag of working people, as well as students and staff from the University on nearby Gilmorehill. It wasn't one of Munro's favourite haunts but Alick

Robertson liked it, largely, Munro suspected, because it was close to home and handy for bed at the end of a night spent drinking.

Alick Robertson greeted him warmly. "Ah!" he cried, smiling hugely. "And how goes the battle for breath, and the search after truth, today?"

Robertson was proud of the northern burr in his voice and made no attempt to conceal it. A small man, developing a paunch, which he refused to reduce, and balding, he enjoyed presenting an aggressively cheerful front to the world. There were times, in the course of their friendship, which had lasted more than twenty years, when Munro wished there was some obvious limit to the energy of the man. About the only thing which stopped Alick Robertson, ever, was too much whisky.

"Fine," Munro replied, accepting the large whisky which had been awaiting his arrival.

"Evidently the office survived without me today," Robertson continued happily.

"Seems like it," Munro replied.

"Nobody's indispensable, you see."

Munro shrugged.

"So what's new?"

"I got a good story from Shinwell today."

Robertson was immediately interested.

"He's going to start using mobile pickets," Munro explained.

"What do you mean?" Robertson inquired, frowning slightly.

"It means what it says," Munro replied. "Men will be sent from one yard to another, depending on where they are needed most."

"You mean if the workforce in one place are refusing to come out, they will be picketed by men from another yard?"

"Something like that," Munro agreed.

"That sounds like intimidation to me," Alick Robertson exclaimed. "Is it legal?"

Munro shrugged. "Can't see why not," he said.

"There could be trouble," Robertson insisted.

Munro nodded.

"Is this Shinwell's idea?" Alick Robertson wanted to know.

"He's the one who's pushing it," Munro replied.

"Men from one yard, where the strike is solid, turning up at another yard, where the men don't want to come out," Alick Robertson continued thoughtfully, "will almost certainly lead to violence. Don't you think so?"

Munro nodded carefully. "It's possible, I suppose," he said.

"If Shinwell and the Strike Committee decide to go ahead with this plan," Alick Robertson went on, "what's to stop them from sending men from the yards, where the strikers are strongest, to the likes of the power stations and the waterworks where they are weakest? Next thing men who have never been inside a pit will be trying to stop miners from working. Fighting could break out almost anywhere. Then the police will be forced to intervene. What happens then?"

Munro shook his head. "Would you like another drink?" he inquired.

Alick Robertson nodded. He sounded thoughtful: "How long will the men be prepared to follow Shinwell?"

Munro attracted the barman's attention and was ordering another drink. "And how far?"

The barman brought them two large whiskies. Munro gave him a ten shilling note and waited for his change. Alick Robertson moved along the bar in search of water.

"Well?" Robertson demanded, returning and adding water to their whisky.

"You know my view," Munro replied. "I think the men are loyal to Shinwell. He has the complete support of the workforce, if you ask me."

"To do what?"

Munro shrugged. "First and foremost they want to win," he retorted. "Obviously. Their target is a forty-hour week and I don't think they'll settle for less. Shinwell won't let them settle for less."

Alick Robertson stared at him thoughtfully for a moment. Munro smiled and sipped at his drink. "I thought you were the one who liked to take things at their face value," he remarked. "Aren't you always telling me to stop going around looking for plots?"

Robertson shrugged. "Are you absolutely certain about Shinwell?" he inquired.

"I've told you," Munro replied, impatiently. "I think he means what he says. He wants a forty-hour week. How many times do you need to be told?"

"That's today," Alick Robertson agreed, his face serious. "But what about tomorrow? Or next week? Next year, even?"

"How should I know?" Munro demanded.

"You spend a lot of time talking to him," Alick Robertson responded sharply. "You must know how he thinks, or at least have an opinion."

His persistence surprised Munro.

"Putting the workers on a forty-hour week won't satisfy the man," Robertson went on. "He has his eyes on other things."

It was Munro's turn to stare.

"The authorities have become very nervous about your friend's activities and intentions," Robertson warned. "I can tell you that Mr Shinwell isn't very popular with any of them."

"He's popular enough with the workers," Munro replied in a voice sharper than intended, "and that's what counts."

Alick Robertson shook his head. "Shinwell is playing with fire," he declared. "What happens if he can't keep the men under control? These so-called mobile pickets, for instance. They're bound to cause trouble. Start fighting in the streets and the police will come down on them hard. And if the police can't cope, take it from me, the government will send in troops," Robertson concluded grimly.

Frank Munro shook his head irritably. "You sound remarkably well informed," he observed. "I presume that the editor and the Chief Constable have been enjoying one of their little off-the-records again?"

Robertson ignored the question. "It's no secret in Fleet Street that some members of the government believe we are on the brink of revolution here," he said. "From all accounts, Churchill for one is obsessed with the idea."

"God help us all!" Munro exclaimed. "Why does everyone keep going on about Churchill? What's it got to do with him? He isn't Secretary of State for Scotland or even Home Secretary."

"No," his friend agreed. "But he is the strongest man in the government after Lloyd George. If he argues for troops, he'll get his way."

Munro nodded thoughtfully. It was his considered opinion that the pugnacious Secretary of State for War and Air harboured no great affection for Scotland. But did this mean a serious confrontation, involving troops and strikers, couldn't be avoided?

"The way you talk," Munro complained, "you'd think that Churchill and all the rest of them in London wanted trouble."

Robertson shook his head firmly. "That's the last thing I intend," he said, reassuringly. "What he has in mind is to prevent it. Churchill believes that the only way the strikers can be deterred from causing more trouble is by providing a show of strength."

Munro sighed. "It'll make a sorry sight on the streets of Glasgow," he remarked. "People in this city are loyal to the Crown, doesn't Churchill realise that?"

"It doesn't take many people to start a stir," Robertson retorted, lightly. Then: "There's a story circulating in London, apparently, that a number of important people think we should shoot the Kaiser."

Munro stared at him, disbelieving.

"It's true," Robertson assured him. "An impeccable source from inside the American embassy reports that senior people in government think it's the only appropriate course of action, now that we've won the war."

"They blame him for the war, presumably?"

Robertson shrugged. "Who else?" he demanded.

"They've been looking at too many posters," Munro suggested drily.

His friend looked shocked. "Do you question the veracity of our propaganda?" he inquired seriously.

"Not for a moment," Munro retorted. "I believe everything the government tells me. Don't you?"

"Of course," Robertson agreed, solemnly.

"Pity about Kitchener," Munro said.

Robertson nodded gravely.

Munro glanced round the bar, to make sure no-one else was listening to their conversation, and grinned.

"You may be surprised to learn that Mr Churchill is against the idea," Alick Robertson continued.

Munro looked genuinely puzzled. "What idea?" he inquired.

"Them wanting to shoot the Kaiser," Robertson told him, mildly exasperated.

"I'm glad," Munro responded. "I imagine the Kaiser will be pleased."

Robertson thought for a moment. "Can you imagine someone descending by accident on that dreadful hat?" he inquired, suddenly.

"He doesn't wear a hat," Munro objected.

"That thing on top of his head," Robertson explained.

Frank Munro treated his friend to a withering look. "That thing, as you call it, is a helmet," he declared.

"Ouch!" Robertson grimaced, imagining himself as the one descending.

"Sore, was it?" his friend inquired, with mock concern.

They both laughed.

"Anyway," Robertson remarked, growing serious, "it appears that Lloyd George isn't so sure."

"About what?"

"That Churchill is right."

Munro smiled happily. "That's good as well," he replied. "Churchill isn't often right."

"People in London say that Lloyd George would be quite happy to shoot the Kaiser."

"Not personally," Munro objected, shaking his head. "I don't believe it."

"That's not what I said," Robertson protested.

"No, it isn't," his friend admitted.

Alick Robertson thought for a moment. "Why shouldn't we shoot the Kaiser?" he asked.

"There would be no point," he was told.

"Do we need a point?"

Munro grinned. "Evidently the Kaiser's helmet needs a point," he said.

"Don't be flippant," his friend ordered. "I am asking you a serious question. Should we shoot the Kaiser?"

"What good would it do?" Munro demanded.

Alick Robertson brushed his objection aside. "Who cares about good?" he retorted. "What about revenge?"

"I discount revenge," Frank Munro admitted.

"Why?"

Munro beckoned to the barman to bring them another two drinks. "I don't like the idea of revenge for its own sake," he explained.

Robertson nodded thoughtfully. "Think what he did to us," he said.

"What did he do?"

Robertson stared at him, disbelieving. "Have you forgotten the war?" he demanded.

"That was him?"

Robertson nodded.

"The Kaiser did that? All by himself?"

"Who else?"

Munro sighed. "What was it you were saying about propaganda only a moment ago?" he inquired.

"I've forgotten," Robertson told him.

Frank Munro shook his head. "I don't have the energy for revenge," he observed. "I'm just thankful the whole thing's finished," he added, putting a hand on his friend's shoulder to prevent him from paying for the extra drinks.

Robertson looked puzzled. "So what do we do about the Kaiser?" he insisted.

"The Kaiser is irrelevant," Munro replied. "Nobody in their right mind cares about the Kaiser."

Then, as Alick Robertson was about to engage in further argument, Munro lifted the newly-arrived whisky and offered a toast.

"Not any more," he said.

They drank.

Alick Robertson smiled. "You're right, of course."

"Of course."

"Come on."

Rain fell in a steady drizzle as they walked to Huntly Gardens by way of Saltoun Street. Munro shivered and cursed quietly under his breath: January always left him with a cold, he thought miserably.

Alick Robertson's house occupied two floors, with a basement, and there was a large walled garden at the rear in which he cultivated roses and where his wife, May, grew vegetables. Munro liked the house but thought it too large for their needs. Robertson opened the front door cautiously, trying not to make too much noise.

"It wasn't my fault," he cried anxiously, as his wife emerged from a downstairs room and came to meet them. "He's the one that was late," Robertson went on, indicating Munro entering the house behind him, and pretending alarm. "Arrived barely five minutes ago. We rushed back straight away. How is everybody?"

Ignoring her husband, May Robertson reached forward to offer Munro a kiss. "Were you late, Frank?" she inquired gently.

"I'm afraid so," Munro admitted. "Perhaps not quite as late as Alick suggests. But I was held up at the office. I'm sorry," he added lamely.

"Don't be," Mrs Robertson smiled. "It's so good to see you."

Munro reached inside his coat and produced a box of chocolates.

"Oh, Frank," his hostess cried, smiling happily. "You shouldn't have gone to so much trouble."

She turned to look at her husband. "I can't think when last Alick bothered to bring me chocolates," she complained.

Robertson glanced at his friend, who shrugged apologetically.

"The others are waiting," Mrs Robertson went on, leading them into the room she'd just left. "Margaret's dying to meet you."

"Bog Irish, of course," Alick Robertson informed him with a chuckle.

His wife turned to rebuke him sternly. "Alick!" she warned. "That's enough! I won't tell you again."

Robertson grinned.

May Robertson sounded determined. "I mean it," she said firmly.

Robertson nodded and shrugged, defeated.

Munro followed Mrs Robertson into the lounge. "Here, everybody!" he heard her cry.

The Robertsons' youngest son, David, was standing in front of a white marble fireplace which dominated the room, talking to a woman in a dark blue dress. David Robertson was twenty-two and studying to be a doctor. Before the war it was his ambition to be a surgeon. Then while serving with the Royal Scots at the Battle of Ypres, in the last full year of the war, he lost his right arm. A few months ago, at a party to celebrate is parents' wedding anniversary, drunk, the boy confided in Munro, "People don't have much faith in one-armed surgeons, I'm afraid." Then he laughed at his own misfortune, thankful that it hadn't been worse.

Now he turned to meet Munro, left hand outstretched. "Uncle Frank, I haven't seen you in ages," he complained.

Munro smiled, reaching out with his own left hand to greet the boy and conscious, as always, of a feeling of deep regret which he managed, somehow, never to reveal.

David's mother pushed between them. "Frank," she said in a gushing voice, and clearly enjoying the moment, "I want you to meet Margaret Armstrong. Margaret, this is Frank Munro, the man we've been telling you about. He's an old rascal, if you want to know the truth, but I think you'll like him."

With some relief, Frank Munro realised that the woman's embarrassment just about equalled his own. He heard himself say, in what sounded a firm enough voice, that he was pleased to meet her. Margaret Armstrong smiled, extending her hand, which he took.

May Robertson beamed at them. "I was so sure you two would like one another," she cried. "I told Alick not to worry, didn't I, Alick?"

Her husband scowled. "You're the one that was worried," he said.

# CHAPTER SEVEN

The tiny ferry sat halfway up long wooden steps which narrowed toward the water; high wooden walls on either side. It was already dark and the steps were lit by a single lamp, which glowed blue against the night, illuminating refuse from the river, bobbing in the quay.

As often happened, the strength of the tide, supported by a cold, sharp wind, tugged at the forward end of the ferry, causing the little craft to shift on the rope which held it, rising and falling against the steps that were wet and dangerous.

Willie McGrandle descended them recklessly, two at a time, ducking to avoid the iron bar supporting the lamp, and jumped the last two feet as the ferry rose to meet him. Safely aboard, he chuckled delightedly, pleased with himself and his small victory, and moved to stand against the engine housing. Located in the middle of the ferry it offered a little warmth, as well as protection from the wind, once they were away from the quay and out in the open river.

McGrandle fumbled in the pocket of his thin jacket in search of his watch. It had a large face, with roman numerals, encased in dull pewter. The meeting he was due to attend had been fixed for eight and McGrandle didn't want to be late. Punctuality was a cornerstone of Willie McGrandle's ambitions. He believed that it indicated dependability and consideration for others: if you were always on time, people noticed. Anyone who made a habit of being late couldn't be trusted to provide dependable leadership; usually it meant they were disorganised and unsure of themselves.

McGrandle wanted to be a politician. More specifically, his heart was set on the House of Commons. Friends, aware of his ambition, thought it an impossible dream; although he had been told that people who knew him well, and admired him for his qualities of honesty and decency, and hard work, when he could find the work, hoped it could be achieved one day; not just to satisfy McGrandle's

57

aspirations to better things, they said, but for the sake of themselves and people like them; which suited McGrandle.

The one thing Willie McGrandle thought he understood perfectly, and believed absolutely, was the notion that all working people, not just in Britain, but everywhere, were the victims of an unscrupulous and self-perpetuating ruling class. They were the ones who controlled the wealth of the country, the land and the factories: what his friend, Derek Taylor, who lectured at the university, called the means of production. The workers owned nothing, not even the houses in which they lived.

McGrandle had been recruited into the Labour Party soon after starting work by a man on the same squad whose best friend was a communist. Their endless talk about politics, voices rising angrily in the course of a debate otherwise deemed to be friendly, fascinated McGrandle; although, later, thinking about what he'd overheard, McGrandle was forced to the conclusion that he couldn't detect much difference in their aims or their arguments.

The reason he settled for the Labour Party, initially, at any rate, was because of Keir Hardie. He had been taken to hear the veteran politician, who had helped start the Labour Party, speak at a rally in the St Andrew's Halls shortly before the war, and left enthralled by the power and personality of the man; and the density of his vision.

The fact that Keir Hardie, a man born in Lanarkshire, who had been sent to work in the pits while still a child, was already a Member of Parliament also impressed McGrandle. It angered him to learn that Keir Hardie attended parliament as the representative of a Welsh constituency, having previously held a London seat: the first socialist to win a seat in the House of Commons should have been a Scotsman representing a Scottish constituency. For as long as anyone needed Scottish constituencies at Westminster, what was wrong with having a parliament in Scotland, anyway? A parliament of Scots speaking for Scots. The idea intrigued McGrandle. But while Westminster was the place to be, then Willie McGrandle was determined to follow Keir Hardie's example.

Joining the Labour Party, which was growing in strength all the time, or so McGrandle judged from the reports in the newspapers, and the talk in the yards, offered the best means to this end. He knew that people liked him. His strategy was to build on this advantage; the rest of his philosophy he was constructing, a bit at a time, with the help of a rare book which had been circulating in the yard recently, called *The Ragged Trousered Philanthropists*, written by a man named Robert Tressell who was said to be dead.

McGrandle himself was twenty-three years old and a ship's plumber to trade. He was currently employed by Alexander J. Stephen, in their yard at Linthouse, where he was originally apprenticed, on a ship for the navy. Although the war in Europe was over, it appeared that the gentlemen of the Admiralty wanted their vessel delivered on time, or earlier, if the yard managers could work miracles, and if the forty-hour strike didn't otherwise get in the way.

Willie McGrandle grinned, picturing the scene in London, and trying to imagine their Lordships' anger. Fat chance them getting the bloody thing on time, he told himself cheerfully, and began to whistle.

The ferryman emerged from the little engine house where he had been ensconced with the engineer, away from the cold. Two men crewed the ferry, one of them minding the engines, which could be temperamental, while the other steered, exposed to the weather. If the ferry moved at a set time, it was a mystery unresolved by its regular passengers, who accepted, without ever making a fuss, that the little craft would cross to the other side when the ferryman was ready and considered it time; and not a moment before.

Heavy traffic made the river dangerous at all times. Huge cargo ships, going at speed and unable to stop, were liable to cross in front of the ferry from either direction. To begin the two hundred yard wide crossing of the river, with the tide running treacherously, and a forty thousand ton cargo vessel approaching, demanded fine judgment, nerve, care and experience, not to mention a good understanding of the ferry's capabilities which were sometimes unpredictable. Being aware of all this, Willie McGrandle was always happy to let the ferryman decide; although his own desire for punctuality made him wish the man would spend less time thinking about it and convey him to the northern side of the river without further delay. Easier to find a snowball in hell than a teuchter in a hurry!

McGrandle cursed silently. He subscribed to a general prejudice, cheerfully accepted, and widely promulgated in Glasgow, that highlanders, as a race, were lazy and not to be trusted. Certainly, there was no doubt in his mind that they were very different people from lowland Scots, particularly native-born Glaswegians, of whom McGrandle was one and proud of it. McGrandle knew nothing of the systematic, and continuing, destruction of the highland way of life by unscrupulous landlords, unhindered by indifferent government, all of whom preferred to leave the land to ruin and sheep. If he had known about the clearances, McGrandle might have thought differently about highlanders generally, and the old ferryman in particular. But all McGrandle knew was what he saw every day: highland families, who had been driven from the islands and northern parts of the country, down to the city, which most of them hated, but needing work, who refused to mix with anyone else, preferring to keep to their own circle of family and friends with a similar background; trying, against all odds, to maintain their own language and, in some cases, their own fierce church.

"It's a cauld night," McGrandle offered, thrusting his hands deep into his trouser pockets. The ferryman stared at him.

"Aye," the ferryman said, unconcerned, "an' it'll get caulder still."

He was a solid-looking man, stockily built, who walked with a slight limp. He wore a thick, heavy coat, which reached to his hips, and gloves. Close-cropped white hair showed beneath a small, peaked cap. McGrandle had been told, by someone who seemed to know, that he was a retired seaman from Uist, a widower, who lived with his married daughter in Partick. The daughter herself had been widowed when her husband was killed, fighting with the Highland Light Infantry at Beaumont Hamel in some of the worst fighting of the Somme, leaving her to raise twin boys and a wee girl.

"Are you in a hurry the night?"

McGrandle nodded. "I'm due at a meeting," he explained.

The ferryman looked at him for a moment. "Aye," he said. "All right, then, let's get started. We won't bother waiting for anyone else. If they're in that much of a hurry, they can always swim," he added with a grin.

Because it gave him something to do, and was part of the ritual of being the only passenger, McGrandle followed the ferryman to the outward end to help check for traffic on the river. To the east, in the direction of the city centre, probably on its way from Queen's Dock, lights on the bridge and mast distinguished the shape of a large cargo vessel against the dark sky. "Need to hurry," the ferryman muttered.

McGrandle returned to his position against the engine house wall on which the ferryman banged twice to indicate that he was ready. The unseen engineer, who was responsible for what went on inside, understood; the engine spluttered, coughed, and was ready. Some reverse thrust took the ferry higher onto the quay steps, helping to release the heavy rope which the ferryman unhitched from an iron pin. He turned and, as the ferry rose on a swell, thin smoke stuttering from its stack, he jumped nimbly aboard.

The ferry was already clearing the protective walls of the quay as the ferryman brushed past McGrandle, heading for the wheel. A wheel at both ends allowed the ferry to be driven forward, from either bank, without having to turn in the middle of the river. Now the ferryman spun the wheel, hard, and urgently fighting against the current which was trying to force them downriver, pulled away from the quay on the opposite side.

McGrandle found himself staring at the safety of the southern bank which they'd abandoned; knowing that, to his left, the approaching bulk of the cargo vessel, no longer a shadow, was growing huge, filling the river. McGrandle knew what was happening: it was a game all the ferrymen played. The freighter, ploughing toward them on its way to the open sea, barked a warning.

McGrandle moved forward to stand with his back against the front of the wheelhouse. He could see figures moving on the bridge, the reflection of lights from crew quarters on the port side, falling on dark, rippling water. The men on the bridge would have seen them: they probably understood the game. But McGrandle knew that there was nothing they could do to save them if the ferryman got it wrong.

Once again, the ship's warning cry carried across the quiet of strike-dead yards on both sides of the river, over the half-finished hulls of ships unborn, and vanished into the city.

It wasn't the first time McGrandle had been involved, as a helpless, committed spectator, with much to lose, in this dangerous game of tig. He knew what would happen if the ferryman got it wrong: a collision would make matchwood of the ferry; the rest he preferred not to think about. Of course, excitement generally stopped short of becoming fear on these occasions because everyone assumed that the ferryman would get it right. In the event of him being on board when one of the half-dozen men who regularly crewed this stretch of river betrayed this trust, McGrandle had long ago discounted any possibility of swimming to safety. Nor, he reasoned, would it be the hull smashing against his head which would kill him; or finding himself caught in the propellers, as he would be dead already. No, he explained to friends with a laugh, one mouthful of the filth-laden Clyde would be enough.

McGrandle understood, of course, that it was the kind of joke people make to discourage serious consideration of real horror; like the kind of thing he was experiencing now. As the bow of the freighter loomed above them, anchors visible on both sides, he felt certain that the old seaman from Uist had misjudged the current, or the distance, or the speed of the approaching vessel, and they were all doomed; himself, the ferryman and the engineer, who was possibly unaware of the danger, and whom he hadn't even seen.

Then suddenly, one more spin of the wheel, one last, desperate lurch, engines thrusting, the current helping now: the Clyde itself was on their side, McGrandle thought; and, finally, they were clear.

Starboard lights flickered on the water: the murderous bow was already out of sight, hidden by the hull. McGrandle found himself cheering, and waving at lascar seamen high overhead, leaning on the ship's rail, and no doubt thinking that the inhabitants of this strange city were mad. The man on the bridge barked his annoyance; or maybe it was admiration, McGrandle thought, considering the old ferryman's cool nerve.

The sound of the engine changed. They were approaching a set of steps more or less identical to those on the southern bank. High wooden walls, the timber splintering, appeared on either side. The front of the ferry bumped against the steps and began to climb. McGrandle lifted the holding-rope, waited for the ferry to settle, and jumped ashore, stopping to drop the loop of the rope across the head of the nearest iron pin. The ferry ran backwards down the steps until it was held by the rope. Then, slowly, it returned to nestle against the lower steps, one side bumping gently against the quay wall. Muck from the river was already collecting around it.

McGrandle turned to look at the old ferryman. "That was close," he remarked, smiling.

"Did you think so?" the other inquired.

McGrandle laughed. "The captain of that big boat must have got a real fright," he said. "Them lascars will have some cleanin' tae dae."

The old man chuckled, enjoying the joke, and turned to head for the engine house. McGrandle called after him, "What about the pilot?" he inquired gently. "Dae ye think he'll put in a report?"

"Why should he?" the old man shouted, without looking round. "He missed us, didn't he?"

McGrandle accepted the logic of the response.

"That's one way of putting it," he smiled.

The old man shrugged.

McGrandle, aware of sounding amused at the ferryman's expense, hoped he hadn't offended the old man. But he needn't have worried. The ferryman turned to look at him. "Enjoy your meeting," he said, with a grin.

McGrandle nodded. "Have a good night," he said.

A young couple in their teens were descending the steps to await the return crossing. The old ferryman disappeared inside the engine house; McGrandle hoped there was a brew on the go.

From Pointhouse Road, with its lumber yards and storage sheds casting strange shadows into the night, he headed towards the fashionable residential district around the River Kelvin and a house in Landsdowne Crescent.

# CHAPTER EIGHT

Following dinner they moved from the dining-room, with its large teak table and uncomfortable, matching chairs, to the lounge, where a coal fire burned in a narrow grate. An expensive-looking, heavily patterned paper, purple in colour, covered the walls and a large plaster rose dominated the centre of the ceiling. A picture rail ran all the way round the room, several oils in ornate frames hanging from it including a seascape by William MacTaggart which Munro much admired. Four lantern shades of frosted amber glass, in a heavy brass fitting suspended from the plaster rose, filled the room with shadows.

Munro and Margaret Armstrong had been persuaded to share a three-seater couch drawn up in front of the fire. Munro could feel the soft cushions shifting under them whenever one of them moved. Margaret Armstrong was in her late forties, Munro guessed. She had dark hair, greying slightly, tied in a bun at the back of her head. The blue dress concealed her figure.

"We have the same trouble at home," Margaret Armstrong asserted in a firm voice, the accent unmistakably Belfast. "It's bound to get worse as well."

"So you expect the whole country to stop work?" David Robertson inquired, thoughtfully. "You think there will be a general strike?"

"It's bound to come," Margaret Armstrong replied, frowning. "Don't you agree?"

The way she kept frowning, concentrating her mind on the issues being discussed, amused Munro. Women who displayed a deep interest in politics were normally quite tiresome, and never vivacious. However, to his surprise, Munro found himself liking Margaret Armstrong. The fact that she and May Robertson, who normally professed no interest in politics, least of all the role of women in the affairs of the state, had been friends at school also surprised him.

Memory making her smile, it was May Robertson who volunteered that Margaret Armstrong's father, now dead, had been a weaver and the family lived in Paisley for a spell. It occurred to Munro that in both places where the weaver had settled with his brood, people took their politics seriously. More than likely, he thought wryly, watching her frown again, Margaret Armstrong's political awareness was developed on her father's knees.

"Of course," Alick Robertson reminded them from his position beside the fire, "Ireland is a different issue. It's a special problem. It has nothing to do with what is happening here in Scotland. On Clydeside," he added, looking at Munro.

"In Ireland religion gets in the way of everything," Munro observed, trying to be helpful.

"Are you surprised?" Margaret Armstrong inquired firmly.

Alick Robertson sounded impatient. "I'd rather we could forget about Ireland," he said. "That's a separate problem. I'm sure Lloyd George will get around to sorting it out eventually. He's got more important things to worry about right now."

"You think so?" Margaret Armstrong responded sharply. "I don't think you should make the mistake the English have made for centuries," she advised, her voice serious. "The problem of Ireland will not go away. Things aren't that simple. People feel maltreated. They want a different life for themselves and their children. They want to be free of Britain, England especially. Do you have any idea how much most people in Ireland actually hate the English? How much they despise them?"

"What do you suggest the English should do about it," Munro inquired, "assuming they care enough to be interested?"

Margaret Armstrong stared at him for a moment, considering the question, and at the same time quite evidently trying to make up her mind about him. Finally, in a low voice, she replied, "Leave Ireland to the Irish."

Munro returned her stare and Margaret Armstrong understood that it was her turn to be judged. He waited for her to finish.

"We'll sort it out," she continued. "The British can never impose peace on Ireland. So long as they are there, the killing will never stop," she added flatly.

"You don't think the British have some rights in the matter?" Alick Robertson demanded, his voice rising.

"No," Margaret Armstrong replied firmly. "None."

"We have people there!' her host protested loudly.

65

"In Ireland what we have are the Irish," she told him quietly. "Anyone else living there is a foreigner with a foreigner's rights. Isn't that the same in this country?"

Munro interrupted.

"If that's what you want," he said, "fine. I wouldn't be surprised if Lloyd George himself agreed with you. I don't think the majority of people in Britain give a damn about Ireland."

"Frank!" May Robertson sounded shocked.

"The trouble is we are stuck with each other," Munro added. "You say the Irish problem won't go away. Well, let me tell you something, neither will the English. They're a pretty determined lot. In fact, we probably know as much about them as you. So long as they want to stay, they'll stay. You can keep producing all those martyrs and it won't make any difference. You can go on killing soldiers and that won't help much either. What you need is a negotiated settlement fairly achieved."

"It is our country, remember."

Munro nodded. "But try telling that to the English," he suggested.

"You are talking about a people with hundreds of years in the business of putting down others," Munro continued. "The fact that you happen to live next door doesn't mean they are going to behave like good neighbours. What you've got, they want."

"Why?" Margaret Armstrong wanted to know.

"Because they are an acquisitive shower of bastards, that's why!" David Robertson responded with a laugh.

Her son being the cause of it didn't lessen May Robertson's sense of shock. "David," she scolded, "that's a terrible thing to say. Especially the way you said it."

David Robertson shrugged apologetically and reached forward to touch his mother's hand. "I'm sorry, mother," he told her gently. "But it is true, you know."

"Of course it is true," Alick Robertson declared impatiently. "Everybody knows it's true, so why mention it, David? It's been our misfortune to have them on our backs since the beginning of time, probably. Sooner or later the bastards will get what's coming to them. But that's not what we are talking about here."

Frank Munro suppressed a smile. The look on May Robertson's face told him everything. His friend could expect a reckoning for his conduct later. For the moment, however, Alick Robertson seemed unaware of the bad time which lay ahead.

"Margaret says the yards in Belfast are about to stop work," Alick

Robertson reminded them. "The same is true here, I dare say. Next thing you know, the trouble will spread to Newcastle, then across the country to Barrow. All the time, if you accept this argument, the power workers and the water workers will be coming out as well. Soon we will be without all the public utilities." He glanced round. "What happens then?"

"Chaos," Munro suggested.

"Then some!" Robertson cried. "Don't forget the docks. The docks are bound to be on the strike leaders' list of targets. Think what a national dock strike would mean! In the end we could all starve," he ended in a doom-laden voice.

His wife gave him a fear-filled look. "Could that really happen, Alick?" she wanted to know.

Her husband shrugged. "This country could never support itself," he asserted. "If the docks close down we'll be in real trouble."

It was David Robertson who offered, "For a start, given a dock strike, most of industry would be forced to close down, anyway."

His father nodded. "From what we know already," he said, "Glasgow will certainly shut down. Belfast, too, I suppose," he added, looking at Margaret Armstrong. "Then comes Liverpool and after that, London. Do you really think the government can stand by, with all that happening, and do nothing?"

The question was directed at Frank Munro, who shook his head. "No," he admitted. "But I've always said that they will be forced to intervene finally."

"How?"

The look which accompanied Margaret Armstrong's question demanded an unequivocal reply. Munro stared at her for a moment. Possibly for the first time, and with a suddenness which surprised him, Munro realised that there was only one answer. "In the end, I suppose, they will use what ever means may be necessary to restore order," he told her.

"Including force?"

Munro shrugged. "If force is deemed necessary."

"Which means using troops," Margaret Armstrong pressed.

"How else could they use force?" David Robertson inquired, puzzled.

Margaret Armstrong shrugged. "There's always the police, I suppose," she replied.

"The police aren't armed," David Robertson objected. "You can't exert force without arms."

Margaret Armstrong nodded. "They might find ways," she argued. "But, no, for all practical purposes, you are right. They would need to use troops."

"And they will," Alick Robertson cried, "you can take it from me, they will!"

His friend's outburst surprised Munro. Alick Robertson rarely became so heated over an issue. Perhaps he was privy to information and briefings he did not share. As deputy editor of the paper it was possible, of course.

"Shinwell and the rest of that gang aren't fools," Alick Robertson continued. "They are bound to know what's in store for them. But what about all those people who are prepared to follow them on to the streets by stopping work? Do they realise what will happen to them when the government finally decides to respond?"

May Robertson looked troubled. "Surely you don't believe they would turn soldiers on our own people?" she protested.

Her husband stared at her for a moment. Then, still addressing Munro, he inquired:

"What do you think?"

Munro considered the question, and its implications, carefully. He was aware of Margaret Armstrong, who was sitting next to him, wanting to speak. Alick Robertson kept her quiet with a glance.

"You can't expect the workers not to retaliate if they are attacked," Munro began. "But I don't believe for a moment that Shinwell for one wants that kind of trouble. What he wants is what he says he wants. There is genuine concern all over the place for the plight of men returning from the forces who can't find work. Go into any pub, or down to one of the yards, and you will find that people care desperately about the unfairness of it all. They want improved working conditions, security of employment, and a decent wage. Not surprisingly, they are furious at the landlords for increasing the rents, but when they talk about the government intervening, they mean, naturally, on their side. They think they have right on their side, remember."

"That's a simplistic argument," Alick Robertson retorted, shaking his head.

"I suppose it is," Munro agreed. "However, so far as I'm aware, it isn't the workers who are trying to make the arguments complex. Nor are they trying to use their predicament for political profit. What they are seeking is what they think they need, the minimum required to survive. You can hardly blame them for wanting a decent life, not on the breadline, for themselves and their families," Munro concluded with a shrug.

His friend looked unconvinced. "You didn't answer my question," he complained.

Munro smiled tiredly.

"Well?"

Munro nodded. "You're right, of course," he admitted. "Most of them don't understand the seriousness of their position."

Margaret Armstrong's tone was sharp. "What do you mean?" she demanded.

Munro shrugged. "I told you," he replied. 'The workers assume that Lloyd George will intervene on their side. They haven't stopped to think what will happen if the government supports the employers."

"Do you think Lloyd George will save them?"

Munro shook his head. "No."

Alick Robertson shifted in his chair. "There are plenty of people about who'll welcome the chance to cause trouble," he declared.

"On which side?" Munro inquired, mischievously.

His friend didn't answer.

"Are the strike leaders any good?"

"Wheatley's the best of the lot," Alick Robertson declared with a scowl.

"Don't forget Kirkwood and Buchanan," Munro reminded him.

"Do you both discount Shinwell himself?" Margaret Armstrong inquired, surprised.

"Shinwell's an opportunist," Alick Robertson declared with finality. "He makes a good speech and that's about the end of it."

Frank Munro shook his head firmly. "It would be a mistake to underestimate him," he warned. "He's the man the workers themselves look to for leadership. If you want my opinion, he's the one they trust."

His friend appeared not to be convinced.

"What about Willie Gallacher?" It was Margaret Armstrong who wanted to know.

"Willie Gallacher?" Munro repeated, genuinely surprised. "Why Gallacher?"

"At least we know he's a real communist," Margaret Armstrong replied, her eyes bright.

"So is John Maclean,' observed David Robertson, with a chuckle.

Munro shrugged. "Talk to Maclean about Gallacher," he said, "and he'll tell you that Gallacher is an anarchist."

69

Alick Robertson burst out laughing. "And Gallacher will tell you that Maclean is as mad as a hatter," he laughed.

Margaret Armstrong frowned. "He's been a good friend to Ireland," she protested.

Alick Robertson nodded, sceptically. "Keep one thing in mind," he advised. "John Maclean's interest in Ireland is strictly limited to what Ireland can help him achieve here. He wants to use Ireland to destroy the British empire. So we can have a separate republic right here in Scotland," he added.

The extent of Maclean's ambitions, and the effrontery of the man, seemed to amaze him. "No, there's no doubt about it," Alick Robertson decided, shaking his head in disbelief, "Gallacher's right. The man's off his head."

The depth of his friend's conviction annoyed Munro. There was always a campaign going to discredit John Maclean, he thought. No doubt Willie Gallacher had his own reasons for wanting to isolate his old comrade. Munro decided against arguing, however. Instead he observed: "One thing is true, anyway. John Maclean's health is certainly failing. You can tell, just by looking at him, that he hasn't recovered from his last spell in prison."

Margaret Armstrong was giving him her full attention, he noticed. "Have you seen him recently?" she inquired.

Munro glanced at Robertson, who grimaced. "I spent a whole day with him last Saturday," he said.

"Are you writing something about him?"

"I don't think so," Munro replied.

"That's a pity," Margaret Armstrong responded, frowning.

Alick Robertson looked at her pleadingly. "I think, if you don't mind, it would be better for us not to start on that particular subject," he warned.

A look of concern clouded Margaret Armstrong's face. "Did the authorities really try to poison him, do you think?"

Munro shook his head. "I very much doubt it," he said.

"His friends claim that's what happened," Margaret Armstrong retorted, refusing to be easily dissuaded. "Why are you so sure it didn't happen?"

She was staring at him intently now, urging an explanation.

"Too many people would have been involved for it to remain a secret for long," he told her. "The risk of discovery was too great. Someone was bound to talk. Which is why the story doesn't strike me as being true," he added with a conviction which, in private, he sometimes questioned.

Alick Robertson snorted aggressively, diverting their attention.

"It's nonsense for anyone to suggest that the authorities tried to kill John Maclean," he told them flatly. "The man isn't dead and, God knows, he' a big enough martyr already. But the fact it didn't happen means they didn't try," Robertson added, giving Munro a sinister look.

David Robertson imagined he could feel the weight of his missing arm. "Do you think Shinwell is dependable?" he inquired.

"The men seem to trust him."

"Are they right to do so, in your opinion?"

"Time will tell," Munro replied.

"You like him, don't you?"

Munro nodded.

"You don't think he 's a hothead?"

"He can be a bit impetuous," Munro admitted with a smile.

"Is it true that the men are frightened of him?" David Robertson went on.

"The kind of men you are talking about, David, aren't easily frightened," Frank Munro rebuked him gently.

"I know what you mean," David Robertson said, smiling.

His father scowled. "Shinwell talks tough, that's all," he declared.

"If that's the case there's nothing for you to worry about," Frank Munro suggested impishly.

His friend gave him a suspicious look.

"The whole thing will just fizzle out," Munro explained, grinning. "For all we know it may be that the workers have surrendered already. Even now, as we consider their plight, they could have decided to accept their masters' terms and returned to their toil, whistling happily."

Alick Robertson shrugged, amiably. "All right," he agreed. "So pigs might fly."

May Robertson sighed. "It would be nice if we could avoid a lot of unpleasantness," she said.

The others listened politely.

"Look what happened in Russia," May Robertson added with a shudder. "All those people killed."

She glanced round the room, an anxious look on her kindly face, and, in a voice which betrayed genuine concern, inquired:

"That sort of thing couldn't happen here, could it?"

Her husband looked, and sounded, exasperated. "For goodness sake, May," he cried, "this isn't Russia. It won't happen here."

"How can you be sure?" May Robertson demanded stubbornly. "I don't suppose the Czar thought he was in any real danger until it was too late."

Alick Robertson turned to Munro for help. "Frank, tell May to stop worrying," he pleaded. "See if you can convince her that the Red Army isn't about to come marching down Sauchiehall Street."

May Robertson refused to be silenced in her own home, however.

"You needn't laugh," she declared firmly. "Anything is possible."

"Don't be daft!" her husband cried, shaking his head at her perceived foolishness. "Anybody who tells you that there could be a revolution in this country is talking nonsense. The people wouldn't stand for it," he added vehemently. "They know what's good for them."

"People have changed," May Robertson responded with a firmness which surprised Munro. "They changed with the war."

"I think I need another drink," Alick Robertson said. "What about you, Frank?"

Munro nodded.

"David, can you get them, please?"

David Robertson rose from his chair and bent in passing to brush his lips against his mother's hair. She acknowledged the gesture with a smile and, reaching out to touch him, her hand fell on his empty sleeve. Thought of it always made her insides turn.

"Does anyone actually believe that people were happier before the war?" Margaret Armstrong inquired of no-one in particular.

The question surprised them.

"Don't you?"

"I can't think of a reason."

May Robertson's voice almost broke as she persisted, "But the war changed everything, surely?"

Margaret Armstrong put her fingers to her face. "May," she said, "I'm sorry."

She glanced at David Robertson bringing drinks one at a time. "I didn't mean to be thoughtless."

David Robertson smiled. "I agree with you," he told her cheerfully. "People blame everything on the war and forget what things were like before it started."

His mother looked upset. He put his hand on her shoulder. "Not many people lived like this, Mother," David Robertson added gently.

"They still don't. No, Margaret's right. Happiness was a scarce commodity even then."

Alick Robertson accepted his drink with a nod of thanks. "You would agree, though, David, that people expected less," he suggested.

"Why?" his son demanded with more aggression than he'd intended. "You're not going to tell me that they knew their place, I hope?"

"Something like that," Alick Robertson admitted, giving him a rueful smile.

David Robertson glanced at Munro and shook his head. "Do you agree with Dad?" he asked.

"Never," replied Munro, grinning.

He turned to Margaret Armstrong. "Do you accept that the less people expect in life the happier they are with what they've got?"

She shook her head. "I've never understood why anyone should think so," she said.

David Robertson nodded. "Except, of course, if you happen to start from a position of privilege and authority." He glanced at his father. "It must be comforting to believe that the poor will always continue to sustain you, never threatening to overtake you, or even replace you."

He found his father staring at him. "I didn't know you were a socialist, David," he remarked casually.

David Robertson helped himself to a drink.

Munro glanced at May Robertson and wondered what she was thinking. She caught him looking at her and offered in a bemused voice, "All this talk about politics. Why can't we talk about something that makes us happy?"

"I haven't decided yet," David Robertson was saying, all the time staring at his father. "But a lot of it does make sense."

"Spare me the details," his father ordered. "So long as you remain unconvinced."

He laughed and turned to look at Margaret Armstrong. "Now I'd say that Margaret is a socialist," Alick Robertson declared in a manner which made his wife wince. "No self-doubts there! Is that right, Margaret?"

"Of course!" Margaret Armstrong replied with great conviction, treating her host to a huge smile.

"I've told you before," Alick Robertson went on, clearly enjoying himself, and turning to Munro, "if we aren't careful the women will end up running the country."

Munro laughed, supporting his mood.

May Robertson, however, was less than pleased with her husband's performance. "Alick," she scolded, "a person's politics is their own business. It isn't fair to embarrass Margaret with such questions."

"Nonsense!" Robertson cried. "Margaret doesn't mind in the least. Do you, Margaret?"

Margaret Armstrong shook her head. "It doesn't bother me a bit," she replied, smiling.

"You see," said Robertson, continuing to affect a light mood. "Margaret's way brings self-assurance. She knows her own mind. Isn't that right, Margaret?"

Munro was aware of the familiar little frown clouding her features. Before she could respond to the question, however, Alick Robertson was already addressing his son. "Remember that, David, when it comes to your turn to decide."

David Robertson understood. "I'll keep it in mind, Dad," he promised.

His father turned on Munro. "And you, Frank!" he shouted in a voice loud enough to make May Robertson jump. "What cause do you support?"

"Oh, politics!" May Robertson wailed. "I didn't want us to talk about politics!"

Munro, who had been eyeing his host warily, expecting an attack, raised his glass by way of salute.

"Alick," he said slowly, his voice serious, "you know that I am a simple seeker after truth and cannot give my support to any single party. Our creed forbids it," he added happily, downing his whisky.

Alick Robertson turned away. "You've no doubt guessed," he growled, looking at Margaret Armstrong, "that the man's a liberal."

She chuckled and gave Munro, who had settled at the other end of the three-seater, a look which he found encouraging. He was already aware that he would like to see her again.

"He wants Lloyd George canonised," Robertson told her. "Imagine them making that one, of all people, a saint."

They all laughed.

"Now you know all about us," Margaret Armstrong said, finally, contemplating her host, "what about you?"

Alick Robertson looked startled. "What about me?" he demanded.

"What cause do you support?" Margaret Armstrong insisted, smiling slightly, curious.

Alick Robertson nodded. "You will agree, of course, that interest in a cause demands an interest in politics?" he inquired.

The reply surprised her. She hesitated, suspecting a trap.

"Well?"

"Of course,' she accepted, doubtfully, and with a frown. "I suppose so."

Alick Robertson smiled. "Then how can you expect me to support any cause?"

Margaret Armstrong looked puzzled. "What do you mean?" she asked.

"Well," said Alick Robertson, "the truth of the matter is that I have no real interest in politics. I thought you might have noted this."

Margaret Armstrong sounded genuinely surprised. "I don't understand," she said.

"Certainly not your kind of politics," Alick Robertson added.

"What, then?" she inquired.

"When you talk about politics," Alick Robertson explained, "what you have in mind is a force for change. You believe in equality, I imagine, and fair shares for all. No doubt, you also believe that given power, you and your friends can produce a programme which will achieve all the marvellous results your hearts desire."

Margaret Armstrong frowned. "That's what people want," she declared.

"Ask them if they would like more and most people will say yes," Alick Robertson agreed. "But follow that road and nothing changes. The problem, which we can all identify, comes when you decide to take something from one group of people and give it to another."

"How else can we redistribute the wealth of the country?" she demanded quickly.

"A pretty problem, right enough," Alick Robertson sighed. "You tell me."

Margaret Armstrong stared at him for a moment. "Would you listen?" she inquired, finally.

Alick Robertson smiled slightly. "I always listen," he assured her.

She nodded. "But do you ever heed the arguments?"

Alick Robertson stared at her, and thought for a moment. "When it comes to people generally, and what they want for themselves, I find them unconvincing," he said, finally.

"I see." Margaret Armstrong responded with a shrug, and looked away.

Frank Munro broke the silence which followed with a cheerful laugh. "You see," he said, trying to reassure Margaret Armstrong, "what we have in our midst is that rare phenomenon, a caring, thinking Tory."

Alick Robertson sounded unrepentant. "It is in order to obtain the best for themselves, and their class, that people generally take an interest in the system which provides it, don't you agree? Tories, and not just Tories, but most people with any sense, if you want to know the truth, will resist any change so long as the status quo is in their favour."

He waited, expecting dissent. When none was forthcoming, he looked at each of them in turn, raised his glass, and continued, "Tories are the only people in modern politics who make any sense."

Frank Munro objected dutifully: "Tories are interested in themselves and other Tories, nobody else."

May Robertson sighed. "The pair of them never stop," she complained, hoping for peace, and rubbing her hands together, fitfully.

Her husband paid no attention. "I don't deny it!' he cried, turning to gaze at Margaret Armstrong and making her frown, a response which Robertson didn't seem to notice, or chose to ignore.

"Don't you think it's a demonstration of the good sense I've just been talking about?" he inquired with a smile.

# CHAPTER NINE

When he arrived at the house in Landsdowne Crescent, where the meeting had been arranged, Willie McGrandle found three other men, representing electricity, water and the tramwaymen, already there. McGrandle had been invited to speak on behalf of the shipyard workers, but unofficially, as only a handful of the men he represented as a shop steward were aware of the meeting taking place.

It was Derek Taylor, their host, who arranged it. Taylor was known to McGrandle and the others for his work on behalf of the socialist cause; although, so far as anyone knew, he wasn't a member of any political party.

Taylor and his wife, and two young children, lived in a large basement house, beneath a smart terraced villa, with access stairs dropping sharply from the level of the gardens in Landsdowne Crescent. Compared to his own home, a room and kitchen flat, which McGrandle shared with his parents, a younger brother, and two teenage sisters, the basement appeared enormous.

An Englishman by birth, Derek Taylor worked as a lecturer in economics at the university. McGrandle could remember meeting him for the first time, shortly before Christmas, following a rally in St Andrew's Hall at which McGrandle was one of the main speakers. The meeting had been organised to focus public attention on the plight of men returning from the war, finding themselves out of work, and the cost of living rising.

Willie McGrandle understood that most of those present despised the bosses, the employers and their toadies, in which category they numbered the managers and foremen; and he spiked his speech with hatred of those who made money from the war. He also made a point of attacking the government and the generals, particularly the commander-in-chief, Field Marshal Sir Douglas Haig, for their conduct of the war.

The war and its aftermath were unpopular on Clydeside and, as McGrandle expected, his audience, largely working class, roared approvingly when he castigated the governing classes as the people responsible for the national misery.

McGrandle had been careful not to go too far, however, and provide the authorities with an excuse to arrest him on a charge of sedition. He had been warned that the Chief Constable's men would be attending the rally in force, patrolling the corridors, and lurking at the back of the hall, just waiting to pounce.

Martyring himself to a long period of imprisonment, amounting to months or even years, wasn't part of Willie McGrandle's plan for the future. That would be time wasted, in his opinion. The great John Maclean had been destroyed by prison. McGrandle was determined the same thing wouldn't happen to him.

He believed, honestly enough, that his place was outside prison, in the yards and on the streets, or making speeches at meetings, large and small, in the St Andrew's Hall, or any place else where people wanted to assemble and listen; recruiting converts to the workers' cause, stiffening resolve and laying the foundations of a movement which would respond spontaneously one day and overthrow the established system. It also occurred to him that with John Maclean out of the way the future leadership of the working class in Glasgow belonged elsewhere. With himself, perhaps.

Following the rally, as the audience gathered in groups in the street, stamping their feet against the cold, Willie McGrandle was standing outside the main entrance to St Andrew's Hall when Derek Taylor approached and congratulated him on his speech.

McGrandle was wary of anyone from a different social class who showed an interest in his opinions, and Taylor's educated manner, and soft English accent, encouraged suspicion. He guessed that Taylor, who was stoop-shouldered and balding prematurely, was in his early thirties; a real pest, in all probability.

Nevertheless, he thanked the other man politely for taking an interest in the workers' struggle, him being a professional man, as he and his friends could see, and the workers needing a lot of support from that quarter; and wondered coldly what else the man wanted.

Derek Taylor must have sensed McGrandle's hostility. He made a point of not being rebuffed, however. Smiling cheerfully against the cold, he informed McGrandle that he thought his speech extremely good; inspirational, as a matter of fact, and certainly one of the best he'd heard from the stage of the St Andrew's Hall.

McGrandle was staggered to be on the receiving end of so much praise. He thought for a moment that Taylor was indulging himself in some elaborate joke at his expense. But no, he decided finally, the man meant it.

McGrandle blinked and glanced anxiously at his companions, feeling certain that they were bound to consider Taylor's response to his speech somewhat overblown, to say the least. However, none of them offered any objections, or attempted to shift Taylor from his golden opinions, and McGrandle tried hard not to look flattered.

Derek Taylor then let it be known that he was encouraged to discover that he and McGrandle shared a common awareness of the supreme irony of recent years: namely, that working people didn't seem to mind being slaughtered in defence of empires whose benefits accrued to people who were already rich. He also disliked the little Field Marshal and thought it ludicrous the way honours were being heaped upon his head; with more on the way, no doubt, Derek Taylor concluded pessimistically.

Willie McGrandle agreed, nodding enthusiastically. Next thing, bet your life, he suggested, and they would be inviting the workers to contribute to his retirement sheet. This remark made everyone laugh.

Imagine someone going round the yards seeking donations for Haig, one of the men suggested. Willie McGrandle chuckled grimly. Poor bastard! He'd finish in the river, sure enough, the other man insisted happily. They all continued to laugh among themselves for a moment. Derek Taylor was conscious now of McGrandle and his friends relaxing a little in his company.

Of course, he continued carefully, while it was true to say that he agreed with almost everything McGrandle said in his speech, there were a number of points on which he would be prepared to take issue.

McGrandle stared at him doubtfully. He was aware of his friends listening carefully, anticipating a joke at his expense, perhaps. Ever since it became generally known that he wanted to become a Member of Parliament, mates from school, and at work, never missed an opportunity to ensure that his feet stayed on the ground; it was their way of reminding him that he wasn't a genius, whatever he liked to think. The women were just as bad, except for his own mother, who believed he could be anything he wanted; but was fearful of seeing him hurt by the failure of so great an ambition. She didn't think it possible that he could reach Parliament, not with his background: in her eyes it was a dream, a boy's dream. But if that's what he wanted, she didn't object to him dreaming, and prayed he might succeed. So Willie McGrandle continued to dream, and scheme, certain in his own mind at least that his ambition would be realised; in time. For the moment, however, he wished his friends would refrain from going into their act in front of a stranger.

It was Taylor who suggested another meeting to discuss the points he had in mind. The development of socialist theory in all parts of the world was one of his hobbies, Taylor explained. At home he kept a library of pamphlets, written by people in England, as well as translations from abroad, which McGrandle might not have seen and would find interesting.

Unsure of his ground, McGrandle was reluctant to commit himself at first. But the other man was persuasive. What he wanted, in particular, was an opportunity to discuss some of his own ideas with McGrandle. He felt certain that McGrandle could bring a different perspective to a number of problems he was currently considering: any discussion was bound to be of benefit to them both, Taylor added. He produced a card on which was printed his name and address. McGrandle told him where he lived in Aboukir Street, Govan. That done, Taylor remained chatting generally for a few minutes outside St Andrew's Hall, before continuing on his way.

McGrandle didn't really expect to hear from him again and was surprised, a day or two later, to receive a short letter inviting him to visit Taylor at his home.

Seated in front of an open coal fire in Derek Taylor's sparsely-furnished front room, McGrandle noted that there were real paintings on the wall and bookcases, loaded with volumes, all the way to the ceiling. Taylor's wife appeared after a few minutes and welcomed him warmly. She was a slim, brown-haired English girl named Susan, who brought them tea in a china pot, with matching cups, and an assortment of biscuits and sandwiches on a silver stand. There was a schoolboy son, aged seven, called William, who attended Kelvinside Academy, and a baby daughter not quite four, named Amanda, they told McGrandle. The children were dying to meet him, Susan Taylor said, but she liked them in bed early, and they were sorry to miss him. He could meet them some other time, perhaps. McGrandle nodded and helped himself to a sandwich.

Susan Taylor smiled. She had been fascinated to learn from her husband that McGrandle wanted to become a Member of Parliament.

Derek believed it was only a matter of time before the workers ruled the country, Susan Taylor continued. She thought Derek would make a marvellous MP, but he didn't agree. Derek Taylor chuckled. Sometimes he thought what his wife wanted was him in London all week, out of the way, he remarked to McGrandle. Susan Taylor laughed cheerfully and invited McGrandle to help himself to another sandwich. McGrandle told them it was a pity MPs were forced to travel to London at all. What was wrong with having a parliament in Glasgow, or Edinburgh, he added, seeing Susan's puzzled look. She nodded and smiled: her husband agreed that a parliament in Edinburgh, considering it was the capital of Scotland, would be a good idea. McGrandle conceded the claims of Edinburgh over Glasgow willingly enough, and they all laughed. Finally, Susan Taylor announced that there was work to be done in another part of the house, and left them to talk, seeking a promise from McGrandle that he would come again sometime and meet the children, on her way out. Derek Taylor yawned and stretched. Whisky? he inquired.

McGrandle let his host do most of the talking. The difference in their education and social background didn't seem to trouble Derek Taylor as much as it bothered McGrandle, especially at first. McGrandle's formal schooling finished at fourteen and there was never any question of him going to university: his family needed him out at work, earning a wage to help feed them. However, there appeared to be no side to Taylor, so far as McGrandle could tell from their brief time together, and he soon felt comfortable in his company.

It was evident that Taylor was a communist. Several times in the course of that first evening and subsequent meetings, he referred glowingly to the Russian leader, Lenin; and his eyes gleamed with satisfaction when Willie McGrandle disclosed that he had been reading a pamphlet based on the teachings of Karl Marx.

They both agreed that what the country needed, starting immediately, was a national strike, lasting a year if necessary. Only then would the workers be able to demonstrate that the authorities were no longer in control of the country after which the socialists could be placed firmly in power.

When Willie McGrandle pressed the claims of Clydeside as a good place to begin, his host surprised him with the ferocity of his opinions. Nothing would begin on Clydeside so long as Shinwell was in charge, Taylor asserted in a voice cold with venom. It was true that there was no better place for the strike to start than on Clydeside, Taylor agreed, and with the country in chaos following the war, the workers would never find a more appropriate time to show their mettle. Except that Emmanuel Shinwell was currently in charge of the Workers' Strike Committee and his heart wasn't in it.

Derek Taylor shook his head bitterly. McGrandle sipped at his whisky and waited for him to continue. Shinwell, the man who had been given the workers' trust, and placed at the head of their struggle to obtain a forty-hour week, and improved conditions generally, was dismissed by Taylor as an incompetent, gutless braggart, interested mainly in his own advancement; a real twister, Taylor finished sharply. He gave McGrandle a hard look, evidently expecting some spirited defence of the strike leader to be forthcoming. Willie McGrandle didn't argue.

The fact that he wasn't close to Shinwell, and didn't like him personally, was unimportant, McGrandle decided; what mattered to him for the moment was keeping certain of his opinions to himself until he and Taylor were better acquainted.

In the course of that first evening together at Landsdowne Crescent, McGrandle and Taylor kept on talking until well after midnight, finishing the whisky, and establishing general agreement between them on all the important issues of the day.

According to Derek Taylor, what the country required above all else was for the workers to take control of the means of production. He itemised his targets one by one – the factories, the foundries, the shipyards, the mines, the banks and stock markets who controlled the money supply, and all the rich farmland, which was presently owned by a handful of families, with a history going back hundreds of years, when the land had been stolen or given to them by some King. When all of that happened, and not a moment before, Derek Taylor concluded sternly, the workers would be in a position to take charge of their own destiny.

It wasn't impossible, Taylor added, seeing a look of doubt spread across Willie McGrandle's face. Hadn't it happened in Russia? Taylor paused. Wasn't it happening in Germany? If it could happen in Russia and Germany, why not in Britain? Willie McGrandle smiled. The idea of all that happening in Britain sounded good to him.

All it required, according to Derek Taylor, and Willie McGrandle saw no reason to question his obvious conviction, was for a few men of imagination and determination, blessed with strong leadership, to emerge and show everyone else the way. One man could be enough, a very special kind of man, admittedly, Taylor continued, but one man could do it. Given a little luck.

Derek Taylor always smiled when he mentioned luck. Don't forget, he was fond of saying, even Vladimir Ilyich Lenin needed luck. McGrandle noted that whenever his host mentioned Lenin in this way he took great trouble to pronounce the Russian name correctly. The subject of Russia was never far from his mind, it seemed. Once he startled McGrandle by declaring that the Bolsheviks were right to murder the entire Romanoff family; an act of needless, and cowardly, brutality which McGrandle abhorred. No, said Taylor: if they had been left alive and allowed to leave Russia, they would have presented a continuing threat to the success of the revolution.

Their meetings became a weekly routine. Willie McGrandle usually made a point of going to Landsdowne Crescent on a Friday after work and, much to the annoyance of his mother, a meal snatched at home. By the third week it had been agreed that it would add another dimension to their discussions if each of them was allowed to bring someone else along: what they wanted were people willing to become active in the movement, as well as enthusiasts like themselves, with something special to contribute, Derek Taylor explained. It became McGrandle's responsibility to find shop stewards, and other interested trade unionists, who wanted to join them; while Taylor introduced colleagues from the university and an occasional visitor from England.

Now, as everyone who had been invited to the latest gathering sought chairs in Derek Taylor's front room, smoke from the fire curled into the chimney and out into the night. The fire, burning slowly, had been well stacked in anticipation of a long evening; and a full scuttle left on the hearth beside Taylor's usual chair.

"If you ask me," someone remarked cheerfully, "it's cold enough for snow outside."

"That's all we need," grunted the man from the electricity workers as he made himself comfortable on a large sofa which filled the centre of the room.

"I hate snow," Willie McGrandle complained.

Derek Taylor smiled tolerantly. "It might be no bad thing," he suggested, "a little snow. Think of the chaos it can cause."

McGrandle shrugged, unwilling to argue.

"Why don't you sit there, Willie?" Taylor went on, indicating a chair on the opposite side of the fireplace from himself. It was the second-best placed chair in the room and everyone understood that the gesture was intended to establish McGrandle's seniority within the group. McGrandle tried not to appear self-conscious as he settled down opposite his host and waited for Taylor to begin.

"I would like to thank you all for coming," Taylor smiled, glancing at each of his guests in turn. "Susan will bring us some tea about nine-thirty, and there's a drop of something stronger for anyone who wants it, including me, if that's all right."

The others laughed, grateful to him for his hospitality: he was a generous host, never mean with the drinks, as all of them knew.

"In the meantime, who'd like to begin?" Taylor inquired.

He glanced at McGrandle, who shrugged. "All we need to know, I suppose, is whether or not we think we are ready," he suggested.

Derek Taylor nodded vigorously. "My own view exactly!" he cried.

The man from the electricity workers shifted his considerable weight against the back of the sofa. He was a big man, with a drinker's complexion. Taylor glanced at him, expectantly.

"My boys are ready to cut off supplies," the big man reported. "They won't let you down."

Taylor beamed and turned to look at the man, who claimed he could speak for the water-workers, and who had unwisely selected an uncomfortable-looking, low-backed chair slightly to one side of him. "Hector?"

The man chuckled. "All we need is for someone to say the word," he declared, making a fist which he used to punch the air.

Clearly delighted, Derek Taylor rubbed both hands together and looked round the room. "That's great news," he cried.

The man from the tramway workers, called Benny, looking gloomy, decided for some reason to abandon his chair and join the man from the electricity workers on the big sofa. Taylor stared at him.

"A lot of my boys aren't sure," Benny reported carefully.

Taylor waited.

"If you want the truth," the tramwayman continued uncomfortably, "I don't think we can depend on all of them coming out at once."

Taylor was watching him carefully. "I see," he said.

The others were waiting for Benny to continue: he shrugged. "There's not much I can do about it," he told them.

"Do they appreciate the importance of their contribution?" Taylor demanded.

Benny looked away.

"We are all depending on them," Taylor added.

The tramwayman nodded. "Once they hear that everyone else is committed, and things start happening, I'm sure they'll be queuing up to join," he replied hopefully.

Taylor sighed. "Can anyone here help?"

"What do you mean?" Benny sounded puzzled.

"Would it help if Willie spoke to them? They all know Willie."

There was no mistaking the other man's annoyance. "Of course they all know Willie," he retorted. "But I don't think they'll appreciate someone from the yards interfering in their decision. No offence, Willie," Benny added, glancing at McGrandle.

"None taken," McGrandle muttered.

Derek Taylor thought for a moment. Then, with a despairing shake of his head, and speaking quietly, he reminded the tramway representative: "We need them with us, Benny. It is essential that the tramwaymen are seen to be out early, right from the very beginning, in fact. We all agree that it is important for us to minimise traffic movement throughout the city. The quickest way to achieve that is to have trams cluttering all the main thoroughfares. Tell a few of them to jump the points," he added with a smile, wishing to encourage the tramwayman. "I want as many as possible left lying about in the city centre: but once we tell them the exact time we want them to stop on Friday, it doesn't matter where they find themselves, we want them to stop. Is that understood?"

Benny sighed, uncertainly. "I can hear you," he replied.

Taylor looked across at Willie McGrandle. "What's the mood in the yards, Willie?" he inquired.

"One hundred per cent," McGrandle replied briskly. "More if you need it."

"Good."

"Work is at a virtual standstill the entire length of the river," McGrandle went on. "The navy are going frantic, screaming for a frigate that's about six weeks late down at Stephens."

"Let them yell," Taylor chuckled.

"It's the same story all over the place," McGrandle assured him. "You needn't worry about the yards."

Derek Taylor showed his excitement. "That's great news, Willie," he exclaimed. "Precisely the sort of thing we want to hear."

The man from the power workers looked concerned. "One thing worries me," he began.

Taylor stared at him. "What's that?" he demanded.

"Shinwell," the man replied.

Derek Taylor scowled. "What about Shinwell?" he snapped.

"What do we do about him and the others?" the man from the power workers inquired. "The rest of the committee, I mean. Everybody thinks they are the ones in charge."

"Ignore them," he was told. "People will realise the truth soon enough. Nobody gives a damn about Shinwell."

They all laughed.

"You're quite certain the government will support the employers?" It was Benny, from the tramwaymen, who wanted to know.

Derek Taylor nodded confidently. "Absolutely," he replied.

"Lloyd George is sometimes unpredictable," the man from the power workers objected, doubtfully.

Taylor shook his head. "Unpredictable or not," he responded with a grim chuckle, "wouldn't you say he's always known which side his bread is buttered?"

"That's true, anyway," Willie McGrandle remarked, raising another laugh.

Taylor stared at him. "There's too much at stake for the government to concede everything that's been asked," he told them. "It would ruin the country. For once Lloyd George is caught in a trap he can't escape. All the charm and determination in the world won't help him now."

"Then what will we do?"

"When we've closed the yards, and stopped the power and water supplies, and the trams aren't running, then we'll bring in the miners," Taylor told them in a clear, confident voice. "Once the miners are with us, we can't fail. The government knows it can never defeat the miners, not if the miners mean business."

Benny shook his head. "That's not what I meant," he complained.

Derek Taylor looked puzzled.

"Afterwards is what I mean," Benny explained.

Taylor nodded, understanding him now.

"We'll introduce workers' cooperatives in all places of employment and use shop stewards to govern the city," he said, addressing Benny. "The biggest works will each send a representative to the supreme council which will meet daily. Other groups will be allowed to vote to choose a delegate in those cases where the workplace isn't big enough to justify a single representative. Once the supreme council is in place, we will then elect a group of seven to make executive decisions, but reporting back to the supreme council, of course."

He looked round.

"Where will the supreme council meet?" McGrandle inquired, offering Taylor an opportunity to revel in his great plan.

Taylor smiled at him. "In the City Chambers, of course," he announced, in a voice anticipating triumph. "Where else?"

There were mutterings of satisfaction all round, except from the representative of the power workers, who looked troubled.

"What if the government used troops to stop us?"

The others became immediately subdued, reminded once again of the seriousness of their intentions. Derek Taylor rallied them quietly.

"They wouldn't dare," he assured them firmly. "We aren't a bunch of coolies causing trouble in some half-forgotten colony on the other side of the world, remember. This is the second largest city in the empire, don't forget."

Willie McGrandle nodded seriously. "All the more reason they won't want to lose it," he suggested darkly.

Derek Taylor, fearing disloyalty, glanced at him sharply. McGrandle shrugged and turned away.

"At this very minute, don't forget, there are troops stationed in Maryhill Barracks," the big man with the drinker's face from the power workers continued stubbornly. "What if they decided to use them to stop us?"

Derek Taylor smiled patiently. "These are Scottish soldiers, Andrew," he protested gently. "Don't tell me you think the HLI would point guns at their own people? This is their city, remember."

The big man refused to be shifted easily, however. "They might if they were ordered," he insisted. "One thing for you to keep in mind," he added, glaring at Taylor. "These men are sojers and proud o' the name."

Willie McGrandle reacted immediately. "Don't be daft, Andra!" he exclaimed. "Derek's right. They'd be pointing the guns at their ain families. They are all Glesga men born and bred. It's unthinkable."

"Exactly!" Derek Taylor cried, feeling better now about McGrandle, and treating him to a brisk, supportive nod.

Hector, who had been listening attentively, appeared unconvinced. "They could always bring troops from the south," he warned. "Give some of them English half a chance and they'd be in among us, bayonets fixed."

"God help us," Benny wailed.

Derek Taylor glowered at him. "I don't think so," he tried to reassure them, conscious of sounding very English himself. "Think of the consequences for the government. People who might otherwise withhold their support would take to the streets on our side. The whole country would turn against them. Lloyd George daren't risk it, " he added firmly.

Hector, who represented the water-workers, sighed heavily. "We'll find out soon enough, I suppose," he offered philosophically. "Anyway, it isn't the sojers that worry me. Nobody's mentioned the polis. Stevenson and his mob of assorted gorillas could give us a bad enough time on their own, without looking for help from anybody's army, if you ask me. How do you expect Stevenson to react when the trouble starts?"

They all stared at him, waiting for him to provide his own answer.

"The polis won't be inhibited like the sojers," Hector continued in a matter-of-fact voice. "What we intend is precisely the kind of thing they are in business to prevent. It's their job, don't forget, and Stevenson won't be slow to remind them. Remember what he did in Belfast."

"We can beat them, don't worry," Taylor encouraged.

"Just so long as none of us forgets that Stevenson's a mean bastard who won't stand on ceremony," Hector warned. "Once our people take to the streets he won't care who gets hurt."

"It's your job to mobilise the men," Taylor told him. "If our people come out in large enough numbers the police won't stand a chance. They've no experience of dealing with trouble on the scale we envisage."

"I hadn't forgotten," Hector grunted.

"Good," said Taylor, glancing round. "Does anyone else have something they want to say?"

There was no response. Taylor nodded.

"Our time is now," he informed them, importantly. "We will succeed."

He paused, enjoying the effect of his words on his audience; Willie McGrandle, especially, appeared almost ready to burst from his chair with excitement. Wishing to rally them further, and almost carried away by his desire to give them a sense of their own importance, and his feeling that each of them had been summoned by destiny, Derek Taylor continued approvingly: "The lives of every man, woman and child in this country will be affected by what we do here in Glasgow. By our efforts, especially, the lives of working families everywhere will be improved. We will be there at the start of a great new beginning, together."

There was a moment's silence, while the others considered Derek Taylor's rousing sentiments, broken finally by Willie McGrandle.

"I've got a slogan," he offered, shyly.

Derek Taylor nodded encouragement.

"Let Glasgow Flourish," McGrandle began.

Recognising the city's own slogan, the others waited, looking puzzled. Willie McGrandle smiled and raised his fist against imagined oppressors everywhere.

"The Workers Tae!" he shouted.

They were all on their feet cheering when the door opened and Susan Taylor entered, smiling, and carrying the first of the tea things. "Has the revolution started?" she inquired with a laugh.

# CHAPTER TEN

James Verdier Stevenson sat, comfortable and confident, in the rear seat of his official car, on his way to a reception in the City Chambers hosted by the Lord Provost. Stevenson enjoyed dressing up and he was particularly happy when the demands of the day required him to don his best uniform, with its heavily embroidered collar, plumed hat and dress sword.

Stevenson had been Chief Constable of Glasgow for nearly seventeen years. He was a handsome man, moustached, with a high regard for himself and a keen interest in his work. When it came to his duties, Stevenson, despite his flamboyant manner, was known to be tough and uncompromising in his outlook; although some people objected to the fact that he wasn't a Scot, but an Irishman, born in County Westmeath and educated in Dublin.

Stevenson didn't mind.

His reputation as a hardman had been well earned, as head of the local constabulary, in Belfast, and rested largely on the ruthlessness with which he tackled an old problem in that unhappy Irish city, sectarian violence.

Troublemakers soon learned that there was little percentage in going against Stevenson's men, who were usually bigger and stronger, better fed and better armed, and more than a match for them in street fighting. People were warned in no uncertain terms that anyone taking to the streets in open defiance of the law, and engaging in violence which threatened lives and property, did so at their peril.

Confronted with widespread rioting, conducted in the name of religion, Stevenson kept his word. He issued orders to his men that they were to protect themselves at all costs. If, at any time, they were attacked, then it was Stevenson's express wish that they should respond with vigour and determination, and sufficient disregard for the niceties of discipline and self-control to ensure a profusion of broken heads and subdued enthusiasm among the rioters for their cause.

His methods attracted antagonism from all sides, but they worked, and Glasgow, the most important police force in the country outside London, soon beckoned. Stevenson knew, of course, that Glasgow was also divided on religious grounds, protestants against catholics, and he wasn't surprised to find that in many districts age-old animosities offered a constant threat to peace in the city. Again, however, he left no-one in any doubt what his response would be if trouble started.

Nobody suggested he was bluffing, not after Belfast, and even people who didn't know him believed that, in the event of serious civic unrest, Stevenson would do everything in his power to crush the lawbreakers.

For the moment, at least, Stevenson could afford to ignore the familiar battlelines of bigotry, however.

His present concern was how best to deal with the army of pickets which stood guard outside all the big shipyards, at the power stations, the waterworks, and the tramway depots, threatening violence and disorder, their numbers increasing daily. Stevenson knew a few of the strike leaders from official functions and other civic events, across the years, and he had viewed all of them at a distance in recent weeks as they went about their unions' business. From the various reports reaching his desk, and other intelligence gathered privately, it appeared that all of them were set on causing maximum disruption, both to the city and the country as a whole. In his opinion, the very least they wanted was a fight; while the worst of them wouldn't stop at employing the most extreme methods in order to achieve their aims.

Stevenson smiled grimly. If, as everyone expected, the strikers took to the streets and resorted to violence in support of their claims, they'd better remember that he would match force with force; and never on equal terms. Nobody could say they hadn't been warned, he thought.

Through the window of his car he noticed a woman in a high hat struggling to control her veil which had been caught in the wind. Stevenson shifted his own plumed hat in his lap and chuckled at the woman's predicament. It was a good job nobody made him walk, he thought with a smile. Damned foolish he'd look if they did.

The woman disappeared from view and Stevenson realised that they were about to enter George Square. The reception which he was due to attend in the City Chambers had been arranged in honour of VAD nurses who had served with the Highland Light Infantry, the city's own regiment, in France. Everyone said what a marvellous job the nurses did in the war, and weren't the girls brave, and Stevenson was looking forward to meeting a few of them and telling them personally how much he admired their efforts.

His driver approached the City Chambers from the north side of George Square, which was heavy with traffic, passing a tram, and drawing into the kerb immediately outside the elaborate Victorian facade behind which the Town Council met each week to determine the destiny of the empire's second city.

Stevenson eased himself out of the car. "Pick me up at two," he ordered.

His driver stood at attention, holding the open door with his right hand. "Yes, sir," he replied briskly.

The Chief Constable straightened his sword and donned the plumed hat.

"Excuse me, sir."

Dressed in a tweed coat, the tall figure of a young man, who had been hovering near the main door of the City Chambers, moved towards them.

The Chief Constable scowled. He considered it beneath his dignity to be accosted by perfect strangers in the street. Besides, as he was fond of reminding himself and his officers, these were strange and dangerous times. People in his position couldn't be too careful.

Stevenson eyed the young man suspiciously. "What do you want?" he snapped.

Henry Wason smiled, encouragingly. "I wondered if I might have a word with you, sir," he said.

Stevenson looked puzzled. "What do you mean?" he demanded. "A word about what?"

Wason glanced round cautiously. "Do you think perhaps we could go inside, sir?" he suggested politely, indicating the huge iron doors of the City Chambers, behind which a green-uniformed attendant could be seen guarding the foyer.

Stevenson hesitated. There was something rather odd about this young man, both in appearance and manner, he thought warily. Also, he sounded English.

"I won't keep you a minute, sir," Wason added, hurriedly.

Suddenly, the Chief Constable spotted a notebook which had been concealed in the young man's hand. A reporter, Stevenson thought, aghast. Didn't the upstart know that he never spoke to reporters? Journalism was a nuisance trade, in Stevenson's view, and its practitioners best avoided, whatever their rank. However, if it was absolutely necessary, he dealt with editors direct. "How dare you speak to me in the street?" he thundered, his temper rising.

Wason was unable to comprehend the other man's fury. "Pardon?" he stammered, going pale.

"I've a good mind to complain to your editor about this," the Chief Constable continued.

"I don't understand," Wason faltered.

"Get out of my way," the Chief Constable ordered and brushed Wason aside.

As he watched Stevenson disappear through the doors of the City Chambers, his temper almost out of control, Wason felt disappointed and perplexed. He hadn't forgotten that he was under orders not to break cover. He assumed that the Chief Constable, whom he recognised immediately from photographs, was reliable, however.

Now, in view of Stevenson's inexplicable behaviour, Wason found himself questioning this assumption. A perfect opportunity for them to meet and talk, offered by their chance encounter, had been lost, he thought.

He turned to find the Chief Constable's car about to depart. The driver was still eyeing him with suspicion. Wason offered the young policeman a bright smile, loaded with confidentiality, and received a withering look in exchange. The smile died on Wason's lips and with it all feelings of comradeship and cordiality.

Finding a place in the stream of traffic, the Chief Constable's driver headed south. Wason assumed, from the little map of the city, showing all the key buildings, which he had drawn in his notebook before leaving the hotel, that the car was going in the general direction of the river and police headquarters in St Andrew's Square.

Wason watched it go with a growing sense of unease. For the first time since leaving London it occurred to him that he was alone. Alone, he thought desperately, in a city which he didn't really know and where, in all probability, a plot to overthrow the elected government was being hatched. If the Chief Constable himself wouldn't even talk to him, where else could he turn?

It was Wason's first visit to Glasgow since his days as a student at St Andrews University years ago. Then he lived at the home of a friend in Park Gardens. The house had a view of Kelvingrove, and the cranes of shipyards to the south, and was once the home of a tobacco lord.

The so-called second city of the empire was never his favourite place and his memories and knowledge of Glasgow, never extensive, were fuzzy. All morning he had been walking the streets, expecting to find, as a result of the war if nothing else, a drab and sullen sort of place, peopled by listless natives. Instead he discovered a city full of confidence and vigour, the unexpectedness of which unsettled him.

It began the moment he left his hotel and walked along Gordon Street into Buchanan Street. The whole area was a bedlam of noise, filled with every imaginable kind of vehicle, and prosperous people who hurried about their business in a most determined manner. The wide range of shops on view, their windows packed with expensive goods, astonished Wason. He was also forced to admit that the main buildings, especially, were just as handsome as anything he had seen in London. Red and brown sandstone, they boasted mock Grecian columns of inspired design, and were splendidly crafted, particularly around the doorways, windows and rooftops. These and all the other buildings which he found himself admiring as he walked around the city, including the magnificent Victorian sprawl of the City Chambers itself, were probably the legacy of businessmen grown rich on the profits of the empire, Wason decided sniffily; men with a strong sense of civic pride and, he suspected, a desire to be remembered.

He looked across George Square. A huge column, with Sir Walter Scott on top, dominated the central garden area, where old men sat about on benches enjoying the bleak winter sun. The flower-beds looked forlorn and empty. This was the heart of the city. If the strikers wanted to impress the city authorities and the government with their strength and determination, they were bound to march on George Square. How many people would it hold? A hundred thousand at least, Wason reckoned, looking round.

When the worst of the traffic stopped he crossed to the gardens and found a deserted bench. Pigeons gathered hopefully, seeking food. An old man in a thin coat sitting nearby became alert and studied him closely. Wason looked away, hoping to discourage him, and considered his next move.

Churchill evidently believed the future well-being of the country depended upon the success of his mission. At the time he thought the Secretary of State for War and Air was laying his fears on a bit thick just to impress him, and make Wason feel important. But now he wondered.

It was true what people said, of course: Churchill's imagination sometimes outran the world around him. There was no questioning the man's obsession with the Bolshevik threat, for example. But what if his instinct was right on this occasion? Were the forces of revolution already gathering in Glasgow?

It occurred to Wason for the first time that if unscrupulous men and women were plotting to overthrow the government, then he was engaged in something extremely dangerous. To his own great surprise, the thought didn't frighten him, however.

He glanced round George Square. Sun glinted from the front of the City Chambers. As headquarters of the civic authority it was bound to be a prime target.

Wason tried to imagine how the rebels would choose to proceed. It would be a simple enough exercise to block off all the main streets leading to George Square. Once in control of the square and the City Chambers they could hold out for a long time, perhaps indefinitely.

The government couldn't afford to go on arguing, or wait for conclusive proof that Churchill was right. Wason could feel in his bones that this was the kind of place where trouble started. The government must be advised to anticipate trouble and let the army assume control of the city immediately. It would be disastrous if the rebels were allowed to move in first and secure the best positions.

He took a notebook and pencil from his pocket and drew a rough map of George Square and the surrounding streets. Then, to remind himself of the main danger areas, he added the location of the most important buildings, chief among them the Post Office, which occupied the southern side of the square at an angle to the City Chambers. Next he made a note of several places, on top of buildings, and on all the main corners, where he thought troops could be stationed to ensure the authorities kept control of the square, as well as access to the City Chambers.

Before leaving London he had been handed a series of departmental briefing notes with strict instructions from his chief that no-one else should glimpse them. The notes contained the names and allegiances of all the leaders involved in the forty-hour strike, together with information concerning the activities of their closest known associates in other parts of the country. Firm evidence existed of serious agitation in Newcastle and Belfast. Liverpool would be next. The basis of a national organisation had been formed which could be used to subvert the lawful government. All it needed was the right leadership to appear, and a successful coup somewhere else, for the poison to spread. Speakers from Glasgow were in great demand at meetings in all the major cities. Churchill was right to be anxious: Glasgow could be the catalyst.

Something else troubled Wason. For years seditious voices had been raised against the war. In his experience those who followed the socialists' foolish creed always sounded particularly vituperative. They claimed that a corrupt ruling class was to blame for starting the war; while something unknown to Wason, which they always referred to as an international capitalism, was responsible for sustaining the years of suffering. The workers, who had nothing to gain from the senseless struggle, had been duped into taking part with siren calls of patriotism and liberty. People of Wason's acquaintance, who employed this argument and claimed to be socialists, generally made a point of insisting it applied to friend and foe alike: the entire working class of Europe had been recruited as fodder for the guns.

Wason had been excused the war. He wanted to volunteer right at the start but his chief wouldn't allow it. Like everyone else in his department, Wason was required for more important duties elsewhere, Colonel Naismith explained, a little brusquely. The idea of being sent out into the field, to the enemy heartland itself, in the company of Sidney Reilly himself, perhaps, appealed to Wason's sense of wanting something useful to do; dangerous, even. But nothing happened.

He spent the whole of the war, safe in London, checking files; and living in dread of being handed a white feather, by some batty old maid, in the street.

But not going didn't stop Wason from holding strong views on the government's conduct of the war. People said it was the fault of Haig that millions of young men perished needlessly in the war, including many of Wason's oldest chums, from school and university. Wason disagreed. He believed the war had been won thanks almost entirely to the single-mindedness and determination of the commander-in-chief, with little support from the politicians. Haig was his hero. It was Haig who realised, better than anyone, that the people of England, with so much committed, and for so long engaged in the terrible conflict, expected the final outcome to be total victory; and would settle for nothing less. Without Haig as their conscience, Wason believed that Lloyd George and the rest of the Cabinet would have caved in long ago.

No-one questioned the final reckoning, apart from a few bickering socialists, who insisted the nation, and most of all the working class, had been sacrificed in vain; whatever happened during the settlement talks in Paris. Only the socialists contended bitterly that there would be no bright new tomorrow, in the land they fought to save, for the men returning from the trenches; or the dependants of those who failed to return. Working-class families would continue to live in squalor, the socialists forecast, the men out of work, their prospects hopeless, while the same undeserving system they had been forced to defend continued as before. But give them power, the socialists promised, and everything would be different: the rich would be humbled and the poor uplifted, on their way to the promised land, a nirvana of plenty which the socialists alone could create in England's green and pleasant land.

Wason found himself chuckling. The socialists, able to promise everything and deliver nothing, were a contemptible lot, right enough! He tried to imagine all those socialists with their grand ideas in government, running things, deciding events, shaping people's lives, determining his own future, for example, and couldn't. It would take a month of Sundays, and a blue moon in the sky, before the Labour Party could hope to win enough seats in the House of Commons to assure them of power. Another thing, he told himself reassuringly, long before power was in prospect, the socialists generally, by which he meant the Labour Party, the Independent Labour Party, the Communists, the Socialist Workers Party, and all the rest of them, could be depended upon to wreck their chance of presenting a cohesive argument to the electorate, against the Liberals and the Tories, by squabbling amongst themselves. Naturally, it was in the best interests of the country to keep them divided, Wason decided with a smile.

In his opinion, the threat imposed by the success of the Bolshevik revolution in Russia required to be viewed differently, however. Wason saw no point in underestimating the danger; or deliberately ignoring the threat to Britain and the rest of Europe: Lenin, the Bolshevik leader, made no secret of his belief that communism would dominate the world eventually. Viewed from Moscow it was only a matter of time, and waiting, Wason thought darkly.

It seemed to him that it was in the long-term interests of the western democracies to stop him now. Wason took it for granted that the chances of an assassination attempt succeeding had been considered within the service and discounted: Lenin would be guarded day and night by a small army of loyal henchmen; impossible for a stranger to infiltrate. Unless, of course, a member of his own staff, previously loyal, could be persuaded to turn against him.

It was the kind of mission, desperate and dangerous, and with little apparent hope of success, to attract Sidney Reilly. For all he knew Reilly could be in Moscow right now, laying plans for Lenin's destruction. Wason dismissed the idea with regret. The west would need to find another way of ridding itself of the troublesome Bolshevik. Perhaps the Prime Minister, together with the other world leaders, was giving the matter some attention, over brandy and cigars, in Paris.

He glanced round George Square. The thought of serious trouble, and troops with guns defending the square against the people of Glasgow, bothered him suddenly. He tried to picture George Square packed with people, all of them intent on storming the City Chambers. How would the troops react? Could they be depended upon to uphold the authority of the government against ordinary citizens?

Wason found himself shaking his head in the direction of the old man on the next bench. The old man shrugged resignedly, and spat. Wason grimaced and looked away.

One thing he did feel sure about: if it became necessary to deploy the army in Glasgow, in order to control the strikers, then whoever was put in charge should insist on using English troops. Wason knew from his briefing notes that a battalion of the Highland Light Infantry was stationed in Maryhill Barracks about three miles from the city centre. The kilted highlanders enjoyed a fearsome reputation from their exploits during the war. It was said the Germans who fought against them in France called them the ladies from hell and the name stuck! It would have been impossible to find better soldiers anywhere in the whole of the empire, probably. However, having spent part of the journey from London considering the problem, Wason was of the opinion that the authorities would be unwise to depend on the highlanders raising arms against ordinary people in the regiment's home city. It would be prudent to include in his report a recommendation that, in the event of serious trouble, either the highlanders were moved to another part of the country, or ways should be found to neutralise Maryhill Barracks. Most of the soldiers would have family and friends living in Glasgow and the chances of a mutiny couldn't be discounted.

The sound of someone approaching made him turn. It was the old man from the next bench. His clothes were wet and filthy from sleeping rough and, by the smell of him, he had been drinking methylated spirits, or worse. The prospect of engaging him in conversation alarmed Wason.

"Excuse me, sir," the old man began, pulling diffidently at his chin. "Do you think you could spare an old soldier a copper for a cup of tea?"

Wason reached into the pocket of his expensive coat and found a penny. "Will this do?" he asked.

The old man shuffled and spat. "To tell the truth, sir, a penny doesn't buy much these days," he replied.

Wason grunted. His fingers searched for a sixpence. "Promise me you'll buy something to eat."

The old man responded eagerly. "I promise, sir, thank you, sir. You're a young man who deserves God's kindness," he added, clenching the money in his fist.

With an unaccustomed sense of pity Wason watched him scamper away. He didn't fool himself for a moment that the money would go on food. But for the moment at least the old man was happy. Wason was prepared to bet the future well-being of the country and fears of revolution didn't rank high in his thoughts. He pocketed his notebook and pencil. It was time to think about his own lunch.

Wason rose and headed across George Square in the direction of St Vincent Street. The prospect of a first-class meal on expenses always heightened his appetite. That and the fact he had been walking all morning made him feel doubly hungry. He walked with a long stride. Being in Scotland some fresh salmon would be nice. Poached, preferably. There was a picture spread in one of the morning papers of anglers in Perthshire posing with several salmon which had been caught the day before at Kenmore on Loch Tay. The season in Scotland wasn't long started and there was an abundance of fish, apparently. Wason enjoyed angling when the fish were running well. The largest salmon in the photograph taken at Kenmore weighed nearly twenty pounds. No harm would come to him if he could only obtain a slice from a beauty such as that! A man he had met in the bar of the hotel the previous evening said there was a good restaurant, Rogano, just off Buchanan Street, which specialised in seafood. Wason hoped the cellar wasn't too primitive: the king of fish deserved decent wine. A good Chablis, perhaps. Considering the risks he faced on this assignment, an acceptable lunch was the very least he deserved.

Statues of long-forgotten dignitaries surrounded the square, standing in line with former heroes of the empire, each of them placed there by grateful contemporaries as a token of their admiration and respect; smug and safe among the leafless trees. Wason approached the pavement's edge. A tram left St Vincent Street and entered George Square, its bell clanging, and a sudden rush of traffic prevented people from crossing the road. It occurred to Wason that worrying about the future kept the majority of people from thinking about the true reality which must be now. What if everyone, politicians especially, spent less time worrying about the future, making promises they would never keep, and concentrated instead on improving the present? Wason glanced at the nearest statue. In the company of these exalted figures his current mood might count as conduct unbecoming a civil servant!

As a break in the traffic provided an opportunity to cross into St Vincent Street, Wason was suddenly aware of people hurrying by preoccupied with their own private thoughts and the concern of their daily lives. And dangerous or not, the idea persisted.

He supposed it was easier for people to worry about the future, even if their idea of the future stretched no further than the next day or the following week, because the present was too readily accountable. For some reason he couldn't fathom, the realisation of this simple truth depressed him. He just hoped his fish was fresh.

# CHAPTER ELEVEN

When Munro arrived at Miss Cranston's Tearooms in Sauchiehall Street at about three o'clock the Room de Luxe was crowded with well-dressed women enjoying the civilising ritual of afternoon tea. A waitress in a black frock, with a white pinafore and matching cap, welcomed Munro and led him to a table by the window overlooking Glasgow's most famous thoroughfare. Munro informed the waitress that he was waiting for a friend, and would order later, and she departed behind a screen decorated with willow-leaf.

The majority of Miss Cranston's other customers sat in groups of three or in pairs at little square tables covered with white cloths on which had been set accoutrements essential to the proceedings. These included cups and saucers and plates that matched, a silver pot containing tea, a sugar bowl with tongs, butter and jam, and two jugs, one large and one small, for water and milk. On every table a three-tiered cakestand laden with bread, French cakes and fruitcake, and empire biscuits topped by icing sugar decorated with small glazed cherries which it would have been considered ill-mannered to remove.

Many of the competing forces, middle-aged or near-elderly, Munro imagined, would remain in Miss Cranston's for the rest of the afternoon, proudly exchanging bits of news which reflected well on their own family, or venturing criticism of mutual friends who were in danger of falling from grace, gossiping happily, while trading darker secrets in cautious whispers, quite oblivious to the slanderous buzz of a hundred similar conversations going on around them.

Munro turned to the window and suppressed a wicked smile. His own mood was good and optimistic. It started the previous day with a telephone call to Margaret Armstrong. Her response had been reassuring. Of course she remembered him from May and Alick Robertson's the other night! No, she wasn't at all offended to receive his call. She had been hoping to hear from him again. The admission surprised Munro and he felt foolish for a moment. Yes, she would be

101

happy to meet him in town, perhaps for tea, Margaret Armstrong continued warmly. Where could they go?

To his own amazement it was Munro who suggested Miss Cranston's Willow Tearooms in Sauchiehall Street. Munro wasn't in the habit of taking afternoon tea in any of Miss Cranston's fashionable establishments, which were a popular feature of the city, or anywhere else for that matter. But the kind of place he preferred was obviously unsuitable for the occasion; not least because women were barred from all his usual haunts.

In addition to providing a superior high tea, said by everyone who knew to be the very best anyone could find anywhere, Miss Cranston's reputation rested on the gentility and social standing of her customers as well as the grandeur of her establishments. The fact that he was the only man in the room unnerved Munro at first. But it wasn't long before he realised most of the women in the room were too preoccupied with their own affairs, and the serious business of demolishing Miss Cranston's famous fare, to bother about him. How many secrets were being exchanged, reputations slandered, whole families gossiped to destruction, in the time it took to pass a cakestand from one wrinkled hand to another?

At a neighbouring table Munro thought he recognised the perfumed totems of a different social order, self-perpetuating and totally ignorant of the problems to be encountered in the outside world beyond the gates of their own precious homes; busy now devouring white bread, thick with butter and strawberry jam, cakes and scones, pancakes heavy with marmalade, a suitable reward, as they approached the end of their days, for whatever time they had been forced to spend mothering a generation of the city's ruthless and selfish merchant class.

The interiors and decor of the Willow Tearoom had been designed by Charles Rennie Mackintosh, a celebrated local architect, about fifteen years earlier, before his career went into decline. In those days, as Munro remembered them, Mackintosh was surrounded by a gang of hangers-on who rejoiced in feeding his own highly-developed ego with their own breathless opinions; most of them worthless. Munro could recall hearing how marvellous the man was, a genius, in fact, pure genius, and wasn't his revolutionary style, which Munro considered eccentric at best, just wonderful and quite extraordinary, revolutionary, in fact; and wasn't it amazing what he did with glass, and all those shapes, quite fantastic. It was obvious then that Mackintosh was working hard, both professionally and socially, to consolidate his reputation which was still growing. Munro saw him often, mostly at functions, and didn't care for his manner, a calculated, hard air of vanity and dismissiveness, which Munro found offensive; and quite often insulting.

Once, near the end of an evening's drinking in the Curlers, he had mentioned his reservations about Mackintosh to Alick Robertson, who responded with interest. His friend, who hadn't met Mackintosh, was in a philosophical mood at the time, and he listened carefully while Munro registered a whole string of complaints against the great artist.

Finally, when Munro was finished, Robertson nodded wisely. "So you don't think much of Charles Rennie Mackintosh?" he inquired dubiously.

Munro agreed with some vehemence that this was true. His friend stared at him for a moment, considering the evidence, nodded and sighed. "Let me tell you something," he confided gently.

Munro shifted in his seat, listening attentively, expecting good advice and hoping for some support for his views.

Robertson's words emerged climbing, rising above the din of the pub, making heads turn, and ended in a roar.

"Charles Rennie Mackintosh doesn't give a fuck about you!" he shouted, laughing, and collapsing in a heap on the bar.

Recalling the moment, and thinking about his friend, and what he would say if he could see him now, Frank Munro shuddered. He knew without doubt that Robertson would have fallen, helpless, into his whisky at the absurdity of him sitting there, in Miss Cranston's Room de Luxe, surrounded by dozens of old ladies, dressed in the height of fashion, stuffing themselves silly with bread and scones and cakes, in one of Charles Rennie Mackintosh's odd little chairs, waiting to keep a secret rendezvous with Margaret Armstrong.

Robertson always insisted his fascination with the romantic activities of his friends was the natural response of an inquiring mind. Finely tuned, he would add quickly, with a serious nod, for the benefit of anyone who might think otherwise. On those occasions when Munro found himself on the receiving end of one of his friend's sharp, inquisitive examinations concerning his own bleak love life, he never bothered to object. The women involved in Robertson's elaborate fantasies were usually people Munro didn't know, or else knew so slightly it made no difference. Robertson could be amusing on the subject of his friend's infrequent romantic ambitions and, in a daft sort of way, encouraging. Munro usually consoled himself with a smile.

103

Robertson, the trained observer, with his inquiring mind, appeared to believe there was hope for him yet and that, at least, was something.

Munro glanced round the ornately decorated room and stifled a chuckle. So long as they stayed within Miss Cranston's exclusive environment, hidden among the regulars, they would be safe from instant discovery. Alick Robertson wouldn't have been seen dead in the place; although he realised his attitude begged the question. What would Robertson make of him seeing Margaret Armstrong? He was bound to find out, of course. Then what would he say?

"Sorry I'm late," she said brightly, approaching from behind, and sitting quickly before he could stand to acknowledge her arrival.

"I hate being late," she went on hurriedly, dumping parcels and looking round. "But the town is impossible today. The worst I've seen it, I think."

She smiled, pulling at her gloves.

She was wearing a navy blue coat with a fur collar and wide-brimmed felt hat, held by a pin. She had a square, pale face, with a large mouth, good teeth, and brown eyes set deep beneath heavy dark brows. Munro found himself liking her a lot.

The waitress who had shown Munro to his table emerged from behind a patterned screen which separated the kitchen from the dining-room.

"What would you like?"

"Afternoon tea is what we're serving, sir," the waitress reminded him pointedly.

Margaret Armstrong smiled. "That will be fine," she said.

"For two," Munro ordered.

The waitress departed, sniffing.

Margaret Armstrong chuckled. "I can't imagine this being your sort of place," she observed.

"Oh, I come here all the time," Munro responded drily.

"With your friend Alick in tow, no doubt."

Munro laughed. "Can't keep him away," he said.

"You must admit it's a most unusual room," Margaret Armstrong remarked, looking round. "Mackintosh is a true original, a genius, in fact. Don't you agree?"

"So they tell me."

She was immediately interested. "Don't you like him?" she inquired, sharply.

"Him I don't like," Munro confessed.

"So you know him?"

"Only slightly," Munro replied. "I'm prepared to give his work the benefit of the doubt. I'll wait and see how he develops. If he develops," he added darkly, turning to help the waitress, who had returned, pushing a trolley. "Anyway, I haven't seen him in years."

"Have I touched a nerve?" Margaret Armstrong inquired, smiling.

"It isn't important."

Margaret Armstrong disagreed. "I've been told that everything concerning Charles Rennie Mackintosh is important," she declared.

Munro shrugged.

"Him and his wife, Margaret Macdonald."

She turned and pointed. "Did you know she was responsible for that panel over there, or that it was inspired by a Rosetti sonnet?"

Munro shook his head.

Margaret Armstrong chuckled delightedly. "You see," she cried, "I can tell you a thing or two about Mr and Mrs Mackintosh."

Munro smiled.

"Is it true," Margaret Armstrong went on, "that they were forced to leave Glasgow because people didn't really appreciate their work? I have been told that no-one would give him a commission, finally. It seems incredible now, doesn't it?"

"Not so incredible," Munro suggested gently, "when you consider that he could be a difficult man to understand, never mind like."

Margaret Armstrong dismissed his objection with a wave of her hand. "You're biased," she retorted. "Didn't you admit as much only a moment ago? Anyway, artists are entitled to behave differently from the rest of us. That's one of the things that makes them special. In any civilised society they are allowed privileges denied to anyone else. And why not? Mackintosh, for instance. His fame will endure. You wait and see. And just remember I was the one who told you so," she added with a smile.

Munro smiled. The question of Charles Rennie Mackintosh's lasting fame would be the business of future generations to decide, he thought happily, and none of his concern.

Margaret Armstrong hadn't finished, however. "Why don't you like him?" she demanded.

"Call it journalist's privilege," he replied, brightly.

"You mean you won't tell me," she insisted.

"I mean you won't find my reasons for not liking him sufficient to establish a case one way or the other," he said.

Margaret Armstrong studied the room. "Where are they now?" she inquired.

"Somehwere in England, I think," Munro replied.

Margaret Armstrong nodded, and shrugged. "Glasgow should be ashamed of itself," she remarked quietly.

Munro waited for her to continue.

"But the fact you didn't like him," she said, "that worries me."

Munro didn't respond.

"Isn't it funny the way we like some people immediately and can't stand others no matter how hard they try?"

"It happens all the time," he told her. "Do you like treacle scones?"

Margaret Armstrong laughed, showing her tongue, and Munro was in no doubt about him liking her; and hoping the feeling would prove mutual.

"I love them," she said.

"That's good," said Munro. "So do I."

He noticed a small brown mole close to her left ear.

"Have you been busy?"

"Keeping up with the strike," he replied. "What have you been doing, apart from shopping?" he added, glancing at her parcels littering the floor.

She grinned. "I was buying a few presents before going home," she explained. "No, this morning I went to Govan."

"You know someone there?"

She shook her head. "Not really," she said. "May introduced me to a minister there. Someone who used to be at Dowanhill, I think. Anyway, I'd better explain," she added, hurriedly. "What I want to do is set up an emergency food service for the strikers' families."

"You mean a soup kitchen?" Munro interrupted.

"Call it a soup kitchen and people think they are one step away from the poorhouse," she objected. "I don't want their pride keeping them away."

"Have you done this sort of thing before?"

She nodded. "I spent most of last year working with a voluntary group in London," she told him.

"I thought you didn't like the English," he smiled.

"The ones I object to are the governing classes," she replied, seriously, "not the poor."

Munro was genuinely curious. "How do people react to someone like you arriving in the neighbourhood with buckets of food?" he inquired, watching her closely.

"Ordinary people find it difficult to understand when the system forces them to starve," she replied. "They hate the fact that our presence is necessary. Can you blame them?"

"I can imagine that in a place like Govan, or anywhere else in Glasgow for that matter, people would rather go hungry than accept handouts from a stranger," Munro suggested, cautiously.

Margaret Armstrong frowned. "In a fight like this there's no shame in accepting a little help," she insisted. "So long as it comes from the right quarter, of course. Nobody wants charity."

Munro nodded thoughtfully. "You aren't just talking politics now, you're participating, supporting the strike," he said.

"Of course," she replied, helping herself to another scone, and reaching for the butter.

"When will you start?"

"This week some time," she told him. "We've been offered the use of an old hall in Golspie Street, not far from the cross. There's a kitchen of sorts and running water, all we need. I've checked on the gas and it's working. Some of the local women have promised to help with the cooking and serving. May and I and one or two others, we'll provide the food."

"You've been busy, I see," Munro commented, admiringly.

"So long as it helps," she said.

Munro looked puzzled. "What I don't understand," he said, "is May Robertson's part in all this. How did she become involved? It isn't the kind of thing you would expect."

"Why not?" Margaret Armstrong inquired, frowning. "May is a sensitive, caring person who is happy to help people less fortunate than herself."

"I can't see Alick being too happy about it," Munro objected, impishly.

"Please don't mention it to him," Margaret Armstrong replied, seriously. "It's got nothing to do with Alick," she added, seeing him hesitate. "May can tell him or not, just as she pleases."

Munro thought for a moment, considering the likely response of his friend when he heard the news that his wife was supporting the families of strikers, using his money no doubt, and chuckled heartily. Munro was prepared to bet a week's salary that May Robertson's right to do as she pleased, contrary to whatever Margaret Armstrong might believe, would be seriously curtailed. Certainly, if she went ahead with her involvement in the project, her participation would be the cause of domestic discord of a high order in the Robertson home. When it came to the emancipation of women, and their right to do whatever they wanted, Alick Robertson was at best a slow starter.

"I won't tell him," he promised.

Margaret Armstrong gave him a satisfied glance. "I want to ask you something," she continued.

Munro waited.

"I couldn't help thinking, talking to those women I met in Govan today, that they were about to suffer a terrible defeat. I could see it on their faces that they thought so. It wasn't so much defeatism as a sense of resignation you could almost feel. Their eyes told you the whole story. They expected nothing," Margaret Armstrong concluded helplessly, "nothing good anyway, to come out of this awful business."

He wanted to help but couldn't think of anything to say. Margaret Armstrong sighed. "Are these women right to despair?"

"They would be sensible not to expect too much," Munro replied, harshly.

"Do you believe the men are being realistic in their demands?"

"They certainly have no hope of winning on the question of the forty-hour week," he told her. "It would be unrealistic to believe otherwise."

"I thought you supported the workers."

"I've been trying not to take sides."

Margaret Armstrong frowned. "Your attitude puzzles me," she said. "You seem so detached from everything. Is it some kind of pose?"

Munro smiled. "I'm an observer," he said. "I'm not a participant."

She shook her head, disbelieving.

"Wouldn't a reduction in the working week mean more jobs for more men?" Margaret Armstrong pressed, finally.

"If you reduce the working week, and bring in more men, then costs will rise," Munro replied. "You could end up paying two men to do the work of one."

Margaret Armstrong glared at him. "You're assuming the profit motive is paramount in society," she snapped.

Munro smiled. "You're the self-confessed socialist around here," he reminded her, gently, "not me."

She stared at him for a moment. "In my opinion the political and industrial leadership of this country has lost its nerve," she declared. "They all but lost the war against Germany and now they are fearful of losing an even bigger war, here at home, against the workers."

Munro shook his head in obvious disagreement.

"Don't tell me you actually believe that the leadership of this country, the social, political and industrial élite, who control all the levers of power, especially finance, are about to rebuild Britain in a way which will guarantee full employment, proper wages and low rents for all the people?"

Munro shrugged. "Obviously it will take time," he replied.

"Let's give them time!" Margaret Armstrong offered, giving him a generous smile. "When will they begin, do you think?"

She was watching him carefully.

"Don't forget that this is already the greatest manufacturing country in the world," Munro protested.

"But how long will that last?" she demanded.

"What makes you think we can't build on it?"

"Because I happen to believe that the so-called governing classes haven't the faintest idea what to do about the future," she replied, vehemently.

Munro glanced round. He hoped none of the dozens of old ladies present was overhearing. Any of Miss Cranston's other customers listening to Margaret Armstrong would require smelling-salts by now; or an ambulance, he thought wickedly.

Margaret Armstrong hadn't finished.

"By that I mean in so far as it will affect the vast majority of people who happen to live in this country. Of course, they have a pretty good idea what to do about saving their own skins, and protecting their own soft-earned money."

Munro shook his head ruefully. "It's an ill-divided world," he replied.

"Working people no longer believe in the God-given right of their masters to rule the world, you know."

"So I've heard," Munro replied, smiling slightly.

"Are you against the workers taking charge?"

Munro shrugged. "I'm against them taking charge by force," he said. "I'm against anyone taking charge by force."

"But you don't mind them using force to protect the status quo?"

Munro said nothing.

"You'd wait until the workers succeeded in sending enough of their own people to Westminster before you thought about changing the world?" Margaret Armstrong added. "Is that what you want?"

She stared at him.

"There's no other way," he told her. "Not for me, anyway."

"How long do you think that will take?"

"It would be foolish to start looking for short-cuts," Munro replied.

Margaret Armstrong sounded impatient. "You've been under the heel of the English for two hundred years," she said. "This could be your chance to drive them out."

Her voice carried to a nearby table where two old ladies abandoned their own conversation to turn and stare, shock on both their faces. Munro offered them a small, apologetic smile by way of comfort. The women continued to stare.

Margaret Armstrong continued, unconcerned. "Well?"

Munro smiled bleakly. "Centuries of oppression have made us docile," he said.

"I thought you Scots were fighters."

Munro chuckled. "Only in other people's wars," he told her. "We are a mercenary race, you know."

Margaret Armstrong frowned. "I'm being serious," she snapped.

Munro endeavoured to keep the conversation under control. "Are you?" he inquired, lightly.

"Don't you think so?"

"I don't know," Munro admitted.

"At least in Ireland people are prepared to fight," Margaret Armstrong observed. She was watching him closely.

"Don't start that again," he ordered sharply.

He could see that the old ladies at the next table were straining to hear. It bothered him that what Margaret Armstrong was saying sounded seditious. Munro tried smiling at them and the old ladies turned away, gasping with fright, and whispering anxiously to themselves. What would they tell their families? he wondered.

Margaret Armstrong appeared unconcerned. "You mustn't let a good chance slip," she warned.

Munro said nothing.

"It's possible, of course, that Shinwell and the others are being used."

Frank Munro refused to accept this idea. "Manny Shinwell isn't the kind of man to let himself be used," he told her.

"He might not know what's going on," Margaret Armstrong insisted.

Munro shook his head.

"There's enough talk," Margaret Armstrong argued. "The city is full of it."

"Don't you think Shinwell knows all about the talk?"

"For all anyone knows," Margaret Armstrong continued, "there could be hidden groups, organised and waiting, ready to take charge the moment real trouble starts."

Munro, hoping to silence her, shook his head stubbornly. "Anyway," he objected, "they would need to be armed."

"There are plenty of people in Ireland who would give them guns," she retorted.

Munro stared at her.

"Or there's the Bolsheviks," Margaret Armstrong added, frowning hopefully. "They could send in arms from Russia easily enough."

"How?"

"You don't believe for a minute, surely, that arms from Russia couldn't be landed somewhere along the coast?" she asked.

Munro looked unconvinced.

"Of course Ireland, being nearer, would be simpler."

"I don't believe it."

"Why not?"

"People here would never support an armed uprising."

"What makes you so sure?"

"I live here, remember."

Margaret Armstrong was warming to her subject. "All it needs is a few dedicated men with the determination and the desire to succeed," she continued briskly. "They take the Post Office, just like they did in Dublin . . .".

Frank Munro was laughing at her, trying to discourage her from going on. "People in Glasgow don't give a damn about the Post Office," he chuckled. "Besides, it's always shut when you want it. The rebels would never get through the door."

". . . or some other important building," Margaret Armstrong, refusing to be diverted from her vision of rebellion, continued stubbornly, "issue their proclamation, just like they did in Dublin, and wait for the workers to join them in their struggle. Why do you think that sounds far-fetched?"

"What I think," Munro responded blithely, "is that anyone who tries it will wait a long time before the workers join them. People here are too sensible to try it. The present trouble is a dispute about pay and conditions, that's all."

"There will be a least thirty thousand men at the St Andrew's Halls tomorrow," Margaret Armstrong reminded him sharply. "How do you think that kind of turn-out must look to the government in London? Don't you think they are bound to be running scared by now, wondering what's going on up here?"

Munro stared at her.

"Well?"

"I hope you're right," Munro replied. "That way someone might do something about settling the strike. It's just a pity Lloyd George can't be in among it."

Margaret Armstrong dismissed his regard for Lloyd George with a scornful snort. "Lloyd George is bound to know what's going on," she said. "The others wouldn't dare not tell him."

"You don't think much of Lloyd George?"

"He'll be on the employers' side, just like Churchill and all the rest of them," Margaret Armstrong asserted. "I don't think you can depend on Lloyd George to help."

Then, when he didn't respond, she startled him by saying:

"Connolly couldn't stand so the English shot him sitting in a chair," adding by way of explanation, "I just want to show that the English can be quite ruthless when it comes to quelling rebellions and discouraging public disorder of any kind. In the event of real trouble the leaders would need to be careful."

"Connolly was executed by the British," corrected Munro. "He was actually born in Edinburgh, did you know that?"

Margaret Armstrong glared at him. "It doesn't matter where a man is born," she retorted sharply, "it's where he makes his mark that counts."

Munro shrugged.

"But isn't it interesting that all of a sudden we're British," Margaret Armstrong went on. "All those centuries of Scottish history, all that nationhood and pride, count for nothing, it appears."

"We gave that up a long time ago," Frank Munro replied tiredly.

"Well, we didn't!" she informed him fiercely. "We might not have much at the moment, but we haven't lost our pride in ourselves or our country, and won't rest until the English are out of Ireland for good."

"Then what will you do?"

"Rejoice!" she cried.

Then she added: "Whatever we do we will be the ones who are doing it. It's called freedom," she added pointedly.

"Scotland joined the Union of its own accord," Munro told her. "There's no going back on it now. Apart from anything else, the English would never allow it. Don't tell me you disagree."

"You could always fight."

"I have no wish to fight," Munro replied.

"Don't you want to be free?"

Munro shrugged. "I don't understand your concept of freedom," he told her. "I can settle for the difference in being Scottish, of knowing that I am not English, without wishing to bring the Union to an end."

"But you have everything you need for self-government," Margaret Armstrong protested.

"Are we talking about self-government or nationhood?" Frank Munro inquired. "We already have nationhood, remember."

"Then why shrink from self-government?"

"Because not enough people want it badly enough to be interested," Frank Munro answered.

Unable to understand, Margaret Armstrong shook her head, bewildered.

"They don't care, you see."

"People need to be led," she replied.

"Most of the strike leaders, including Shinwell, aren't nationalists." Frank Munro went on. "Shinwell is a hard-headed pragmatist who wants to make a deal. Don't be fooled. He'll be the first to recognise the best he's going to get the moment it appears. And then he'll grab it with both hands."

"But Shinwell isn't alone in this," Margaret Armstrong objected. "The rest of the leadership, the men themselves, will want to have a say in the final decision, surely? Whatever offer the employers make will require to go to a vote. Some of the people I've spoken to tell me that Shinwell isn't even the real leader of the Clydeside movement. What about Gallacher, or the likes of Buchanan and Wheatley, even John Maclean, although I know you think he's past it?"

"I happen to believe they'll take their lead from Shinwell," replied Munro. "The men will certainly want to follow Shinwell and they'll accept what he tells them. But he'll be a good judge, don't worry."

Margaret Armstrong helped herself to another scone and reached for the butter. "I've often wondered why the Scots and the Irish, who should be so much alike, are in fact so different."

"Perhaps its the water between us that makes the difference," Frank Munro suggested easily.

"The Irish have never stopped fighting against the oppression of

England," Margaret Armstrong continued, buttering a scone and frowning. "But the Scots don't seem to mind."

"We enjoy being patronised."

Margaret Armstrong sounded shocked. "I don't believe you," she said.

"It's one of the great unspoken truths of our time," Munro affirmed.

"It could explain a great deal," Margaret Armstrong observed, frowning.

"For instance," Munro explained cheerfully, "we like to kid ourselves that the English depend on us to rule the empire. It's rubbish, of course. But have you ever seen a Scotsman preen, his little tail wagging, whenever an Englishman says so?"

Margaret Armstrong stared at him for a moment. "Are you bitter?" she inquired finally.

"I hope not," he replied.

"But you don't like them very much, do you?" she asked.

"I try very hard to like them, as a rule," Munro replied, "but it can be difficult sometimes."

Margaret Armstrong frowned. "Why bother?" she inquired.

"I want to try and understand them," Munro explained.

Margaret Armstrong chuckled grimly. "You'd never hear an Irishman admit that he spent any time at all trying to understand the English."

"Perhaps that's the difference between us," Munro suggested, grinning.

"We understand that the English are in Ireland, where they don't belong, and that's all we need to understand about the English," she said.

Munro beckoned to a passing waitress and asked her to bring them another pot of tea. "Anyway, I hope you like it here," he said.

"Oh yes," Margaret Armstrong replied, looking round, "it's very nice."

Munro lowered his voice. "You realise, of course, that the two ladies at the next table are quite horrified," he whispered.

Margaret Armstrong didn't seem to mind her voice carrying. "Serves them right," she replied, "they shouldn't be listening."

Munro chuckled. "Don't you ever listen to other people's conversations?" he asked.

"Of course. All the time," she confessed.

"Me too," Munro admitted.

"Doesn't everybody?" Margaret Armstrong wanted to know. "I can't help it," she added brightly.

"In my case I suppose it comes with the job," Munro suggested, enjoying himself immensely now. "What's your excuse?"

"I've never bothered to look for one," Margaret Armstrong admitted, smiling carelessly. "Is that a terribly sinful thing to say?"

"I shouldn't think so," he replied.

"How do you like your tea?"

"As it comes," he told her.

"You don't want the milk in first?" she asked, accepting a fresh pot from the waitress.

"I don't care," he assured her.

"It's all a terrible fad," Margaret Armstrong observed. "Don't you think so?"

Munro nodded. "Though some people can be quite fussy about it," he said.

He studied her closely, watching her looking at him, openly staring at her in fact, following every movement of her hands and eyes. Margaret Armstrong didn't seem to mind, however. "It's lovely being friends," she said, "isn't it?"

Frank Munro didn't know what to say.

"There's no point being shy," Margaret Armstrong added, giving him a smile, "is there? Not at our age, anyway."

"I suppose not," Munro admitted, conscious of his own excitement.

"Do you think I am too direct?"

Munro shook his head. "No," he replied, "I don't think you are too direct. Anyway, I don't mind you being direct."

"I'm glad. Some people don't like it. You're sure you don't mind?"

"I don't mind."

"Do you object when I tell you what I think about politics?" Margaret Armstrong continued.

"Why should I object?" Munro inquired.

"Men usually don't like it when women talk about politics," Margaret Armstrong replied, frowning. "They think we don't know enough about it to express an opinion."

"I'd say you were entitled to your views."

"I'm glad about that too," she said, and smiled.

The two women at the next table were preparing to leave, Munro noticed. "Let's hope they don't call the police," he whispered, grinning.

"Wouldn't that be fun!" Margaret Armstrong exclaimed, turning to look at them, and provoking them with a smile.

Going out one of the women paused and glared at her. "I've never ever heard such terrible talk," she declared in a voice shaking with anger. "Never in all my life," she added, looking round.

Margaret Armstrong stared straight ahead, disregarding the woman and her outburst, and said nothing.

"I've a good mind to report you to the authorities," the woman continued, her voice rising, attracting the attention of people at other tables.

"Oh! Did you have any particular authority in mind?" Margaret Armstrong inquired politely.

"You sound Irish," the woman shouted, looking round the restaurant and finding everyone staring at her. "You should have heard the pair of them," she went on, as if addressing an audience. "They were talking treason against the government."

Frank Munro half rose from his chair. "That's enough," he said in a quiet voice. "I think you'd better go."

"Are you threatening me?" the woman screamed.

"Pay no attention to them, Elizabeth," her friend advised, looking frightened, and hoping to steer her towards the door.

A small woman, who appeared to be the manageress, arrived to quell the disturbance. "What is the meaning of all this noise?" she asked sharply, staring first at Munro, and then at the departing women.

"There was some kind of misunderstanding," Munro explained. "It's settled now."

"We are just leaving," the second woman said, obviously embarrassed, and clearly anxious to be away.

Her companion was unrepentant, however. "You should have heard what they were saying," she cried.

The manageress looked stern. "Please leave these premises at once," she ordered.

Margaret Armstrong, staring straight ahead, and paying no attention to the rumpus, giggled. The manageress eyed her stonily.

Everyone else in the restaurant appeared to be watching them, talking in whispers, speculating. There was also a good chance, Frank Munro thought anxiously, that the two women who had been the cause of all the trouble would stop the first policeman they could find and tell him God-alone-knows-what rubbish.

Silently cursing everyone in sight, and himself most of all for not stopping Margaret Armstrong earlier, he tried to attract the attention of a waitress to give him a bill. "We'd better go."

Margaret Armstrong nodded and sighed. "Weren't they nice," she said. "Such lovely people."

# CHAPTER TWELVE

I t was the doorman who guarded the entrance to the Central Hotel against intrusion by rougher elements of the city's population who suggested that Wason should try the Theatre Royal if he was in search of entertainment. People said it was a good show, the doorman added, enthusiastically.

Dressed in a long coat and top-hat, with white gloves and spats, and the look of an old soldier, the doorman's territory extended from the top of the steps which led to the hotel from the street to the edge of the pavement, beyond which he refused to venture.

Yes, the doorman told him, smiling broadly, he knew exactly what was playing there. Little Red Riding Hood, he beamed, showing teeth. Wason nodded appreciatively. Being a Wednesday, the doorman went on, there would be a matinee at two. The gentleman had plenty of time to walk to the theatre before the performance started. Everybody said it was a good show. It had been running since before Christmas. Glasgow loved its pantomime. No, he couldn't remember who was in it. But he could assure the gentleman, sir, that the Theatre Royal enjoyed the highest possible reputation. And wasn't Glasgow famous the wide world over for the quality of its theatres, each of them a wonder in itself, especially the ones which specialised in pantomime and music hall, the greatest of all the popular arts, the doorman added seriously.

His accent puzzled Wason, who thought he knew about accents, having just spent a month at a secret address in Wiltshire, attending a regional accents identification course. Wason had been taught how to recognise essential characteristics of tone and rhythm, as well as basic speech patterns peculiar to different parts of the country. The course had been designed to assist personnel who might find themselves operating in the field one day.

Yes, the doorman agreed, nodding seriously, he would certainly recommend it, if that was the kind of thing the gentleman appreciated. He hoped to go to the Theatre Royal himself before the end of the week.

"It's the best there is, sir," the doorman concluded with an air of absolute conviction.

Perhaps the man was foreign, Wason thought. Many of the words he favoured sounded foreign.

It wasn't much of a walk, no sir, the doorman assured him, smiling, and pointing to the head of Hope Street, which he could almost see from where they were standing. Ten or fifteen minutes at the most, the doorman added, and he could admire all the wonderful buildings on the way. "Don't forget to look up, sir," the doorman said.

Wason smiled appreciatively. "Have you lived in this country long?" he inquired, giving the doorman a silver sixpence for his trouble.

The doorman stared at him uncomprehending. "I don't know what you mean, sir," he replied.

Wason smiled. "I was wondering which country you came from originally, that's all," he explained. "I can guess, if you like."

The doorman looked hurt. "You think I'm a foreigner, sir?" he asked. "Let me tell you something, sir, I've never been abroad in the whole of my life. No wish to go, sir. What's there for us to want? No, sir, everything I need is here. Then, when the time comes to retire, I'll away hame to Banff."

Wason laughed nervously. "I was joking, of course," he remarked, trying desperately to recover his composure.

The doorman regarded him uncertainly. He turned the silver sixpence between his fingers and watched him go. Wasn't it true what people said? It took all kinds, right enough. But what a strange young man, the doorman thought.

Hope Street rose in a marked, cobbled incline, fine-looking buildings on either side. A tram heading north on the far side of the street proclaimed its destination as Normal School. What was normal about it, Wason wondered curiously, and what was wrong with the rest of Glasgow's schools?

Struggling against the gradient other trams were headed for places with unfamiliar names like Camlachie and Springburn; while on the near side of Hope Street, only yards away from the pavement where he was walking, trams going south raced downhill, swaying murderously, ready to leave the rails, warning-bells clanging just in case, on their way to other unheard-of destinations like Dumbreck and Bellahouston.

At the junction with West Regent Street a brewer's dray occupied the middle of the road, an ancient, blinkered horse between its shafts. While the horse rested other traffic piled up as far as the next corner and beyond. The carter, an old man wrapped in a filthy blanket, slumped in his seat, evidently asleep; or dead drunk, more likely. Wason made to walk in front of the horse and almost missed the carter coming alive, snarling and lashing at him with his whip. Moving instinctively, and yelping with fear, Wason jumped back out of the way, and narrowly missed being run down by a tram going south.

Having reached the pavement, he clung to a lamp-post, gasping and trembling with fright. The carter, displaying a mouthful of broken teeth, laughed uproariously at his discomfort; clearing his throat and hawking into the street.

Black fury almost overwhelmed Wason. He felt tempted to haul the ruffian from his perch and give him a good hiding. The carter, unaware of the danger, was laughing, still; jeering at him, black teeth showing spittle, frosting his stubbled chin.

Wason controlled himself with difficulty.

Good sense made him cautious. He didn't want any trouble which might involve the police. He couldn't risk exposing his cover. The whole operation might be jeopardised.

Then what would Churchill say?

The old horse shook its head and snorted, wearily. The carter waved his whip. Head low and swaying as the harness bit, the horse began a slow, sweeping turn to the right. All other traffic was forced to a halt. The carter fell back in his seat, cursing.

Wason watched them go. He felt sorry for the horse. The poor beast's days were obviously numbered. How many more times would it survive that killing climb of Hope Street?

Wason grunted. Pity the local knacker's yard didn't deal in foul-tempered, Glaswegian carters, and not just horses, he thought murderously.

A large crowd, which included a good many children, spilled across the pavement outside the Theatre Royal. It occurred to Wason that the show might be a sell-out and he would be unable to obtain a ticket. Despite his encounter with the venomous carter, he had been looking forward to a pleasant and undemanding afternoon.

Wason harboured no pretensions about the theatre. His tastes were popular and uncomplicated. He loved plays by J.M. Barrie, and thought he had seen them all, as well as the more stirring kind of stuff which had been left to the nation by Gilbert and Sullivan. Wason absolutely adored the Pirates of Penzance.

Now he hurried to find the box office, doubly anxious that he might miss the curtain going up. He hated going into a theatre late.

The clerk who stared at him from behind the tiny box-office window indicated that there was a single ticket available in the dress circle. Wason glanced at the seating plan, which was kept under glass in front of the window through which tickets were purchased, and satisfied himself that it looked a good seat. Then, with great care, he counted out four shillings and ninepence exactly in silver and copper coins, and pushed the money towards the waiting clerk. The clerk took the money, separated the different coins into a drawer according to their value, and, finally, gave Wason his ticket. Wason took it, checked the date and the price, thanked the man, who gave him a cheerful little nod by way of acknowledgement, and went in search of his seat.

There was little room to move in the crowded foyer. A queue had formed on the stone staircase leading to the dress circle. Wason allowed himself to be jostled gently towards it. From the babble of conversation going on about him, he heard a woman's voice, indignant with disbelief.

"You would think we were made of money," the woman was saying. "Do you know what happened today? The shop steward appeared in William's office this morning and said the men wanted another sixpence an hour, starting right away. There would be no negotiation. That's what he said. You're right, said William, there won't be. Threaten me again and you're all dismissed. He's given them until tomorrow morning to make up their minds. Can you imagine?"

Wason looked round, hoping to catch a glimpse of her, but he was unable to identify the woman in the crowd. He would have enjoyed meeting her husband. Evidently this unknown Glaswegian knew how to handle trade union bully-boys. Give them a dose of their own medicine, that's what, Wason thought with a grin.

At the top of the stone stairs Wason entered the dress-circle through a curtained door. A middle-aged usherette in a blue smock sold him a programme for twopence. Another woman, also dressed in blue, showed him to his seat, which was five rows back, near the middle. He had an elderly couple, stiffly dressed, with the look of a retired merchant pair, on one side; and a pretty girl, in her late teens, who appeared to be accompanied by her parents, on the other. There were few empty seats and it looked a good house.

The first half was an unsettling experience, however.

When the performance started, and Little Red Riding Hood appeared, in the beguiling form of Miss Maudie Francis, the presence of the girl in the next seat was at first annoying, then alarming, and finally disturbing.

The moment the house lights dimmed she took possession of the seat arm they were meant to share and pressed her shoulder warmly into his side. Once, as she shifted in her seat, her left knee bumped against his thigh He tried looking at her, without shifting his eyes from what was happening on stage, until the strain of what he was doing made him stop.

At the interval, as the curtain fell, Wason rose to go to the bar. He could feel the girl's knee against his legs. Concerned that he himself might somehow be at fault, Wason turned to apologise.

The girl ignored him.

She was already chattering to her mother about the performance, and looking round, intent on spotting friends. She no longer commandeered the arm rest, sitting now with her hands clasped on her lap, and gave no sign that she was even aware of Wason's presence.

The sound of a man coughing made him turn.

It was the girl's father, who had his legs drawn back, and was scowling at him, wanting him to hurry. Wason apologised again and pushed past them into the aisle. When he found the bar he thought about ordering champagne as a special treat, thought better of it, and settled for whisky. "A large one, please," he added, "with ice."

From half a crown the barman gave him a shilling change. Wason considered the drink expensive and thought immediately he had been overcharged. He was about to complain when he noticed his glass was fuller than usual. Then he remembered that bars in Scotland specialised in large measures. It was something he'd better watch, Wason thought, pocketing his change and thanking the barman. He didn't want to end up legless.

He found a corner beside the bar, beneath a portrait of Harry Lauder. The photograph on the wall showed Lauder, wearing comic highland dress and brandishing a strange-looking stick, smirking, self-satisfied and confident of his fame. Wason had seen him perform at the Palladium in London and, with his strutting, bouncing style and infectious smile, thought him a wonderful turn.

But thinking of him now Wason couldn't push from his mind other pictures of Lauder which he had seen recently, circulating within the department, of him crying in France, on a visit to the trenches and the grave of his son; just one man among millions who paid grievously for the war.

Wason sipped at his whisky and glanced round the crowded bar; noting for the first time a scattering of junior officers parading their uniforms. The rest of those present probably included more than a few employers and landlords who were responsible, in a way, for him being there. It occurred to him that many of them must have made fortunes in the war. Not that Wason cared. Didn't his mother's sister's husband manufacture billy-cans? How much did he make from the war? A lot, Wason imagined; and for a moment bitterness at his uncle's meanness towards the rest of the family clouded his judgment. Finally, however, Wason was forced to conclude that his uncle, and men like him, contributed a great deal to the war effort.

He was totally out of sympathy with socialist intellectuals who were forever complaining that the people who profited most from the war hadn't themselves fought at the front; or slaved in munition factories, working all hours, in the shipyards, or on workbenches elsewhere. They were the lucky ones, Wason reasoned, because they were able to exploit the system. Not many people, given the chance, would turn their backs on such an opportunity.

The thought made him smile, conspiratorially.

A woman standing about a yard away smiled back. Wason stared at her, uncertain how to react. The woman smiled again. She was aged about fifty, and was with a group of friends, a number of whom seemed to acknowledge Wason in a friendly way, without actually saying anything to him. It was the woman who spoke.

"Excuse me," the woman said. "Don't I know you?"

Wason shook his head. "I don't think so," he replied.

"I'm sorry," the woman apologised. "I though perhaps you were at university with my son."

"I don't think so," Wason told her.

"Have you enjoyed the show?"

Wason nodded enthusiastically. "Very much," he said.

"It is fun, isn't it?" the woman agreed. "Much too good just to be left to the children."

"Yes," said Wason, "I suppose so."

"We come every year," the woman added, with a guilty chuckle. "I hate to think I may be depriving some poor child of a seat."

Wason smiled. "It's my first time," he admitted.

The woman nodded absently. "I hope you enjoy the rest of the show," she said. "It is fun."

Wason finished his whisky and returned to his seat. It had been an instructive afternoon, he thought.

He glanced at his programme. A giant electric chicken was on its way to the village of Nick Nock, where no evil could reside for long, to deal with the big bad wolf, it seemed. Wason smiled at the stage. Serve the bastard right!

The curtain began to rise and Little Red Riding Hood and her friends were back on stage before Wason noticed that the girl who had been sitting next to him earlier was no longer there.

Looking round he found himself being glared at by her father. They must have changed places during the interval, Wason thought, and tried not to panic.

# CHAPTER THIRTEEN

The huge, hand-painted safety curtain dropped slowly into place behind the proscenium arch. Using hydraulics, it was raised in the presence of the audience before the start of each performance, and lowered at the interval and end, in case of fire. Most of the advertisements which decorated its surface, in simple, gaudy style, were for soaps or cures of one kind or another, encouraging Henry Wason to conclude that Glaswegians were unusually concerned with cleanliness and the state of their health. The idea made him smile. It was an image of the hard, northern city, to which he had been despatched by the bullying Churchill, and without much choice, he hadn't considered before.

Wason no longer felt guilty about taking the afternoon off from tramping the streets looking for revolutionaries, real or imagined, and going to the Theatre Royal instead. He was forced to admit, to himself at least, that he was having a good time. It was nice, being able to enjoy the afterglow of an undemanding performance, recalling the laughter of the children, at ease with the world for the first time in days, he thought happily.

Wason hadn't the faintest idea what he wanted to do with the rest of the evening. It occurred to him that he might find a public house and treat himself to a drink or two before dinner. He had been warned that going to a strange bar in Glasgow might be risky, but at least it wouldn't be dull, Wason thought with a shrug. He wanted to avoid spending another evening alone in the dismal surroundings of the lounge in his hotel. Besides, he reminded himself seriously, thinking about his mission, he might learn something of interest from the talk going on around him in a pub. At the very least it would give him an opportunity to study ordinary citizens at close range and off-guard, he decided with a purposeful nod, glancing round at others in the audience now dispersing towards the various exits, and whatever fresh entertainment appealed to them, and was on offer in the city at that time of day. Wason chuckled. Judging by the number of children present, most of the adults accompanying them would be on their way home to a quiet family dinner, and an evening in front of the fire, the latest P.G. Wodehouse for company, if they were lucky. That would be the limit of their excitement for one night, Wason guessed wryly.

His own next course of action determined, Wason started to move. Then he remembered the girl who had been the cause of so much alarm and embarrassment during the first half performance, and slumped down in his seat again. Girls like that, strangers, could be a load of trouble, Wason thought, coughing quietly, and glancing round nervously, half expecting to see her standing somewhere, in the company of the theatre manager perhaps, pointing at Wason, accusing him.

Of what? Wason didn't know.

Wason enjoyed the company of women his own age and younger, so long as they didn't try and take the matter of them being together too seriously. He took the view, formed as a result of close and careful scrutiny, that women are unscrupulous creatures, totally unpredictable, and always liable to behave badly given the slightest excuse. Breeding didn't help, Wason reminded himself grimly. Girls whom he knew well, or encountered at society parties, appeared to have their hearts set on marriage at whatever cost to friendship; a circumstance Wason was determined to avoid, despite the compensations offered by their presence on those occasions when they wished to be genial. Whenever his mother complained about his attitude, which she maintained was particularly distressing to her personally – as she expected him to do his duty and continue the family line by giving her a grandson, whom she could treasure and adore – Wason always pleaded that the exigencies of the service, and the demands of his career, prevented him from doing so. Quite often the strength of his resolve made his mother cry, and Wason was forced to struggle hard to stop himself feeling sorry for her; and thus find himself engaged to whatever hungry young miss happened to be in favour at the time. However, as she quite often made clear, it was a battle of wills his mother was determined to win, and one which, in his darkest moments, Wason expected to lose.

Now Wason shuddered, recalling the girl's father glowering at him in a most disconcerting and uncompromising fashion, as the family pushed past him into the aisle, following the final curtain, and as soon as the applause ended, when the company didn't bother to reappear; their performers' smiles and departing waves an indication that they were well satisfied with the results of another day's work, happily received, and generously acknowledged by the departing audience.

Fearful of being challenged, and anxious to avoid an unpleasant scene, Wason remained in his seat while the audience continued to disperse. Not until he found himself alone in the dress-circle, apart from two usherettes, who were busy tipping seats, and looking for articles left behind, did Wason decide it was safe to depart.

He found the foyer jammed with people, crowding into Hope Street, and jostling for places on a tram already packed with workers going home. The weight of the crowd carried him to the right where Hope Street ended on a corner. It was already dark and beginning to rain.

A street sign told Wason that he was on the corner of Hope Street and Cowcaddens. Tenement houses stretched away on either side of what appeared to be the outline of a church black against the evening sky. The name Cowcaddens puzzled Wason. What on earth could it mean? he wondered and shrugged, half expecting to find himself trampled underfoot by rampaging cattle.

From the other side of the street he could hear the unmistakable sounds of a public house on a busy night. Wason hesitated. He had been told countless horror stories of the dangers facing any stranger foolish enough to enter a public house in Glasgow on his own: worse still, Wason remembered, when the stranger happened to be an Englishman.

He frowned at his own nervousness. Churchill wanted him to prove that a revolution was being planned in the city: he would be furious with him if he failed. How else did he expect to find out what was going on without taking risks?

His sense of duty, coupled with an obstinate anxiety about what Churchill would say if he felt let down, prevailed. Wason crossed Cowcaddens and stopped outside the door of the pub. A sign said WOMEN NOT ALLOWED. He grunted approvingly. Serve them bloody well right, he thought, pushing the door open, determined now that he would face whatever danger was waiting to greet him.

The noise was deafening. Bedlam, thought Wason, unable to believe his ears. If these people were friends, God help their enemies. Who could think in such a din? Men wearing caps and scarves under their coats stood shoulder to shoulder, talking at one another in loud angry voices, and drinking earnestly. A hundred different arguments, exploding all at the same time, threatened to hurl everyone into the street. Wason stayed by the door for a moment, adjusting his ears to the noise, and his eyes to the smoke.

Something brushed against his legs, making him jump, and almost producing a fearful yelp. A little man standing beside him stared at Wason across the top of his pint. "Don't worry," the little man grunted. "He won't bite."

Wason glanced down and saw the skeletal shape of a dun-coloured whippet, which the little man appeared to be holding on a lead in his pocket, pressed against him. The little man's lips never moved from his pint. "Anyway," he went on in a thick, flat voice, and an accent Wason barely understood, "if he does have a go at ye, take my advice and just run."

Wason stared down at the dog, puzzled. The little man cackled quietly. "Mister," he said, "the bugger'll never catch ye."

Wason smiled uncertainly, sensing a joke.

"There's never been wan ran slower than this," the little man confided, matter-of-factly. "In fact, if you've a use for him, you can take him wi' pleasure. There's naebody else wants him. Would you look at him," the little man added, giving the whippet a contemptuous look and tugging on his lead.

A mean-looking brute, with pointed teeth, and a large tongue which hung from the side of its mouth, its breath coming in rapid gasps, the whippet was so thin Wason could count the ribs. But he didn't feel compelled to touch it. Having gathered from its owner that the whippet lacked racing pace, he couldn't help thinking the animal might respond sharply enough if someone stood on it. In the crush of feet surrounding them this could happen at any moment. He moved away, pushing towards the bar, nodding at the little man as he went.

"See you," the little man said.

The bar was a long counter, with a high, wooden-and-glass gantry behind it, and three men serving. One of the men, who appeared to be the oldest, wore a black alpaca jacket denoting that he was a charge-hand. He finished giving a customer some change before turning to look at Wason, inquiringly.

"Yes, sir?"

"Can I have whisky, please?"

"Any special kind of whisky?"

"I don't think so," Wason answered.

"Do you want Scotch or Irish?" the barman inquired.

The question surprised Wason.

"A lot of people who come in here like Irish," the barman explained roughly.

"I see," said Wason, doubtfully. "I think I'll stay with Scotch, if you don't mind."

"We've got Bushmill's red and Bushmill's green if you prefer it," the barman added.

"I don't think so," Wason said.

The barman nodded and glanced at the gantry. "Any special kind of Scotch?" he asked.

Wason shook his head. "Why don't you recommend something?" he suggested.

"Large or small?"

Wason hesitated. "Large, I think," he said finally.

The barman brought a bottle of Ballochmyle from the gantry and showed it to Wason for his approval. Wason nodded. Although the name meant nothing to him he was quite happy to accept anything the barman offered. He was then shown a pewter measure which the barman filled to the brim in front of him without spilling a drop. Wason sensed that the barman wanted him to admire his expertise and he chuckled admiringly. The barman held the measure in front of him for a moment, keeping it steady, not spilling anything, enjoying the ritual, showing off a little, finally upending the whisky into a short, stubby glass in a single, confident flourish.

"To you, sir, that'll be one and tuppence," the barman said. "Cheap at the price, eh?"

"Do you have any ice?"

"We don't keep ice, sir," the barman replied.

Wason decided against making a fuss about the lack of ice.

"There's a fishmonger just across the road by the Queen's Arcade," the barman told him. "Have you thought about trying there for some ice?"

His tone wasn't unfriendly and Wason grinned. "Do you think I could have some water?" he asked.

"There's no shortage of water," the barman muttered, pushing a dirt-stained jug towards him, and leaving him to his drink.

Wason filled the little glass almost to the brim before trying the whisky for taste. A little more water and it would be fine, Wason decided, praying desperately that whatever lived in that jug wouldn't survive the whisky for long.

Paler now, the amber fluid trembled on the edge of the glass as

Wason raised it to his lips, and tried the whisky for taste once again. It still tasted stronger than the whisky served in his club in St James but he decided to drink it anyway. If he kept on adding water to the little glass someone might notice and consider his behaviour strange. The last thing he wanted was to draw needless attention to himself. The question of how best to behave in his present surroundings was a source of some worry. He was conscious of looking different from everyone else in the bar. However, as far as he could judge, no-one was paying any special attention to him. The other customers were too busy drinking and shouting at one another to brother about him, he thought, grunting.

A large man in a tweed suit emerged from behind a lead and glass partition, which concealed what appeared to be a little office, at the far end of the bar. He behaved like the owner, Wason thought, sensing that he had been spotted as a new face in the crowd. The man was heading towards him when someone to Wason's right reached across the bar and stopped him. Wason couldn't hear what was said but the big man responded with a smile. "Let's wait until Saturday," Wason heard him say. "Saturday could decide the league. Celtic aren't out of it yet."

He approached Wason and stopped. "Good evening, sir," he offered.

"Good evening," Wason replied, liking his manner.

"Have you been to the theatre?"

Wason nodded, surprised. "How did you know?" he asked.

The tall man smiled. "I hadn't seen you here before, that's all. Quite a lot of strangers come in for a drink straight from the theatre," the tall man added. "I'm always glad to see them."

"Are you the landlord?" Wason inquired.

He nodded.

"Is it always this busy?" Wason went on, adding with a smile, "Not to mention noisy?"

"I'd say this is about average. Fridays and Saturdays are our best nights."

He appeared to sense what Wason was thinking.

"We try and keep them in order."

Wason smiled uncomfortably.

"Is this your first visit to Glasgow?"

Wason shook his head. "I was here as a student," he replied.

The landlord showed interest. "At the university?" he asked.

"No," said Wason, "I was at St Andrews, actually. But I came here several times with a friend who lived in Park Gardens."

The landlord grunted. "I don't have many customers who live in that part of town," he said.

Wason shifted uncomfortably.

"Are you just visiting?"

"No," said Wason, "I'm working."

"Really."

"I'm a journalist," Wason explained.

"With one of the London papers?"

Wason shook his head. "I'm with an agency," he said.

"Here to write about the strike, I suppose?"

"Yes."

"One of my regular customers is a journalist," the landlord said. "In fact, he was in earlier. He's probably still here," he added, looking round. "Would you like to meet him?"

Wason would have preferred time to consider the offer. Being introduced to a real working journalist might prove hazardous, he thought nervously. However, he told himself, his mind racing wildly, it might appear odd, not to mention ill-mannered, if he refused.

"Yes, there he is," the landlord cried, spotting his quarry, and beckoning him over.

A pink-faced man with thinning hair pushed towards them. He appeared to be scowling slightly and the thought crossed Henry Wason's mind that he might have been responsible in part for dragging the other man away from an interesting companion or an important conversation. The landlord was the one who had been quite insistent in wanting the man over and Wason had no wish to impose himself, or appear a nuisance, to some total stranger. At least women weren't allowed in the pub so he couldn't be blamed for interrupting anything in that line of activity.

"Frank, I want you to meet a fellow journalist," the landlord said.

He turned to Wason. "I'm sorry," he said, "You didn't tell me your name."

Wason told him.

"This is Frank Munro. Frank's with the Examiner," the landlord said.

They shook hands. Munro noted the good London clothes and the kind of manner which, in his experience at any rate, was usually associated with a moneyed background and an expensive education.

"Who are you with?"

"I'm an agency man," replied Wason.

"Which one?" Munro inquired, unable to resist the thought that agency reporters were notoriously underpaid, while admiring the other man's splendid coat.

Wason shrugged apologetically. "It isn't one of the big ones, I'm afraid," he replied. "We're a small outfit who specialise in doing background features for overseas markets."

Munro looked interested. "Really?" he said. "What's brought you to Glasgow? The strike, I suppose."

Wason nodded eagerly.

"It's a good story," Munro observed, watching him closely.

"Frank's been writing about nothing else for weeks," the landlord remarked, smiling.

"I don't suppose you'd let me pick your brains?" Wason smiled.

"This is a hard game," Munro replied.

Wason nodded ruefully.

"What did you do before?"

"I worked in America for quite a long time," Wason told him. "My father has business interests there."

"I see," said Munro. "So you'd miss the war?"

"I'm afraid so, yes," Wason answered.

"So did I," Munro admitted. "They didn't want me."

He turned to the landlord. "Can I have another drink please, Willie? What are you drinking?" he added, glancing at Wason.

"No, please," Wason protested, "let me buy this."

Frank Munro scowled. "I'm buying," he insisted.

Wason, not wishing to risk causing offence, nodded quickly. "Can I have a whisky, please?"

"Any special kind?"

"The same as last time will be fine," Wason replied.

Munro stared at him for a moment. "Don't you know what it was called?"

"The barman knows," Wason said, conscious of feeling foolish.

"I've never met a whisky drinker who didn't know the name of what he was drinking before," Munro observed drily. "Considering the price of it nowadays, you should make a point of knowing. Willie," he went on, giving the landlord a serious look, "will you kindly ask John, or whoever it was served Mr Wason last time, to let him have the same again. And I'll have another pint."

"The gentleman is drinking Ballochmyle." It was the chargehand, who had served Wason before, and who was now pushing past the

131

landlord on his way to another customer, who spoke. "A large one," he added, winking, and treating Munro to a small, compassionate smile.

"Ballochmyle," he repeated mournfully. "A large one."

"A small whisky would be fine," Wason said.

"A large one's been ordered," said Munro.

Munro put both hands on the bar. "Where do you expect to sell?" he inquired casually while they waited for their drinks to arrive.

"I understand the New York Times may be interested."

"Really?" said Munro, impressed. "That's big stuff."

Henry Wason shrugged diffidently. "You know Americans," he said. "Europe is fashionable at the moment. Having saved civilisation from the crazy hun, and sent President Wilson to sort out all our future problems, there's an almost insatiable appetite there for information on what's going on over here."

Munro looked interested. "Including Glasgow, you say?"

Wason nodded enthusiastically. "At the moment Glasgow is big news worldwide," he declared.

"I suppose so," Munro agreed, thoughtfully.

When their drinks arrived Wason noticed with dismay that he had been given another small glass. He needed a tumbler, for all that whisky, but was afraid to ask.

"Is it the water you like?" Frank Munro inquired roughly, watching Wason fill his glass to the brim, and obviously wanting more.

"I find the measures a bit heavy," Wason admitted.

Munro shook his head emphatically. "That's because of the daft wee measures you'll be used to in London," he said. "What you get there doesn't deserve to be called a drink. You could lose it in your eye," he added, scornfully.

Henry Wason sipped cautiously at the whisky, fearful of spilling most of it on the sawdust-covered floor.

"Anyway," Munro went on, "if you want all that water, why don't you ask for a bigger glass? John," he shouted, attracting the chargehand's attention, "can you give this man a bigger glass, a tumbler, or something?"

The chargehand brought Munro a half-pint glass. "Is this wan big enough?" he inquired, scowling.

Wason took the glass gratefully. "This will be fine," he said hurriedly.

The chargehand glanced at Munro and moved away, muttering something under his breath. Munro smiled. "I don't think he's used to seeing anyone drinking whisky out of a half-pint tumbler," he remarked, "even here where you will find a number of gentlemen who are more than a little partial to partaking of the water of life."

Wason grimaced.

"It isn't a bad idea, if you want something, to just ask for it," Munro added.

Wason smiled apologetically.

Munro gulped at his beer. "Slange."

"Pardon?"

"It means cheers," Munro explained, licking froth from his upper lip.

"Oh," said Wason. "I see. Cheers."

Frank Munro was studying him carefully, sizing him up, Wason realised, his heart beginning to pound.

"Anyway, I'm more interested in the idea that you are in Glasgow, on behalf of the highly prestigious *New York Times*, intending to write about our big strike," Munro said.

"I'm not really here on behalf of the *New York Times*," Wason corrected him carefully. "What I meant was that my agency think they can interest the *New York Times* in one or two articles on the strike and the city generally."

"What do you know about the strike?"

"Only what I've read in the London papers," Wason admitted.

"You can't depend on them," Munro told him firmly. "They're out of touch. You should go to the Mitchell Library in the morning and see what you can find in the Scottish papers."

"Which ones do you recommend, apart from your own, of course?"

"You should try the *Record* and the *Herald*," Munro told him. "Both of them know what's going on. While you're at it, you should also keep a lookout for the Strike Bulletin being issued by the workers themselves. They'll give you some idea of what the men are thinking."

"That's a good idea," Wason responded enthusiastically. "Where can I find them?"

"You'll see them on sale anywhere there's a large meeting."

"That's useful," Wason said.

"Rather than send someone who doesn't know the city, or any of the people involved in the strike, didn't your agency think about asking someone local to do you a piece?" Munro inquired, pointedly. "Quite a few of us do lineage for the PA, for instance. I'm sure one of us could have given your people what they wanted."

Wason tried to look apologetic. The idea that he might be treading on local toes, by denying Glasgow-based journalists an opportunity to make extra cash, hadn't occurred to him before.

"I think the idea was to look at the city with a different eye," Wason explained, cautiously.

Munro drank his beer and nodded. "Colour pieces," he said, thoughtfully.

"That's right," agreed Wason. "Colour pieces."

"What kind of colour pieces?" Munro wanted to know.

Wason hesitated. "Articles about the city, how it's facing up to the strike, profiles of the leaders, what the ordinary people think," he said finally.

"Won't you need an angle?"

Wason suspected a trap. "What do you mean?" he inquired, cautiously.

"The Americans are bound to want you to come up with something different, surely?" Munro explained, frowning.

"I suppose so," Wason admitted nervously, conscious suddenly that his knowledge of what an American newspaper might want in the way of a story was somewhat scant.

"On the other hand," Munro continued cheerfully, "as the Yanks generally don't know their arse from their elbow, you might be able to sell them any old rubbish."

Wason smiled weakly. "Don't you rate American journalism very high?"

Munro shrugged. "It's all right, I suppose, although there are reporters working in this city I'd back against anyone," he said.

Henry Wason accepted this assertion willingly enough, pulling at his ear, and nodding wisely. His new acquaintance might prove useful before long and Wason didn't want to risk upsetting the man by giving him an argument. Wason sipped at his whisky, murmuring encouragement, and waited for Munro to continue.

"Anyway, there's a lot of stuff about," Munro went on obligingly.

"I'm glad to hear it," replied Wason, looking relieved.

Munro treated him to a wicked smile. "So long as you can find it, of course. You won't want to miss anything," he added, pointedly.

Wason grimaced. "No," he admitted, feeling vulnerable.

"It's easily enough done," Munro reminded him gloomily.

"Don't I know it," Wason agreed.

He downed his whisky with a nervous gulp. "Let me get you another drink."

Frank Munro chuckled. "A few more of those and what you don't know you can always make up."

"Same again?"

Frank Munro nodded. "I don't want a heavy night, not tonight. I thought I'd just coast," he said.

"It's quite a story, isn't it?"

Frank Munro scowled. "Outside the war it's the biggest challenge this country has faced in years," he said.

Wason tried not to look too excited. "You really believe it's that big?" he inquired, keeping his voice casual, and handing Munro a fresh pint which he took from the barman who served them last time. Although he would have preferred something else, a soft drink even, he ordered another large whisky for himself. This time, without being asked, the barman brought him his drink in a large glass. Frank Munro smiled bleakly. "As you can see, people learn fast around here," he remarked.

"I didn't want to cause a fuss."

"Some fuss," retorted Munro.

Wason nodded and smiled.

"Do you know anyone in the city? Any contacts, I mean?"

"Not really," Wason said.

"It won't be too easy starting from scratch," Munro warned.

"I don't suppose so," Wason admitted.

"You shouldn't have any trouble with the strike leaders," Munro told him. "They'll talk to anyone."

"At least that's something," Wason replied.

"Shinwell, especially, is always good for a quote," Munro went on. "So's Gallacher."

"What about the employers?"

Munro grunted. "They're an unhelpful bunch, generally," he replied. "They work on the principle, least said, soonest mended."

"That may be the sensible thing for them to do," Wason suggested, cautiously.

Frank Munro stared at him over the top of his pint. "Interesting you should think so," he said.

"Aren't they the ones with most to lose?"

"That's what they say," Munro replied with a grim chuckle.

"What the men are seeking is more money for fewer working hours, as I understand it," Wason continued quickly. "One or other would be reasonable, perhaps, but not both, surely?"

"Is that what you think?"

"Don't you?"

"I don't know," Munro replied

"It sounds a bit greedy to me."

Munro nodded. "How do you feel about the employers wanting to cut wages?" he asked.

Wason sensed he was heading for trouble.

"Or the landlords raising rents to a level the workers can't afford because the employers, who are often the landlords in a different guise, won't pay them enough?"

Wason was reminded suddenly of the minister he met on the train. Why were these damned Scots so bloody quarrelsome?

"As I understand it, whatever way you dress things up, the argument is about more people being needed to do the same amount of work, and all of them demanding more pay," Wason said.

"And?"

"That's bad business," Wason complained.

"Would it be good business if the workers went on a prolonged strike which brought the entire country to a halt?"

"The employers would need to fight," Wason told him.

"Of course they'd fight," Munro agreed. "I am simply trying to respond to your point about an increase in wages being bad for business. A lot worse things could happen to business."

Wason didn't answer. Munro continued:

"Anyway, with the war over and all those men returning from the trenches looking for work, don't you think high unemployment could be the cause of real trouble eventually?"

Wason sighed. "Everyone feels sorry for the men who fought in the war," he replied.

"If there was an increase in productivity, so that we were able to sell more abroad, wouldn't that be good for business?" Munro suggested. "Also, presumably, the more people who are in work, the more money they have available to spend on themselves. Isn't that good for business?"

"I'm not an economist," Wason mumbled.

Frank Munro grinned. "Neither am I," he conceded. "But as an argument it does seem to make some sense. So why doesn't the government tackle the problem from that end?" he added.

"What's it got to do with the government?" Wason objected.

"You don't think the government is entitled to some say in the prosperity of the country?"

"I don't think they should be expected to interfere in the way a man runs his business," Wason replied.

"Even if the national interest is being threatened?"

Henry Wason saw his chance. "In London," he said, sipping at his drink, and choosing his words carefully, "a lot of people seem to think that this strike is only the start of something worse."

Munro nodded grimly. "A lot of people here will tell you the same thing," he replied.

"That's interesting," Wason said. "What do you think?"

"Shinwell would put a stop to it."

Wason sounded surprised. "People in London think he's the worst of the lot," he said.

Frank Munro shrugged. "If you ask me," he retorted, "the employers, and the authorities generally, are lucky to have Shinwell."

"What about the rest of them?"

"Gallacher's probably a bit wild," Munro admitted. "He's the main organiser, of course, not Shinwell."

"Gallacher's a communist, isn't he?"

Munro nodded.

"Him and John Maclean together?" Wason said.

Frank Munro frowned. "What does that mean?" he asked.

"I've read a lot about John Maclean."

"You make him sound quite sinister," Munro observed. "Is that what you want?"

"Not at all," Henry Wason tried to reassure him hurriedly. "I'm just looking for background, that's all."

Frank Munro drank from his glass and waited for him to continue.

"It's interesting what you say about Shinwell," said Wason. "I must try and meet him."

"You'll find him hard as nails, with a mean temper," Munro warned. "He's been around Glasgow a long time, of course. The family originate from London. His father was a tailor in the East End who came here looking for work. Shinwell's fond of boasting that he was only eleven years old when he started work himself. He's been a full-time union official for years. You should ask him about the time someone tried to assassinate him on the Suspension Bridge."

"Really?"

"A bit of a bully-boy when he isn't getting his own way," added

Munro. "But the man's a realist and, if you want my opinion, I think his heart's in the right place."

"He sounds interesting," Wason remarked. "I must make a point of meeting him."

Munro gave him a hard look. "I'd say it's essential," he said.

Wason hoped he hadn't allowed his cover to slip. He was conscious suddenly of beginning to feel drunk. All those whiskies, he thought; not enough water.

"Shinwell is due to speak at a big rally in the St Andrew's Halls tomorrow," Frank Munro continued. "Come along and you can meet him afterwards. I'll introduce you."

"That would be good of you," Wason replied, trying not to sound shaky.

"Are you all right?"

Wason shook his head. "Not entirely," he admitted. "Would you say that's a particularly strong whisky I've been drinking?"

Munro chuckled. "I thought you understood about the measures," he said.

"Obviously, from the way I feel, I must have misjudged them," Wason confessed.

"Where are you staying?"

Wason told him.

"Really?"

In similar circumstances, Frank Munro couldn't help thinking, his expenses would have stretched to a good commercial hotel at best; but never anything as grand as the Central, the biggest and most expensive place in town.

"Anyway, you're lucky," Munro told him. "From here it's downhill all the way."

"That's good," Wason sighed.

Munro chuckled. "Come on," he said, finishing his pint, "I'll point you in the right direction at least."

He said goodnight to the nearest barman and waved to the landlord, who was at the far end of the bar counter talking to a customer.

"It looks like being a dirty night," Munro remarked as they crossed Cowcaddens and turned into Hope Street. "There's a been a lot of fog recently."

"I hate fog," Wason said.

"It's a fact of life in Glasgow," Munro grunted.

"London too," Wason said.

"At least you haven't far to go. Hug the wall and try not to wander off on the crossings. There's quite a few of them, so be careful."

Frank Munro stopped on the pavement outside the main entrance to the Theatre Royal. "I live over there," he said, pointing across the street to a red-sandstone tenement with shopfronts underneath.

"That's handy," Wason said, and shivered.

"You could wait for a tram but you would be quicker walking," Munro advised. "You'd better hurry before the fog thickens. Only the other night, I finished up lost on the other side of the street, right outside the close where I live. Have you ever felt damned stupid?" he added ruefully.

They shook hands. "I am grateful to you for offering to introduce me to Shinwell," Wason said.

"When he finds out that you write for the *New York Times*, and a lot of other foreign papers, besides," Munro told him, "you won't need any help from me."

Henry Wason nodded gravely. If he could fool an experienced reporter like Frank Munro, why not Shinwell next?

Deception was easy, he thought fuzzily.

# CHAPTER FOURTEEN

St Andrew's Halls, an elegant building of light brown sandstone, fronted by a magnificent colonnade consisting of sixteen Ionic columns, occupied the main part of an island site to the west of North Street and to the rear of the Mitchell Library. Arriving there, intent on locating Willie McGrandle and hearing his account of Shinwell's speech on the employers' latest response to the workers' demands, Derek Taylor found the area around the hall blocked by a huge crowd whose numbers he put at not less than thirty thousand; including a white-haired woman who was waving a red flag and shouting, "Down with the bosses!"

The St Andrew's Halls provided a favourite venue for important meetings and political rallies in the city. Derek Taylor could remember being there, three years earlier, at the height of the war, when Lloyd George had been shouted down by an audience of munition workers, furious with him for wanting to recruit unskilled workers, and pay them the same as skilled men, to work in munitions. Looking confident, almost smug, the Prime Minister misjudged the mood of the men completely. When he talked in an over-aggressive manner about his dream of building a land fit for heroes after the war, the audience, not trusting him, grew restless; and, finally, as he left the platform the boos of the workers were ringing in his ears. Derek Taylor could also remember thinking then that the people of Glasgow would wait a long time before they could expect any help from that particular quarter in future.

Now, as he went in search of Willie McGrandle, he could see that those who occupied Granville Street extended in an unbroken mass on to the front steps of the building and into the foyer; and from there, no doubt, right into the main building where another three thousand people would be listening to Shinwell. He wasn't surprised by the size of the crowd. It had been evident for weeks that the strike leaders commanded the attention of the men. Only the employers, and perhaps the government, believed otherwise.

Derek Taylor couldn't help thinking, however that those nearest to him appeared depressingly cheerful and not at all threatening: a mixed bag of ages, but mostly men in their thirties and forties, who exchanged slogans and bantered insults at one another while they waited for their mates inside to come out and report. Taylor consoled himself with the thought that, when the time for real action arrived, their mood would change.

"What do you think Shinwell's telling them right now?"

The question came from a tall, pale-faced lad who had been pushed against him in the crowd. Taylor, not wishing to commit himself, shrugged. His inquisitor wore a cap and scarf and kept his hands buried in his pockets.

"He must be telling them something."

Taylor nodded thoughtfully, hoping to discourage him.

"Shinwell's all right, isn't he?" the lad persisted stubbornly.

"Of course," Taylor told him.

"So what do you think will happen?"

"I don't feel too optimistic," Taylor replied.

"Don't you? Are you on strike as well, then?" the lad inquired, staring.

Taylor was aware of other people listening. "No," he admitted, feeling trapped. "I work at the University. I'm a sort of teacher.'

"Does that mean you're clever?" the lad inquired, grinning.

Taylor tried not to sound foolish. People in the crowd were nudging one another, nodding in his direction. "Not particularly," he replied.

The lad laughed. Derek Taylor tried to exclude himself from his company. With the crowd pressing against them it wasn't easy, however.

"This one says he works at the uni," the lad said to a friend. "He says Shinwell's wasting his time. He doesn't think we'll be offered anything worthwhile. That's what you said, isn't it?" the lad added, glowering at Taylor.

"I don't think the employers will want to give much away," Taylor agreed. "Certainly not at this stage."

"You see," the first lad said to his friend.

"Does that mean we could be out on strike forever, then?" the second boy wanted to know.

"If that happens we'll starve, won't we," his companion remarked matter-of-factly.

"It won't be too good for the bosses either, will it?"

The first lad was grinning now, nudging Taylor. "Anyway, what do you know that we don't know?" he inquired happily. "Just because you work at the uni doesn't mean to say you know everything, does it?"

"What's he doing here, anyway?"

Derek Taylor shifted uncomfortably. He was beginning to feel threatened. But he was unable to move because of the crowd.

"This is our fight," a big man with a mottled face announced. "It's got nothing to do with the likes of you," he added, scowling at Taylor.

The remark angered Taylor. Didn't the fool realise that appearances could be misleading? He was as much one of them as any of them, Taylor thought. In the end, Taylor believed, it would be his brains and determination and planning which would change their lives.

"Him and his kind should keep away," the big man continued, looking round, seeking support.

"It's got nothing to do with them, you're right," someone else agreed.

"If you ask me, he looks too damned pleased with himself for his own good," the big man observed darkly.

The first lad, invoking comradeship, nudged Taylor in the ribs. "Why don't you come out on strike with us," he suggested earnestly, "instead of just watching? What do you think would happen if everybody at the uni went on strike? Would anybody miss them?"

"I don't think it would help," Taylor replied uneasily.

"We won't know if you don't try, will we?" the lad insisted stubbornly.

The big man with the mottled face was scornful. "People like him are all talk," he remarked.

The big man looked dangerous, Taylor thought.

"He wants to cause trouble," the big man continued, looking round those who were close to them in the crowd, "that's what he wants."

Derek Taylor could see that people, previously not involved, were craning towards them, staring at him, muttering dangerously; exchanging the little information they possessed on the subject of himself, Taylor realised, most of them talking in nods and grunts which encouraged alarm. It was with an enormous sense of relief, therefore, that he spotted Willie McGrandle leaving the St Andrew's Halls by a side door.

"Excuse me!" said Taylor, grateful for an excuse to be rid of his tormentors. "Excuse me!' he repeated, forcing a path through the crowd and shouting for McGrandle to wait.

"I didn't think I'd find you," Taylor said when they were together in the middle of the street. "What's happening?"

"Everybody's going to the City Chambers," explained McGrandle, eyes bright with excitement. "Shinwell is demanding to see the Lord Provost."

"What for?"

"He wants the Lord Provost to send a message to Downing Street insisting that the government comes out on our side."

People struggling to separate themselves and form up in marching order, pushed against them. Taylor could see Shinwell, accompanied by Davey Kirkwood, making his way towards the head of the procession; and the woman with the red flag talking to Gallacher.

Conscious suddenly of his own excitement, Taylor contemplated the effect on the authorities of all those people arriving together in George Square prepared, in the name of justice, to confront no less a dignitary than the Lord Provost himself. As well as being head of the Town Council the Lord Provost acted as Lord Lieutenant for the City of Glasgow, in special service to the King, and probably felt safe in the City Chambers; a feeling of security well justified in the past but no longer, perhaps: the idea was intriguing, Taylor thought.

"What makes him think the Lord Provost will oblige?"

"Shinwell says he doesn't have any choice. If the government refuses to make the employers settle on our terms, then Shinwell wants a national strike. The country would be ruined," McGrandle added, shrugging.

The idea appealed to Taylor. "What are the employers saying?" he asked.

"They won't budge," McGrandle replied.

"I don't give much for Shinwell's chances with the Lord Provost."

McGrandle shrugged. "I suppose it's worth a try," he replied. "Are you coming?"

"I'd like to see what happens," Taylor admitted.

"Let's try and stay close to Shinwell," McGrandle suggested.

A young man in an expensive-looking coat appeared beside them. "I thought I'd lost you," the young man gasped.

Derek Taylor didn't know him. However, Willie McGrandle nodded recognition and explained off-handedly:

"Derek, this is Henry Wason. He's a reporter from London."

"I'm with an agency," Wason said, shaking hands.

"A reporter I know on the *Examiner* asked me to look after him," McGrandle added, eyeing Taylor.

143

"From London, you say?" inquired Taylor.

"Yes," said Wason. "I work for an agency which specialises in selling material overseas, in America mostly. I'm here to write about the strike."

"He wants to interview Shinwell."

Taylor nodded. "Presumably he'll want to talk to reporters once he's seen the Lord Provost."

"I hope so," Wason told him.

"We'd better hurry or we'll be stuck at the back," McGrandle warned. They tried pushing their way towards the head of the procession.

"That's Willie McGrandle," someone said. "Better let him through."

Some of the men were starting to sing. McGrandle grinned. "Ever hear that before?" he asked.

Wason shook his head. He could barely make out the words.

> I don't like the factor,
> his rent I won't pay
> Three cheers for John Wheatley,
> I'm striking today!

"Maxton wrote it," McGrandle told him.

"I see."

"Listen!"

His singing voice was weak and tuneless. Wason tried not to appear embarrassed. McGrandle and the others didn't seem to mind the noise he was making, however. They were obviously enjoying themselves immensely; and totally committed to the words of the song which they interpreted with all the strength and passion they could muster.

> To hell with the landlord,
> I'm not one to grouse
> But to hell both with him
> And his bloody old house!

"Willie, that was great, just great!" one of the men cried in a choking voice as soon as McGrandle had finished. "Will you stey an' sing it again?"

McGrandle slapped the man on the shoulder and shook his head cheerfully. "No' this time, Hughie," he replied. "I'm due to march at the front beside Shinwell."

"Oh, aye, of course, so you will!" said the man. "Tell him from me there's nothing fur him tae worry aboot. He can depend on us tae back him a' the wey!"

McGrandle pummelled at the other man's shoulder by way of

acknowledging the depth of his commitment. He was a riveter at Fairfields, a strong union man, married with three kids, who lived in Govan.

"He knows that, Hughie!" McGrandle cried. "We all know it! Don't you worry! You're one of the best, I tell you!"

The other man grinned, delighted to have his importance recognised by one of the strike leaders in front of his mates. He looked round happily. "Let Willie McGrandle through!" he shouted. "He's needed at the front!"

Some of the men stared curiously at Wason, who looked considerably out of place in the crowd, as he followed on McGrandle's heels. But no-one tried to stop him or interfere with his progress in any way. There was no mistaking the affection with which the men regarded the young shop steward. Some of them made a point of calling out encouragement to McGrandle, raising their fists in support, and slapping him on the back, as he pushed past them on his way to the head of the procession.

Shinwell, who was already in his accustomed place at the front, saw McGrandle approaching through the crowd and waved. McGrandle nodded and pushed towards him, gesturing for Wason to stay with him.

"Do you know Shinwell quite well?" Wason inquired.

Willie McGrandle nodded.

"I hope I'll get a chance to talk to him later."

"Why don't you try and grab him now?" McGrandle suggested.

"Won't he mind?"

"He likes the publicity," McGrandle grinned. "Manny," he added, attracting the strike leader's attention as the march was about to begin, "this is a reporter from London who would like a word."

Shinwell appraised Wason with a quizzical look. "Can you walk and talk at the same time?" he inquired jauntily.

"I think so," Wason replied as the marchers left Berkeley Street on their way to George Square.

Shinwell's step was brisk. "Are you here to write lies or do you propose reporting the truth?"

"The truth, I hope, Mr Shinwell."

"Do you suppose that you are able to recognise the truth when you see it?"

"I hope so, sir."

"Why do you call me sir?" Shinwell asked.

The question unsettled Wason.

"Reporters aren't generally so polite," Shinwell added.

Wason kept in step as they marched along Bath Street towards the city centre, and didn't answer.

Shinwell smiled wickedly. "I don't mind reporters as a rule. Sometimes they take themselves far too seriously and their idea of ethics leaves much to be desired. One reporter of my acquaintance actually admitted to me that he didn't believe in letting the truth get in the way of a good story. Isn't that a shocking thing to say, Mr –."

"Wason. Henry Wason."

"I hope you aren't that kind of journalist, Mr Wason."

"I hope not, Mr Shinwell."

"Of course, the people I totally detest and despise are the editors and the proprietors," Shinwell continued.

Wason stared at him.

"It doesn't much matter whether a reporter is honest or not," Shinwell explained. "You must be aware that newspapers in this country are controlled by a handful of quite unscrupulous men, Mr Wason. They will never allow the truth to appear if it happens to conspire against their own best interests. They will do everything in their power to suppress it, or distort it, which, sometimes, when you are dealing with the truth, is by far the most damaging thing you can do."

He glanced at Wason. "You don't deny that this is true?"

"I'm sure it happens sometimes," Wason answered cautiously.

Shinwell, having set his trap with care, smiled cunningly. "What is the name of your newspaper, Mr Wason?" he inquired.

Henry Wason tried not to sound smug. "Actually," he responded, with only the slightest trace of triumph, "I work for an agency."

Shinwell responded with interest. "Then your work appears widely?" he remarked.

Wason nodded enthusiastically. "Most of our customers are overseas," he replied. "We send stories and articles to quite a number of papers and magazines in the United States, for example, as well as all the principal countries of the empire, naturally."

"I see."

"What do you expect from your meeting with the Lord Provost?" Wason asked.

Shinwell glanced at Davey Kirkwood marching beside him. "Mr Wason wants to know what we expect to get from our meeting with the Lord Provost," he said. "What do you think, Davey?"

A scowl crossed the big man's friendly face. "From that yin, not much," Kirkwood replied.

Shinwell smiled at Wason and turned to look at the huge crowd marching in step behind them. "There's your answer," he said.

Then, treating Wason to a mischievous wink, Shinwell added, "We'll give him something to think about, though, won't we?"

"Is it your intention to deliver an ultimatum to the civic authorities?"

"I intend to advise them of the seriousness of their position," Shinwell told him. "These men," he went on, indicating the marching strikers, "have been extremely patient, Mr Wason. They have behaved lawfully at all times. They have not resorted to force to further their claim. They have behaved reasonably. Wouldn't you say they are entitled to expect the authorities to respond in a similar manner? You may think that this is entirely a matter between us and the employers. But when we know that government policy is on the side of the employers, and against us, that Lloyd George is willing the employers to resist our demands at almost any cost, then who can blame us for turning our backs on the employers and going over their heads to the government itself? If the employers are merely puppets in a wider show, why deal with them when we can deal with the puppet-master himself, Lloyd George? Of course," Shinwell went on, as they left Cathedral Street and turned towards George Square, "we all know that Lloyd George has little regard for Glasgow. But we also know that he has a highly developed awareness of what's good for Lloyd George. Don't you think he would rather avoid the prospect of the whole of Britain being forced to a standstill because working people everywhere refuse to work? Don't forget, he is a vain man who says he wants to rebuild the country and make it a land fit for heroes. A nice phrase, certainly, but what does it mean? Who are these heroes? You can bet, I suppose, that his heroes aren't mine. What we can be sure about, however, is that Lloyd George wants to be remembered as something more than the questionable victor in an utterly wasteful and unnecessary war."

They were approaching George Square now, marching in disciplined columns twenty abreast, those at the rear more than half a mile behind the leaders. Through sheer weight of numbers all traffic had been forced to a halt along the entire length of the main route followed by the marchers: then, as the resulting chaos spread to feeder streets, the whole of the city centre had been paralysed. It would be interesting, Wason thought, to learn how citizens not involved in the strike reacted to the demonstration: people who were out of sympathy with the strikers, regardless of the issues, were bound to find the disturbance intolerable.

Shinwell appeared to be reading his thoughts. "Anybody who didn't know there's a war on knows now," he smiled

As they entered George Square from the Queen Street end, the leaders kept to the main road, dividing round several trams which blocked their approach to the boastful Victorian bulk of the City Chambers; while many of those following behind spilled out across the central garden reservation, heading for the far side of the square and a good view of Shinwell entering the headquarters of the Town Council for his confrontation with the Lord Provost.

"Gladstone won't like that," Willie McGrandle chuckled, pointing.

Shinwell had broken away from the front of the procession and, showing a total lack of respect, scrambled on to a statue of the fierce old man who had been four times Prime Minister of Britain; and which occupied a place of honour in front of the City Chambers.

People pouring into the square cheered wildly as soon as they spotted Shinwell clinging to Gladstone's arm. Eyes gleaming with excitement, and cheering himself hoarse, Willie McGrandle couldn't help marvelling. Designed to infuriate anyone watching from the first-floor corner windows of the Lord Provost's room across the street, it was a masterstroke, McGrandle thought.

The marchers, wanting a speech, surrounded the statue, and shouted at Shinwell to begin. The chairman of the Workers' Strike Committee grinned at them from his place of triumph and, throwing punches at the sky, appealed to his followers for silence.

"Behind those windows," he cried, and pointed to the City Chambers, "there are frightened men."

Henry Wason felt someone nudge him in the ribs. He glanced round and saw Willie McGrandle gazing at Shinwell with an intensity of feeling which startled Wason. There was an awful possibility, Wason thought, feeling aghast, that the young shop steward, to whom he had been introduced less than an hour ago, was about to start shedding tears of joy at the sight of Shinwell on his plinth.

"Isn't this bloody marvellous!" McGrandle whispered.

Henry Wason glanced round the crowd and saw faces alive with hope.

"Not everyone likes Shinwell," McGrandle continued, "but like him or not, you must admit the man's got balls."

Wason nodded. He was aware of Derek Taylor watching them, with an air of disapproval, Wason realised with some surprise. He turned and smiled. Taylor looked away.

"I intend telling them that we mean business!" Shinwell cried.

The crowd greeted his words with a roar.

"Whether they like it or not, and I don't suppose they will find the idea in any way appealing, I will make it plain to them that we will settle for nothing less than total victory!" Shinwell promised, his gaze sweeping the crowd, discouraging dissent. "When I see the Lord Provost," he added menacingly, "I propose reminding him that, as titular head of the city, he has a duty to be concerned about the welfare of all its citizens."

He paused, allowing his words to register. All around him the crowd growled their support.

"Of course, I can understand why the Lord Provost feels an obligation towards the employers and the landlords. They are his friends and I admire a man who supports his friends," Shinwell explained.

He waited while the expected laugh rippled round George Square. Henry Wason smiled grimly. Shinwell's performance was pure theatre.

"When I see him I must tell him how much we all admire his efforts on behalf of his friends," Shinwell continued effortlessly. "It may be, of course, that the Lord Provost doesn't realise they are the same unscrupulous men who have been for so long resisting the legitimate claims of the citizens he purports to lead."

His ironic manner worried Wason.

"Well, comrades," Shinwell continued, "each one of us has friends, more friends than the Lord Provost, I'll wager! The man standing next to you is your friend. Turn and look at him. Remember his face. He is a true friend, comrades! All of us here are friends! Please believe me, comrades, when I tell you victory is certain! So long as we stand together we cannot lose this fight. You'll see, the workers will triumph in the end!"

"We're with you, Manny!" someone shouted.

"Good old Manny!" another voice cried.

People were applauding him warmly, cheering and shouting slogans. "I say down with the bosses!" yelled the white-haired woman with the red flag.

"That's right, comrade!" a man standing nearby encouraged. "Down with the bosses!"

"Who is that?" Wason inquired, indicating the woman with the flag.

McGrandle grinned. "Her name is Mrs Reid," he replied. "She never misses a meeting. She made that flag herself," he added, admiringly. "Isn't it a beauty?"

Shinwell was about to finish his speech. "Comrades," he declared, "the labour movement has embarked on a great crusade. We have a duty to eradicate all the iniquities which afflict our people. This is only the beginning."

He looked round the crowded square and his voice rose to a roar. "Glasgow can show the world!" Shinwell cried. "We must not fail! We shall not fail! Are we together, comrades?"

A murmur of approval swept George Square. "We're with you, Manny!" came the cry.

The strike leader descended briskly from his perch, leaving Gladstone to brood alone on his plinth. "Go on, Manny!" someone shouted.

"You tell the bastards!"

"We'll show them!"

People were cheering wildly and shouting encouragement. Someone grabbed the red flag from Mrs Reid and threw it over the heads of the crowd. As it fell to the ground someone else standing only yards away from Henry Wason propelled it in the direction of the City Chambers. Billowing high into the air, to the great amusement of the crowd, and the consternation of Mrs Reid, who realised she was in danger of losing her precious flag, it caught on the glass bowl of an ornamental street lamp, where it remained a vivid symbol of the strikers' determination to impose their will on the civic authorities.

Wason watched, with growing private concern, as, cheering and applauding, encouraging their leader, assuring him of their support, the huge crowd divided in an orderly fashion to let Shinwell approach the entrance to the City Chambers unmolested. Of course, being a member of the Town Council, he was entitled to enter the building at any time in his own right, Wason realised. But in the present circumstances, he thought grimly, the chairman of the Workers' Strike Committee would be as welcome on the other side of those huge ornamental front doors as a rapist in a convent. After hearing him speak in George Square there was no longer any doubt in Wason's mind that the workers of Glasgow would be prepared to follow Shinwell in whatever direction he chose. What he needed to learn, therefore, and with all possible speed, was the extent of Shinwell's commitment to the idea of revolution. Then, hopefully, he could inform Mr

Churchill of his findings in good enough time to prevent a disaster.

"Wasn't that something?"

Willie McGrandle turned to stare at Wason, demanding an answer.

"He's very impressive," Wason conceded.

"You think so?"

It was Derek Taylor who spoke. Wason nodded carefully.

"Didn't you think he was in great form, Derek?"

Taylor glanced at Willie McGrandle and shrugged.

"He has a certain exuberant style, I suppose."

Wason couldn't help thinking that this was a man who looked out of place surrounded by strikers. Taylor hadn't been introduced as a journalist or anything and from his appearance and manner Henry Wason concluded that he was probably an academic. What was he doing there, and what was his relationship with Willie McGrandle?

"I get the impression," said Wason, "you don't think much of Shinwell."

Derek Taylor shrugged. "Mr Shinwell is a man who needs to be watched."

"I don't understand."

"It would take too long to explain."

"Some people will tell you that Shinwell has an eye on the main chance all the time," McGrandle remarked, grinning.

Wason nodded. "Do you think so, Willie?" he inquired.

"Any time I'm in his company," McGrandle chuckled, "I like to know where he's standing."

"What do you think of him," Derek Taylor inquired, watching Wason closely, "now that you've met him and seen him in action?"

"I thought he spoke well," Wason answered carefully.

"He can be splendid on his feet," Derek Taylor agreed drily, "no question about that. But did you feel there was any real substance to the man?"

"It's hard to say when you don't know someone personally," Wason said.

Derek Taylor nodded.

Something about Taylor's manner, and his presence at the demonstration, excited Wason. "You didn't say, but I gather you aren't a journalist?" he ventured.

"No," said Taylor, "I lecture at the university."

Wason smiled knowingly. "Politics, or social subjects?" he inquired.

"Economics," replied Taylor.

"Now I understand your interest in the strike," Wason remarked. "The economic implications of a long stoppage are pretty horrific, wouldn't you say?"

"Certainly."

"Can it be avoided?"

"What do you think?"

Wason shrugged. "This does look impressive," he conceded cautiously.

"So why aren't you impressed?"

"For all I know it might not amount to much more than a boisterous day out for the lads," Wason ventured.

Taylor chuckled. "When did you arrive in Glasgow?" He asked.

"Earlier this week."

"I'll be interested to learn what you think once you've been here another few days," Taylor told him.

Wason looked round the crowd. "You really believe they mean business?"

Derek Taylor nodded. "Of course," he replied.

"Victory at any price?"

Taylor stared at him for a moment. "I can't imagine them wanting to settle for anything less," he replied.

"That's interesting. However, if they go outside the law, and the authorities are forced to take action against them, it could really turn nasty," Wason argued.

"Don't you think Shinwell's thought of that?" Taylor inquired.

"I'd say he was playing with fire," Wason observed.

Taylor shrugged. "I'm sure you're right," he agreed.

Wason glanced round the crowd waiting patiently for Shinwell to reappear.

"How far will they go?"

"Your guess is as good as mine."

Frank Munro approached them through the crowd. Margaret Armstrong followed close behind.

Willie McGrandle, who had been talking to a group of workmen, excused himself and turned to address Munro. "Not a bad turn-out, eh, Mr Munro," he remarked cheerfully.

"I'd say it's pretty fair."

McGrandle smiled impishly. "I don't think your editor will like it."

Munro grunted. "He's a hard man to please. By the way, Miss

Armstrong is a close friend of my deputy editor, so be careful what you say. Everything all right?" he added, glancing at Wason.

"Everything's fine," Wason told him. "Willie introduced me to Shinwell."

"Did he tell you anything I should know? I don't want you scooping me in my own town," Munro added, half seriously.

"I don't think so," Wason answered before continuing hurriedly, "Are you from Glasgow, Miss Armstrong?"

"No," she replied, "Belfast."

"I haven't met many women journalists," Wason went on.

"I'm not a journalist," Margaret Armstrong responded coolly. "I'm on holiday, if you want to know."

Wason appeared disconcerted. Munro chuckled and turned to McGrandle. "Is it true that three thousand men are being sent to Pinkston for a showdown with Dalrymple?"

"I don't know the exact numbers," McGrandle replied evasively. "It'll depend on who's available."

"Three thousand sounds like an army," Munro told him.

Willie McGrandle looked uncomfortable. "It might not be that many. I told you, it depends."

"Don't tell me you are seriously considering trying to take the place by force?" Munro demanded.

McGrandle shrugged.

"What's Pinkston?"

Munro sighed. "The main power station serving the trams," he explained. "A man by the name of James Dalrymple, who is the tramways manager, is locked inside with some of his men. Dalrymple is determined to keep the trams running at all costs."

"Can he succeed?" Wason asked.

"In the end, obviously, it will depend on the drivers," Munro observed, "but whatever they decide, the trams can't run without power."

"He sounds interesting."

Munro grunted. "You'd better not say that to Shinwell," he advised.

"You're right, of course," Wason added. "Three thousand men marching on the place sounds like the most awful intimidation."

Willie McGrandle was unrepentant. "We aren't looking for trouble," he insisted fiercely. "All we want is for them to see sense and come out. What do they think they're playing at, barricading themselves inside the place like that?"

"You know Dalrymple," warned Munro. "He's just as stubborn as Shinwell. He won't abandon Pinkston without a fight."

McGrandle shrugged. "If there's trouble," he declared, "they'll be the cause of it. All we want is a peaceful demonstration."

"We'll see," said Munro.

He glanced at Derek Taylor. "I don't think we've met."

"He's a friend of mine," McGrandle explained. "Derek Taylor."

Munro nodded.

"Here comes Shinwell."

The chairman of the Workers' Strike Committee was smiling broadly as he made his way through the crowd and ascended the plinth, shouting for silence and spreading his arms to embrace the crowd. Word that he was out spread quickly and people began to cheer.

"Comrades!" Shinwell cried.

The men continued to cheer.

"Comrades!" he repeated.

The cheering died away.

"I have been to see the Lord Provost and told him of our demands."

There was an outbreak of cheering. "Well done, Manny!" someone cried.

Shinwell, who was clearly enjoying himself, grinned.

"Of course," Shinwell added, "it would be a mistake to imagine that he is now on our side."

The remark encouraged laughter. Shinwell paused. The crowd waited. Wason couldn't help admiring the skill with which the strike leader commanded his audience.

"However," Shinwell told them, "he has agreed to send a telegram to Downing Street informing the government of our demands."

The men cheered wildly.

"I have given him until the end of the week to come back with an answer," Shinwell added above the din.

"What will happen then?" Wason whispered. Frank Munro shrugged. Shinwell continued:

"He has been left in no doubt that unless the government agree to our demands for a forty-hour week we will bring the whole of Clydeside to a standstill. Make no mistake, it is in our power to do so, comrades."

"You tell them, Manny!" someone shouted.

The mood of the crowd was unmistakable, Wason thought. On all sides men were shouting their support, and pledging themselves to follow Shinwell. How far would he take them?

Shinwell pointed to the City Chambers and heads turned to stare.

"I informed the Lord Provost that we would prefer to achieve our aims by constitutional means," Shinwell declared. "But if Lloyd George chooses to ignore our demands, or the Lord Provost fails to convince him that we are serious, then no-one should doubt for a moment that we will take whatever action is deemed necessary to succeed. I have given the Lord Provost until Friday to come back with an answer."

There was a growl of approval from the crowd. Shinwell continued:

"What I propose, comrades, is that we reassemble here on Friday morning in order to hear the government's reply. In the meantime we must redouble our efforts to ensure that the strike continues in strength. You've all heard of Mr James Dalrymple, I suppose?"

Shinwell waited for the resulting laughter to subside.

"Well, then, you will be interested to learn that we propose paying him a visit. What we have in mind is an orderly procession," Shinwell explained amid fresh laughter. "We will go to Pinkston and seek a meeting with Mr Dalrymple. I don't suppose we can expect much help from Mr Dalrymple himself," he added, grinning. "But it may be we can persuade those of his men who are occupying the premises to join our cause. Can you imagine Mr Dalrymple trying to run that big power station all by himself?"

His mood became serious. He looked round the crowd, who quietened to hear him. It was a superb performance, Wason thought, and glanced at Frank Munro, who was busy making notes.

"Didn't I tell you he was good?" Munro remarked, looking up.

"He sounds very effective," Wason agreed, grimacing.

Munro chuckled. "You won't find many like him in London."

"Is that bad?"

"I told you," Munro replied, "his heart's in the right place."

Shinwell hadn't finished. "Comrades!" he cried, and the crowd listened attentively. "Victory is in sight!"

His voice rising above the cheering, and the applause of the men which now filled George Square, Shinwell continued savagely:

"Our enemies are in retreat because our cause is just!"

Then, arms outstretched to embrace them, he assured the men: "We shall prevail!"

The crowd cheered wildly as Shinwell descended nimbly from plinth to pavement and was immediately surrounded by well-wishers wanting to congratulate him on his performance. Hoping for a glimpse of their leader, people beside Henry Wason began pushing and shoving towards him. From the looks on their faces Wason didn't doubt they would follow Shinwell anywhere. The man was amazing, he thought; and dangerous.

Reading his thoughts, it seemed, Frank Munro chuckled. "His bark is worse than his bite," he said.

They found themselves being borne towards Shinwell by the sheer weight of the crowd.

"What do you think will happen at Pinkston?" Wason asked.

"Dalrymple could be a match for Shinwell," Munro replied. "It all depends on whether or not Shinwell is bluffing. If he tells his men to storm the gates there could be real trouble. Let's ask him."

By the time they reached Shinwell he was already talking to a group of reporters. He had been given cause for offence by one of them, it seemed.

"What we have in mind is an orderly procession," Shinwell protested, speaking quickly, a pained expression on his broad face. "That's all. There is no question of us taking the law into our own hands. The way you put it you would think we were going out of our way to cause trouble. Why would we want to do any such thing?" he added, looking round with an air of innocence.

"Mr Dalrymple says he is determined to prevent you from entering the works. Don't you think there's bound to be trouble?"

Shinwell smiled, reassuringly. "I give you my word," he replied. "There isn't going to be any trouble. Yes, Mr Munro?"

Munro began cautiously. "Mr Shinwell, as you must know, the Prime Minister is out of the country."

Shinwell smiled. "According to what I read in the newspapers the acting Prime Minister is Mr Bonar Law," he replied. "Presumably, if he is acting Prime Minister, he is in a position to act. Wouldn't you say so, Mr Munro?"

"Do you feel at all that Mr Bonar Law might be more sympathetic to your claims than the Prime Minister?"

Shinwell glanced at the others. "Mr Munro," he replied finally, "it is my impression that nothing happens in this government which is against the wishes of the Prime Minister. As he is in Paris, no great distance away, and not on the other side of the moon, I am certain he can be consulted if his colleagues consider it necessary to do so."

It was Derek Taylor who spoke next.

"I'm not a reporter, Mr Shinwell, but I am interested, naturally. You seemed to be saying in your speech that you would resort to something drastic if the government didn't intervene to help settle the strike. What did you mean?"

"I don't mind you not being a reporter. You'll hear the truth from me direct. What did I mean? Exactly what I said," Shinwell told him.

"What do you have in mind?" inquired Frank Munro.

Shinwell shrugged. "You don't really expect an answer to that question, Mr Munro. We are discussing tactics," Shinwell said.

Henry Wason saw his chance. "People are afraid there may be an increase in public disorder, Mr Shinwell. As chairman of the Workers' Strike Committee surely you can't ignore their fears," Wason argued.

Shinwell shrugged. "We have until Friday to hear from the government. We'll see what happens then," he said.

# CHAPTER FIFTEEN

Wason thought he was on to something. "Your question intrigued me," he said.

"I asked you what you would like to drink."

Wason laughed. "I meant the one you put to Shinwell," he said.

Derek Taylor shrugged. "Let's sort out the drink first," he suggested.

"Can I have a half pint, please?"

They were in an almost empty pub, with a horseshoe bar, in a lane off Queen Street. A large man with a bluebird tattooed on the left-hand side of his neck was serving. "Would you like to touch it?" the man asked, leaning forward to confront Henry Wason, who was staring at the bluebird, mesmerised.

Wason shook his head.

"Lots of people do," the barman continued helpfully. "They think it will bring them luck."

"No thank you," Wason replied.

"One night, on the caur gain' hame, a bloke gave me ten bob just for lettin' his wife touch it. I don't mind," the barman added. "You're sure you wouldn't like to touch it?"

"I'm sure," Wason told him.

The barman gave them their drinks and shrugged. "Suit yourself," he said. "It's due to fly south next week. Goes to Tanganyika, or one of them other hot places, I expect."

Taylor took his change and they moved to a table near the door.

"I wish I could go to Tanganyika," the barman added, grunting. "Better than this hell-hole of a place on a cauld winter's day. I went to Mombassa once. But that isn't Tanganyika, that's Kenya."

Derek Taylor smiled. "I hope you don't mind me saying so," he remarked, "but your face is a picture."

Wason grimaced. "What an extraordinary fellow," he replied.

"He's playing at being a Glasgow character," Derek Taylor

explained. "The city is full of nutcases. He'll realise you're from London, of course."

Wason nodded. "It was quite well done, I thought."

"What?"

"His tattoo."

"Don't tell me you want one?" Taylor chuckled.

Wason shuddered. "No thank you," he replied.

They both laughed. Wason went on: "Thanks for finding the time to talk."

Derek Taylor shrugged. "It's a pleasure," he replied.

"I want to talk to as many people as possible while I'm here," Wason added. "Obviously, if I just talk to people who are totally committed, like Shinwell or Willie McGrandle, I would go away with a terribly distorted picture of what's going on here."

Taylor nodded. "Of course. Perhaps I should warn you, however."

Wason waited.

"It would be a mistake to imagine that the strikers don't command wide public support," Taylor told him. "Sympathy might be a better word. But I'd say Shinwell is generally popular. He has shown himself realistic on the question of hours, don't forget. The original claim for a thirty-hour week was unrealistic. Forty was a reasonable compromise."

Wason thought for a moment. "I met a minister coming up on the train who told me that support for the strike spread across all social classes," he said. "Would you agree?"

Taylor laughed. "Don't tell me he thought the employers and the landlords were on Shinwell's side?" he asked. "Or the people who sit on the Town Council? I suppose the merchants might have a vested interest in the workers having more money to spend," Taylor said, shaking his head. "But I can't believe they would support them because of the wider risks."

Henry Wason was immediately interested. "What do you mean?" he inquired. "What wider risks?"

Taylor stared at him. "The merchant classes are an endangered species," he declared, "didn't you know? Victory in this strike would demonstrate the workers' strength. They would be in a position to dictate their future terms. By doing so they would become a political force. Do you really believe it is in the best interests of all those people with power over them at present, the employers, the landlords, the merchants, the kind of people who sit on town councils, and generally fill parliament, to let the workers succeed?"

159

Wason didn't answer.

"No," said Taylor, "in my view, they will do everything possible to ensure that this doesn't happen."

"The way you talk you would think the whole country was on strike," Wason objected.

Taylor shrugged. "There could be a national strike on the back of this," he said. "It's time the workers forced a showdown."

Wason looked puzzled. "How can you contemplate the prospects of a national strike so easily?" he demanded.

"It may be what's needed," he said.

"For what?"

"Commonsense dictates that the workers must take control of the country sooner or later," Taylor declared. "They represent the majority, don't forget. So long as they have the will to succeed it's only a matter of time."

"Are you a socialist?"

Taylor smiled. "I prefer to avoid labels," he replied. "I'm an academic, remember."

"You sound like a socialist."

"Why?" Taylor demanded. "Because I face facts?"

Wason stared at him for a moment. "The question you put to Shinwell," he said finally.

"What about it?"

"Do you believe Shinwell would sanction force if everything else failed?"

"Force may be necessary, I suppose."

"But at heart, people tell me, Shinwell's a constitutionalist," Wason argued. "Isn't that right?"

"Don't forget," replied Taylor, "that he could be overtaken by events. His attitude could change."

"Could he be replaced?"

"I'd say his position was quite secure for the present. But the strikers expect results," Taylor told him.

Wason nodded. "Shinwell looks like a man who enjoys power," he observed.

Taylor chuckled.

"Don't you agree?"

"He revels in it, I'd say," Taylor declared with a laugh.

"Which means he might be prepared to go to extremes to keep it," Wason suggested cautiously. "In London," he went on, "people believe that the strike is politically motivated. What do you think?"

"Shinwell denies it," Taylor answered. "He is often at pains to explain that the strike is about pay and conditions, and nothing else."

"Do you believe him?"

"Why not?" Taylor demanded.

Wason smiled. "I'm the one looking for answers," he replied.

Derek Taylor downed a third of his drink in a single gulp. "You'll find there's no shortage of people with opinions in this town," he grunted.

"What I must try and do is convince people in London and abroad that lots of people who aren't on strike actually sympathise with the strikers," Wason went on. "Most people don't seem to mind being inconvenienced, for instance."

"People here are clannish," Taylor explained.

Wason nodded. "I think I know what you mean," he said.

Taylor shook his head. "I'd advise you not to start from any preconceived position," he warned. "Shinwell is an extremely complex man. He is being forced to balance and contain a good many conflicting opinions, don't forget. For example," Taylor explained, "quite a few of his colleagues would like nothing better than to see him forced into a position where his only available option was to engage in some serious confrontations with the authorities."

Wason stared at him. "Really?" he said.

Derek Taylor nodded. "There are some people who would like to see pitched battles in the street," he observed.

Wason looked shocked. "Are you being serious?" he asked.

"This is a violent town at the best of times, Mr Wason. It wouldn't take much of a spark to light the fuse," Taylor added, smiling slightly.

Henry Wason sensed that he was being teased.

"I'm here because some quite senior people in London are convinced this city is on the brink of revolution," he said.

Derek Taylor couldn't stop his eyes from gleaming. "I can imagine how that would upset them," he remarked unkindly.

Henry Wason stared at him for a moment. He had been prepared to dismiss the opinionated minister encountered on the train as some kind of religious freak concerned about the rights of man; and anxious, Wason thought gloomily, because the meek weren't inheriting the earth fast enough for his liking. But a lecturer at the university, who professed no party allegiance, calmly contemplating the idea of revolution, and showing no evident concern for the danger, was an entirely different matter. It would be a mistake not to take the man seriously. Wason shook his head and smiled admiringly.

161

"You should be in politics, Mr Taylor. Have you ever thought about running for the town council, or parliament, even?"

Derek Taylor shrugged. "Not many people can afford the time for that," he replied.

"Still," said Wason, "you're interested. What do you think will happen now?"

"I don't know," Taylor told him. "But people in London are right to be worried."

"To what extent?" Wason asked.

"This whole country suffers from a history of neglect," Taylor informed him roughly. "London isn't really interested in Scotland's welfare. Or what happens to its people. So long as they don't cause trouble or inconvenience their neighbours to the south in any way."

Wason didn't answer. Taylor continued:

"Clydeside was at the heart of the industrial revolution, remember. But the mass of ordinary people didn't benefit. Have you seen how most of them live?"

Wason shook his head.

"In squalor!"

Wason remembered his father insisting the Scotch were a rebellious lot, of extreme political views, who always needed watching. The old man had been a good judge of character. It was a shame he was never made general. Wason missed him more than he cared to admit. What would he say about his present predicament? First the minister on the train, and now a lecturer at the university, educated men with a social conscience: the old man would have described these two as the worst kind of trouble. The fact that Derek Taylor had been born and educated in England only made his position worse. The man was a renegade.

Wason sighed. "From what you say the government could be in serious trouble."

"But it's hard to feel sorry for them, wouldn't you say?" Derek Taylor added.

"I thought people in London were exaggerating the dangers," Wason told him.

"If the government decides not to assist the strikers, then the chances of real trouble could be worse than fifty-fifty," Taylor claimed.

Taylor believed the quickest way to power among the workers was by way of the shop stewards, which probably explained his friendship with Willie McGrandle. The men depended on the stewards to protect their interests against the more ambitious of the wider leadership, some of whom they didn't trust, Taylor explained. There was bound to be a struggle for power between the stewards, operating from inside the yards and factories, and the centralised control offered by the likes of the Clyde Workers' Committee and Glasgow Trades Council. What happened next would depend, more than anything else, on the outcome of that particular struggle. He was betting the stewards would win. Revolution remained a possibility.

Henry Wason gave him his full attention. He was no longer in any doubt that, in all probability, hidden groups, plotting in secret, were active in Glasgow. Derek Taylor, an educated man employed in an important post, who supported the workers' cause and was prepared to offer them all possible assistance, certainly sounded dangerous. Churchill would need to be informed immediately.

"Do you believe some kind of organisation already exists?" Wason inquired recklessly. "Presumably, from what you say, the leaders could be just waiting to say the word. What's to stop a revolution beginning here, in Glasgow, right now?"

Derek Taylor was watching him carefully. Wason felt compelled to continue. "Could the men find arms, do you think?"

Derek Taylor grunted. "There are stories circulating all the time about guns coming in from Ireland," he said. "Nobody pays much attention to them. But I don't think finding guns would be difficult. And there's no shortage of men who know how to use them, remember. It could be the last legacy of the war," he added in a matter-of-fact voice which shocked Henry Wason.

"Would you mind if I write some of this?" Wason inquired. "I'm sure people would be interested to know your views."

"I'd rather you didn't use my name," Taylor replied cautiously.

"Being from the university, a professional man, makes them particularly interesting," Wason said.

"I can see that," Taylor smiled. "But the university might not like it. I don't mind giving you my impression of what's going on, and helping you in whatever way I can, but I wouldn't want to be quoted."

"If that's what you prefer –" Wason began.

"It would be safer, I think," Derek Taylor interrupted.

"I'll respect your wishes, naturally," Wason assured him. "Don't worry," he went on, seeing Taylor hesitate and treating him to a small, conspiratorial smile, "you can trust me. I won't let you down."

# CHAPTER SIXTEEN

The Prime Minister and his Secretary of State for War and Air eyed one another suspiciously and shook hands warmly.

"How are you, Winston?"

"I feel fine," Churchill growled. "You look very well, I must say, Prime Minister. Paris agrees with you, or so it would appear."

Lloyd George stifled a chuckle. "I remember it as a place of happy distractions," he replied wistfully. "Unfortunately, that was long ago, and I am no longer permitted such genial pursuits."

Churchill laughed.

The two men understood and valued the high regard they shared for one another. It was something they rarely felt the need to disguise, and certainly never in private, where it was easier to ignore the political rivalries which sometimes caused a shadow to fall between them.

The Prime Minister gestured for him to sit and Churchill chose a straight-backed, winged armchair, beside a window, through which he could view the garden, surrounded by pines, and a lawn wet with frost. The Prime Minister had been given the use of a large, expensively furnished, oak desk where he now seated himself with the air of a man who owned the place. In fact, the château where their meeting had been arranged in the utmost secrecy was the property of one of the oldest noble families in France. They had been related to the Churchill family, through marriage, for more than two hundred years; an irony not lost on Churchill, or on Lloyd George either, Churchill wagered silently. The thought made him scowl.

"Paris, as you are bound to appreciate, Winston, will be the ruin of us all," Lloyd George remarked in a tired voice.

He was toying with a large paperweight, which he had lifted from the desk, and which Churchill recognised as a piece of mounted coral brought from St Helena.

"Anyone who tries to argue otherwise, Winston, you can tell them from me that nobody won this war," the Prime Minister continued gravely. "It was a war everyone lost, including Woodrow, whatever he likes to think, and whatever the American people have been led to believe. I can understand, of course, how it is important to them to believe that, having come in so late, they were the true victors. It's nonsense, of course, although without them goodness knows how long the whole terrible business might have lasted. We can all be thankful now it's finished."

The Prime Minister sighed heavily. Churchill waited for him to continue. Lloyd George stared at the paperweight in his hand for a moment, considering its history, perhaps. Churchill smiled quietly.

"If anyone emerges from the whole débâcle with anything it will be the Americans, of course. I understand your feelings for them, Winston," he added quickly, "but please be aware that the scent of influence and power in Europe has turned poor Woodrow's head. He imagines himself to be a man of destiny, you see, the first President of the United States to have found himself in a position where he can actually wield real power in Europe. The prospect of sweeping away all the old frontiers, dismantling entire nations, destroying ancient empires, excites him beyond reason, I'm afraid."

Lloyd George grinned.

"He can't be a bigger nuisance than the French, surely," Churchill objected, trying hard not to sound annoyed.

Lloyd George shrugged. "So long as Germany is emasculated, and the glory of France restored, the French will be quite happy," he replied. "As you know, Winston, there is nothing in this life which is more important, to the French at least, than the greater glory of France."

The Prime Minister sighed heavily.

"They are being most unhelpful, as you can imagine, I am sure. What they want is for Germany to be destroyed, once and for all, I think. Of course, I can see their point of view. Without the Channel between us I might be encouraged to agree with them. But everyone else can see that it would be folly for us to treat the Germans too harshly. Eventually it would mean another war in Europe, at a time convenient to Germany, of course."

The Prime Minister stared at Churchill for a moment. Churchill waited. Lloyd George shrugged.

"You understand what I am trying to say, of course. A time convenient to Germany must mean a time when they think they can win against all-comers."

Churchill busied himself with a cigar. "What you must do, surely, Prime Minister," he reflected gravely, "is convince the French that in victory one must be magnanimous. It is the only way," he added firmly.

Lloyd George shook his head doubtfully.

"If they are reluctant to accept this point of view," Churchill persisted stubbornly, "you might wish to advise them that there is no other way for truly civilised people to behave."

The Prime Minister vetoed this suggestion drily. "I have never met a Frenchman yet who could be described as magnanimous by anyone, even another Frenchman," he said.

Churchill chuckled.

"So how can you imagine for a moment that I might encounter this Gallic paragon in Paris?" Lloyd George inquired. "Not forgetting that there will be a German present and they will be discussing who is the rightful owner of Alsace-Lorraine."

Churchill drew on his cigar. "Prime Minister," he conceded lightly, "the point is won."

Lloyd George responded by giving him a sour look. His old friend smiled mischievously.

"I have an idea," Churchill smiled.

Lloyd George waited, his eyes narrowing suspiciously.

"Tell them we'll take it," Churchill suggested brightly. "I am always attracted, as you know, to the idea of us increasing the size of the empire. To do so at the expense of both the French and the Germans, and of both at the same time, is an opportunity not to be missed."

The Prime Minister scowled. "What would we do with Alsace-Lorraine?" he inquired wearily. Then, before Churchill could attempt an answer, he ordered, "No, don't tell me! We have enough problems of our own."

Churchill grinned, obviously unrepentant.

"However, for you to come here in such secrecy, Winston, you must be very concerned about events at home," the Prime Minister continued.

Churchill spread his hands and nodded gravely. "Indeed, you may say so, Prime Minister," he agreed.

Lloyd George stared at him. "Well, what is it?" he demanded.

Through the window Churchill could see a robin dancing on the lawn.

"Is it a plot against me?"

The huge, familiar features adopted a vexed expression. Churchill

166

shook his head firmly, wishing to reassure him. "Of course not, Prime Minister," he replied. "No-one would dare stand against you."

Lloyd George shrugged moodily. "Wouldn't they?" he inquired thoughtfully, eyes narrowing.

"Your position is quite secure, Prime Minister," Churchill assured him, nodding.

"For the moment, perhaps," Lloyd George responded with a sigh. "But we both know, Winston, that one day it will happen. My support in the House will turn against me and I will be alone. It may be that you –"

He stopped.

Churchill looked uncomfortable. He was conscious of Lloyd George studying him closely. The entire Cabinet knew that the Prime Minister was obsessed with the idea that a group of his colleagues might unite to oust him. Churchill was not alone in thinking that any such scheme would be doomed to failure, for the foreseeable future, at least.

"Prime Minister, there is no suggestion of a plot being hatched against you," Churchill insisted. "I am here on a different matter entirely."

The huge head shook slowly. "I am sorry, Winston," the Prime Minister told him. "Please continue with your business."

Churchill knew from long experience that dealing with the Prime Minister when he was in a mood to suspect colleagues of conspiring against him required care. However, he was determined not to be rushed and felt inclined to nourish his own indulgence for a moment. The contents of the over-furnished room in which they were sitting were worth more than a passing glance, Churchill thought with a secret smile, rising from his chair to examine them: priceless paintings and several ancient tapestries decorating the walls, a pair of Louis VI chairs, which he'd long coveted, placed with relaxed precision in the centre of the richly carpeted floor.

"For goodness' sake, Winston, will you stop wandering about the room and sit down," the Prime Minister interrupted, ill-humouredly. "Then perhaps you might tell me why you have come all this way, and insisted on bringing me from Paris."

Churchill put his hand on the back of one of the Louis VI chairs. "I have always thought that these chairs would look rather nice at Blenheim," he remarked.

Lloyd George scowled. "For goodness' sake, Winston, what's the matter with you?" he growled.

Churchill shrugged. He sensed it was time to begin: the Prime Minister was clearly becoming impatient; and Lloyd George in a foul temper was one man Churchill preferred to avoid. He returned to his seat.

The Prime Minister nodded. "Having completed your perambulation about the room, and made an inventory of those items you would like to transfer to your own historic pile, perhaps you will be good enough to tell me what this is all about."

Churchill shrugged. Much of his time, on the journey to France, had been spent ruminating on how the Prime Minister would react to his interpretation of what was happening on Clydeside. Everyone else in the Cabinet evidently believed that he was indulging in some foolish fantasy, Churchill realised glumly. However, he felt certain that Lloyd George, alone among his colleagues, would be prepared to listen seriously; and give his report the consideration it deserved, at least. Having reached this conclusion, Churchill decided also that it would be pointless to keep his worst fears from the Prime Minister, whatever the risk of ridicule.

"I believe we are facing the most serious crisis," Churchill began.

"Go on."

Churchill paused.

"It is my considered view, Prime Minister," he continued finally, "that our nation is on the brink of revolution. The forces of disorder are gathering and preparing to move against us."

The Prime Minister thought for a moment. Finally, in a calm voice, he inquired: "Starting in Scotland, I suppose."

Churchill nodded gravely.

"I see."

Churchill waited.

"No doubt, having convinced yourself of this threat, you have some hard evidence, Winston?" the Prime Minister inquired.

"Of course," Churchill replied calmly.

"Something upon which we would be entitled to act, I mean?"

Churchill responded sharply.

"Do you think I would have made the journey, deflected you from the onerous work you are required to perform in Paris, unless there was sufficient evidence to justify my concern, Prime Minister?"

Lloyd George shook his head apologetically. "I am sorry, Winston," he countered. "Tell me, how much do we know about the plotters' intentions, and how was this information obtained?"

"We know a great deal about them," Churchill replied.

"How?"

"I sent an agent to Glasgow," said Churchill.

The Prime Minister appeared startled. "Why were you inspired to do such a thing?" he inquired, unable to keep the surprise from his voice.

Churchill looked pleased with himself.

"Intuition, Prime Minister," he replied with a smile. "I felt for months that real trouble was brewing there. In my opinion events reached a stage where we were in urgent need of reliable intelligence, so it seemed the simplest means to employ."

"You didn't feel the need to consult any of your colleagues in this matter?" Lloyd George inquired gently.

Churchill shook his head. "There was no point," he grunted. "Who else would support me?"

Lloyd George grunted admiringly. "Imagination and determination, Winston," he remarked, "are two of your finest qualities."

Churchill accepted the compliment gratefully. "Thank you, Prime Minister," he replied.

"Were you able to procure the services of Mr Reilly?" Lloyd George asked.

"He's in Russia, or so I was informed," Churchill told him.

"The man's mad," Lloyd George observed with a sigh.

"But brave," Churchill asserted, admiringly.

"Yes," Lloyd George agreed quickly.

"However," he continued briskly, "tell me about this other man."

"Wason," said Churchill. "His name is Henry Wason."

"Whatever he's called." Lloyd George waved aside any interest in the name. "Tell me what he learned."

"He established beyond any doubt that the forty-hour strike is politically motivated," Churchill told him.

The Prime Minister scowled. "We didn't need to send an agent all the way to Glasgow to find that out," he complained.

Churchill shrugged. "When its aims have been achieved in Scotland, and all the main services have been disrupted on Clydeside, it is the strike leaders' intention to move the strike into other parts of Scotland, finally engulfing the whole of Scotland, before turning their attentions to England," he said.

The Prime Minister nodded. "We were aware of this before," he said.

Churchill stared at him. "It appears that an agent of the Bolsheviks has been operating in Scotland," he said.

"How was he received?"

"With interest, certainly," Churchill replied.

Lloyd George nodded. "I have heard of this man," he said.

"You are aware also, Prime Minister, that known troublemakers like John Maclean have been travelling widely in England, addressing large audiences, encouraging unrest?"

"Maclean!" the Prime Minister snapped. "I thought that last spell in prison was supposed to have finished him? I was assured we had heard the last of him."

"Obviously not," Churchill shrugged. "But he isn't the worst. There's a whole gang of them loose in Glasgow who are perfectly capable of bringing the entire country to its knees. Make no mistake, Prime Minister, they can certainly organise themselves in a way which will threaten the stability of the central authority."

The Prime Minister stayed silent for a moment, giving careful thought to Churchill's fears. Finally, he told him:

"All of this sounds bad enough, admittedly. But are these really the seeds of revolution, Winston?"

Churchill nodded determinedly.

The Prime Minister sighed. "I know you have no wish to be alarmist, Winston," he said.

Churchill scowled, fearing a reprimand.

"I realise that you express these fears from the best of motives, of course," the Prime Minister added, "and a genuine desire to protect us from the worst excesses of the people who are behind this highly disruptive strike. However – "

Churchill interrupted him with a growl. "Assuming the strikers find that they can withhold power and water supplies, close the shipyards, at great inconvenience to the Royal Navy, don't forget, and paralyse the mines, Prime Minister," he argued grimly, "don't you think it would be a mistake for us to imagine that they wouldn't want to go further, much further, Prime Minister?"

Lloyd George eyed him bleakly.

"Aren't we entitled to imagine that it is their intention to usurp the lawful government of the country?" Churchill continued darkly. "If they can demonstrate they have the power and the organisation to accomplish all of these things, wouldn't we be foolish to deny or ignore the possibility? Didn't it always seem likely that the Bolsheviks would wish to begin their attack on us in Scotland?"

The Prime Minister sighed. What Churchill said was true, of course.

"I hate Glasgow," the Prime Minister remarked gloomily.

"I try to avoid the place," Churchill admitted. Then:

"What do you propose doing about this business, Prime Minister?"

Lloyd George understood that he was being pressed: Churchill wanted to return to London having won his support. He remained unconvinced, however.

"We must be careful not to over-react, Winston," he cautioned the younger man gently.

Churchill snorted impatiently. "What would be worse?" he demanded. "That or not reacting at all?"

The Prime Minister thought for a moment, nodded. Churchill felt heartened: there was some agreement between them at last, he thought.

Lloyd George addressed him quietly, choosing his words with great care: "For the present what we have on our hands in Clydeside is an extremely damaging, and potentially disastrous, strike. It would be calamitous, of course, if we were unable to stop it spreading to other parts of the country."

Churchill, sensing victory, nodded vigorously.

"However, and this is the important point for us to consider now, Winston," the Prime Minister continued, "it is essential that we take every precaution to ensure that we don't make matters worse by some precipitate action on our part."

Churchill scowled.

"You disagree?" Lloyd George demanded sharply.

"About what, Prime Minister?" Churchill inquired, moodily. "Obviously, it is not my wish to make matters worse. I seek to prevent any further deterioration in our present circumstances which are troubled enough. However, I am also convinced that, the way things are in Scotland, we could soon arrive at a point where we are no longer in control of events. The country could become the preserve of an unelected tyranny," he warned seriously. "None of us wants that, Prime Minister."

Lloyd George stared at him.

Churchill shrugged. "I assume you are not suggesting we do nothing, Prime Minister?"

Lloyd George responded patiently. "Winston, if you are absolutely convinced that we are on the brink of revolution, please tell me this: Who would be its leader?"

"Shinwell is chairman of the Workers' Strike Committee," replied Churchill.

"Don't forget that Shinwell worked well on our behalf during the war," the Prime Minister objected. "Why should he turn against us now?"

Churchill didn't answer.

"Without him who knows what trouble we might have encountered on Clydeside."

Churchill grunted, but didn't argue.

"No," said Lloyd George, "I don't believe he would hurl himself against the elected government of the country, the House of Commons itself, not forgetting the King, in so desperate a fashion."

Churchill refused to be shifted.

"Shinwell is an ambitious man, jaundiced by socialism," he argued, "who courts the working class, hoping they will carry him to power one day."

"A number of potentially dangerous people are well known to us," Churchill replied, defensively. "Maclean is still on the prowl, don't forget."

The idea that John Maclean could pose a threat to the realm was dismissed with a wave of the Prime Minister's hand. Churchill continued cautiously: "Several other people are being investigated as a matter of the utmost priority. For example, we have become most interested in the activities of a man named Derek Taylor, a lecturer at the University of Glasgow, and a known Marxist, who has established a close association with some of the more active and younger shop stewards. He figures prominently in our agent's reports. It would appear that he is attempting to provide some kind of alternative leadership to Shinwell and the official committee.

Lloyd George frowned, evidently interested. Churchill added hurriedly: "However, it cannot be emphasised too strongly, Prime Minister, that it remains our opinion that Shinwell is the only man who has emerged so far who could provide the kind of leadership you have in mind. Indeed, it is my view that Shinwell is probably the most dangerous man in the country at the present time."

Lloyd George chuckled grimly. "I hope you excluded us from the reckoning, Winston."

"I mentioned the activities of a man named Taylor," Churchill went on. "He is an educated man, an economist by training, who is going out of his way to cultivate contacts among the younger shop stewards. He is particularly close, it appears, to a young man from the shipyards called McGrandle, who is described as a natural leader with a large following.

McGrandle has been gaining a considerable reputation as an orator recently."

Lloyd George smiled. "You can't be afraid of a little competition, surely, Winston?" he inquired wickedly.

Churchill ignored the interruption. "It concerns me that groups of highly motivated men, representing all classes, are meeting in secret, outside the control of the Workers' Strike Committee, and almost certainly conspiring against the central authority," he said.

The Prime Minister nodded, indicating he understood the seriousness of what Churchill was saying.

"Allowing that the official strike leadership is prepared to proceed in what we shall call an orderly fashion, you will appreciate, Prime Minister, that we have little way of knowing who may be hidden from sight, their preparations complete, just waiting for the strike to proceed to its next stage before they emerge to take advantage of the chaos which will surely ensue."

Lloyd George grunted. His mood appeared to be changing. Churchill sensed he might be winning.

"How would they organise themselves in order to run the country?" the Prime Minister wanted to know. "It would be impossible for them to be successful in this, at least."

Churchill shrugged. "According to the report submitted by our agent there is open talk in Glasgow of how government could be conducted, starting with the shop stewards, through a series of committees, with a worker-controlled council at its head," he replied. "It is suggested that the so-called Supreme Council could sit daily, using the City Chambers in Glasgow as its base."

Churchill shook his head in evident despair.

"What would happen as disorder spread, I have no idea," he said. "Nor do they, I suspect."

"You make it sound like a bad business," Lloyd George told him.

"I think we require to treat the matter most seriously, Prime Minister."

Lloyd George nodded.

Churchill added: "Sooner or later, I suppose, there will be a suggestion that a parliament of the Scottish people should convene in Edinburgh. Can you imagine what that would mean, Prime Minister?"

Lloyd George rebuked him sharply. "Never underestimate the Scots' deep-rooted sense of national identity and pride, Winston. They are a very different people from the English, remember. As are the Welsh," he added with a slight smile.

After a moment the Prime Minister went on: "What else do we know about these people?"

"They are all known socialists, mainly involved with the trade unions, and well known in the area," Churchill told him. "You know the sort of thing: writing pamphlets, addressing meetings, some of which attract large audiences, I am told, and generally making a nuisance of themselves."

"Theory, Winston, theory," Lloyd George protested wearily. "We've heard it all before. Nothing ever comes of it. At the first sign of real trouble the police will soon take charge."

"The police are unarmed, Prime Minister."

Lloyd George looked startled.

"Are you trying to tell me that the strikers have access to weapons?"

"Weapons are easily found once the will to use them has been established," Churchill replied sternly.

The Prime Minister nodded gravely. "God knows," he muttered, "there are enough men available who know how to use them."

"Exactly!"

Lloyd George lifted a piece of flawless crystal from the desk and studied it carefully. Light from a chandelier above Churchill's head danced on the ornament's impeccable surface. Lloyd George turned the crystal slowly in his hand and warm shafts of light darted about the room, hunting spirits, he thought, and chuckled; his grim mood lightened for a moment.

He grinned at Churchill, who rose from his chair and stood by the window, looking out. France always looked so different from England, Churchill mused. But, then, there was no other place in the world which looked like England. It was a difference worth defending, he reminded himself fiercely.

"It appears that nothing can be done to alter the course of events in Russia."

Without turning from the window, Churchill grunted. His views on the subject were well known to the Prime Minister. Wasn't he the one man in the whole of the Cabinet, with everyone else against him, including the Prime Minister, who wanted to send an expeditionary force marching on Moscow, and drive the tyrant Lenin from his lair? The Prime Minister, sensing his mood, ventured patiently: "Winston, I know you disagree with me on this, but in my opinion, now that the revolution in Russia is a fact of life, our main concern, so far as the Bolsheviks there are concerned, must be how we can learn to co-exist."

Churchill glowered. "That great Russian bear will cause us trouble yet," he warned. "It means to devour us, Prime Minister, make no mistake."

"The threat of revolution in Germany is a different matter entirely," Lloyd George continued gravely. "We must do everything in our power, summon all the forces at our command, to prevent it, Winston. It is possible, of course, that we are already too late and nothing can be done about it. The war lasted too long, cost everyone too much, and now we may find that it diverted our attention from an even greater peril."

"Revolution in Germany would be the final catastrophe," Churchill agreed darkly.

Lloyd George nodded, deep in thought.

"Let that happen and there is little we can do to stop the fever from sweeping across the Channel and infecting us too," Churchill warned.

"The point is not lost on me, Winston," the Prime Minister muttered, glaring at him.

"Obviously it would be impossible for the German government to approach us looking for help."

"It's a nice idea," Lloyd George conceded, chuckling grimly. "But I hardly think it's likely. In fact, if it was left to some of their generals presently in Paris hostilities between us would recommence immediately."

Churchill returned to his chair.

"These are dark days, Winston."

"If the revolution in Germany is successful, we can expect France to suffer a similar fate," Churchill said. "Italy will be next, I imagine. Then the Low Countries. Nothing can stop them being swept away."

"What will the Americans do, I wonder?"

"From what you say, Woodrow will be tempted to take a hand," Churchill retorted.

Lloyd George nodded. "But will American public opinion allow it?" he wondered.

Churchill shrugged. "Without their assistance there is little we can do to prevent the whole of Europe falling to the Bolsheviks," he said. "Our first task will be to save ourselves."

Lloyd George turned to face him and light from the crystal ornament fell across Churchill's forehead, making him frown. Lloyd George smiled at his friend's irritation. "Forgive me, Winston," he said, returning the ornament to its rightful place on the desk.

It was evident from his manner that there was something else he wanted to say. Churchill waited. He was generally quite happy to support Lloyd George, privately, and in public in times of crisis: without him the war would have been lost, in Churchill's view. He sometimes thought, however, that time could make them rivals. How would they compare in the great roll of honour, to be written by history, and still to be decided?

Churchill pushed the question from his mind. Lloyd George was looking at him thoughtfully.

"We both know that so much will change as a result of the war," Lloyd George said. "There are forces now working in society which it will be impossible for us to suppress. Perhaps, in trying to win the war, we encouraged people to expect too much from the peace. My abiding fear is that we will be unable to give them enough. I feel heartily sorry for the men who have been to the war and returned home to find themselves without jobs and nothing to encourage hope. We must dedicate ourselves to rebuilding the country, and with it the lives of our people, Winston. Between us, once everything else is settled, we can provide the leadership to make the nation strong again, confident, and proud."

Churchill accepted the responsibility with a nod.

"But what we need now, more than anything else, is a period of stability so that we can embark on a programme of controlled development," Lloyd George went on. "We need investment; money and men. There is no point in having one without the other, Winston. It is the task of government to find the money, either by way of taxation, or, better still, by encouraging people with funds to invest in industry for the future good of the country. It is also the responsibility of government, supported by the employers, to ensure the availability of a reliable workforce, well-trained in the skills of modern industrial methods."

He paused. Churchill had been listening carefully. Lloyd George shrugged. After a moment he continued seriously: "However, in my opinion, for the foreseeable future at least, we require to maintain the existing social order. Without order and discipline at every level of society the country will disintegrate."

"I agree," said Churchill.

"This could be the greatest change in our history," Lloyd George added.

Churchill knew agreement had been reached. "What do you propose, Prime Minister?" he inquired anyway.

Lloyd George rose from his chair and walked to the front of the desk.

"We will heed your advice, Winston," he replied sadly. "We will arrange for troops to be sent to Glasgow, as an emergency measure, so long as any request for assistance comes from the Lord Provost acting as Lord Lieutenant of the city. I am anxious that we don't appear to be taking this action against the wishes of the people who are responsible for maintaining order there."

Churchill nodded, well pleased with his morning's work. It had been worth the early morning crossing of the Channel, and the long journey by road to the remote château, deep in the valley of the Seine, near Rouen.

"What about tanks, Prime Minister?"

"Subject to what I have said about the local authorities being involved," the Prime Minister answered, taking his arm, "do whatever you consider necessary, Winston."

Churchill rose from his chair. "Thank you, Prime Minister," he responded gravely.

"You are absolutely right, of course," Lloyd George added, steering Churchill towards the door. "From the sounds of it the situation in Glasgow, and on Clydeside generally, is extremely serious. We must do everything possible to ensure that the trouble is contained."

Churchill hesitated. "We will require to inform the King, of course."

"Naturally."

"How will he react, do you suppose?"

"What do you think?" the Prime Minister inquired.

"He won't like the idea, I fear," Churchill replied.

"I don't care much for it myself," Lloyd George responded wryly.

Churchill stared at him. Lloyd George smiled conspiratorially.

"Don't worry, Winston," he said. "I think we are entitled to assume that His Majesty will be anxious to ensure the stability of the realm. Apart from anything else," the Prime Minister added, with a wink, "from what we have seen of them elsewhere, revolutionaries tend to dispense with the service of monarchs at the earliest opportunity. No, I doubt if it is in the King's best interests to go against us" he concluded cheerfully.

Churchill didn't want to upset the Prime Minister's good mood. He grunted, and said nothing.

"Frances accompanied me from Paris in order to see some of the countryside," Lloyd George went on, opening the door and steering Churchill out of the room first. "She hopes to see you before you leave. I am sure she would be happy to join us at lunch."

Churchill nodded.

"How is Clementine?"

"In the very best of health," Churchill replied.

"Good," said Lloyd George.

A small woman appeared in the corridor ahead of them.

"Ah!" said Lloyd George, smiling. "There's Frances. You must say hello."

# CHAPTER SEVENTEEN

It had been raining during the night and George Square was wet and muddy underfoot as thousands of marchers, carrying banners and waving flags, cheering and singing to the accompaniment of district bands, converged on the square from all over the city to hear the government's response to the Lord Provost's appeal. Made up largely of men, with a scattering of women visible here and there, the crowd behaved like people on a day out who expected it to end with the promise of certain good news. Their mood was infectious and Frank Munro wished he could embrace the celebrations. But he couldn't suppress the feeling that he was in the company of men and women about to be sorely disappointed beyond reasonable understanding; and what Munro felt was pity for people who deserved a better fate.

Munro was accompanied by Alick Robertson, freed from his desk for the morning and behaving like a tourist, Munro thought irritably, and Margaret Armstrong, who was determined not to miss anything.

"Have you ever seen such a crowd?" Margaret Armstrong inquired, her face shining from excitement. "They all look so happy! How many people are here, do you think?"

Munro grunted. "It's impossible to say," he answered. "Fifty or sixty thousand anyway, I'd guess."

Alick Robertson shook his head. "There'll be more than that," he declared. "Look," he added, pointing, "they're still pouring in from all sides. Who would believe that it was against the law to assemble in George Square?"

Margaret Armstrong looked surprised. "Is it?" she asked.

Munro nodded.

"The police will have a hard job controlling them if they decide to cause trouble," Alick Robertson muttered darkly.

Frank Munro sighed. In his opinion the huge police presence which had been assembled in George Square and all the surrounding streets was unnecessary; and could itself become a source of real trouble.

Everyone knew there wasn't much love lost between workers and police in the city and the Chief Constable was foolish to risk a serious confrontation.

Shortly after Munro and the others arrived in George Square they witnessed James Verdier Stevenson leaving the City Chambers to confer with a group of senior officers who stood, heavily guarded, on the pavement in front of the main entrance to the building.

"Doesn't he look smug?" Margaret Armstrong remarked unkindly, as the Chief Constable went to the edge of the pavement to survey the square. "You'd think he wanted trouble."

"That's unfair!" Alick Robertson protested sharply. "It's his responsibility to keep the peace, remember."

Frank Munro sighed. "You must admit, the man's a worry," he said.

Alick Robertson glared at him. "I refuse to admit any such thing!" he cried.

His friend chuckled drily. "Don't worry about it, Alick," he replied.

Frank Munro considered it an astonishing achievement that Shinwell had been able to persuade more than a hundred thousand men to join the strike in the course of the last few days. The leadership's one major setback had been its failure to stop the trams from running. Mr James Dalrymple, General Manager of the Tramways Department, and several of his men, still refused to abandon their occupation of Pinkston power station; while enough drivers and conductors reported for duty each day to allow the service to continue without undue interruption.

The tramwaymen enjoyed a reputation in the city as a stubborn lot generally, with a liking for independence, and their manager was widely regarded as a hard man who refused to countenance any interference whatsoever in the running of his department. On a visit to Pinkston the previous day Frank Munro found a mass picket, totalling at least three thousand men, with Shinwell himself in command, threatening the gates. Shinwell chuckled grimly when Munro and several other reporters suggested that the presence of so many men amounted to intimidation of the worst possible kind. Nor did it mean much to be reminded afterwards by big Davey Kirkwood, one of Shinwell's closest cronies, that the strikers hadn't stormed the gates; and, Kirkwood added earnestly, the reason for them not taking Pinkston by force was because Shinwell was against the idea.

The one man who didn't seem to mind all the fuss was James Dalrymple. He remained inside and refused to emerge although invited to come out and talk by Shinwell shouting at him through the gates. In a report for his newspaper Frank Munro noted grimly that Pinkston had been turned into a fortress which the tramwaymen appeared determined to defend at all costs. Those who opposed the strike and needed heroes responded happily to the name of James Dalrymple: when his report appeared Frank Munro discovered, with no sense of satisfaction at its elevation, that what he had written had been accorded a special place at the top of the page; and was accompanied by a leading article, signed by the editor, which applauded the efforts of the tramwaymen and proclaimed their leader as the kind of man the country needed if ordinary people everywhere were to be saved from the bully-boys of the trade union movement.

From the point of view of Shinwell and the other members of the Workers' Strike Committee the main effect of the strike had been to paralyse the shipyards and close down most of the major factories and steelworks in the area. However, reports reaching the city from elsewhere were discouraging. It was becoming clear that workers in other parts of the country were refusing to join them in sufficient numbers to sustain the hope that Glasgow was the first step on the way to a national strike. Instead, it was obvious to anyone not blinded by over-commitment, that Clydeside was in danger of becoming isolated from the rest of the national industrial community. Frank Munro numbered among those who believed that anyone wanting change on a national scale couldn't succeed without nation-wide support.

He offered Shinwell an opportunity to comment and was treated to a broad smile followed by a stern rebuke. The country expected leadership, Shinwell informed him coldly; and that leadership, he continued fiercely, would be forthcoming from Clydeside. Once the rest of the country witnessed what could be achieved by determined leadership, and the utilisation of strong industrial muscle, workers everywhere inspired by their example, would be rushing to support them. Frank Munro thought that this analysis was flawed and some-what optimistic; but he chose not to say so. He realised, of course, that Shinwell would construe his silence as evidence of yet another argument won against unpredictable odds. Munro didn't mind. It meant that they parted with the strike leader still in a jovial mood and good relations maintained between them.

Munro smiled. Margaret Armstrong stared at him. "Is something wrong?" she asked.

Munro shook his head. "It's nothing," he replied.

181

Alick Robertson nodded. "Here comes Shinwell now," he remarked.

Accompanied by several colleagues, including Davey Kirkwood, and a local Member of Parliament named Neil McLean, the chairman of the Workers' Strike Committee could be seen pushing his way through the crowd towards the City Chambers. Munro immediately recognised the mood adopted by Shinwell in preparation for the day. Whenever he wanted to impress his followers and intimidate the other side, Shinwell always made a point of presenting a carefully manufactured look which combined an appearance of grim determination with an air of smouldering belligerence. Munro was forced to concede that the trick appeared to work. Anyone who saw him in action couldn't possibly doubt that Shinwell was ready for a fight whenever, and in whatever conditions, his opponents cared to suggest. Munro grunted. So far, in the present difficult circumstances, in the whole of Glasgow, only Mr James Dalrymple, the General Manager of the Tramways Department, had been prepared to accept Shinwell's challenge, he remembered.

Munro shook his head thoughtfully. Not forgetting the Chief Constable, of course. And forgetting the Chief Constable would be a mistake, Munro reminded himself grimly.

He could see the stern and upright figure of James Verdier Stevenson watching carefully as Shinwell made his way through the crowd. Everyone knew his reputation and no-one in the city believed for a moment that the Chief Constable would flinch from the prospect of a fight. Indeed, many people representing both sides in the argument, together with neutral observers who had been following the progress of the strike with particular interest, expected him to intervene sooner or later; and, if anything, most of them were surprised he hadn't made his presence felt more forcibly already. Frank Munro for one accepted the popular consensus that everything known about the man supported the view that he was just waiting, biding his time, and hoping with ill-concealed impatience for an excuse to involve himself in the proceedings. Munro felt certain that the presence of so many people loose on the streets, demonstrating openly against the established order, was the worst possible affront to James Verdier Stevenson's most cherished sensibilities; not to mention his understanding of what constituted law and order within an organised and settled community.

He glanced round George Square.

Everywhere demonstrators were singing loud enough to make their lungs burst, drowning all attempts by the assembled bandsmen to make themselves heard above the din, cheering wildly now, whistling and chanting slogans, shouting support for their leaders, encouraging one another, arms reaching for the sky, no longer questioning the impossible dream, for victory was assured, their faces aglow with pleasure, knowing everything was worthwhile, all the pain and anger, in return for the realisation that this was the best morning of their lives!

Munro could see Mrs Reid, the white-haired woman with the red flag featured in all the newspapers following the march from St Andrew's Halls earlier in the week, standing in the middle of the road, red flag waving, her face a picture of joy.

"Isn't she wonderful?" Margaret Armstrong cried.

Munro chuckled. "What do you think, Alick?" he inquired.

His friend scowled irritably. "You know what I think,' Alick Robertson replied.

Munro nodded. "Anyway," he continued cheerfully, "seeing this for yourself you can't deny that Shinwell's got them going."

Alick Robertson shrugged and muttered, "We'll see."

Smiling at his friend's obvious displeasure, Munro turned away. "This is really something, isn't it?" he remarked to Margaret Armstrong.

"I think they are all positively inspired," she told him, breathlessly.

"I think that's going a bit far," Munro objected.

"I don't."

Munro laughed lightly. "Alick will never forgive you," he warned.

Margaret Armstrong nodded. "I know. Alick's out of step with the world," she declared.

"That's true, anyway," Munro conceded with a smile.

Shinwell was about to enter the City Chambers when Frank Munro heard him tell Willie Gallacher to wait behind and occupy the crowd while he went inside to hear from the Lord Provost. By now the noise of the assembled strikers, convinced that they were on the brink of a famous victory at the expense of the government and the employers, could be heard miles away on the far side of the city. Munro felt no special concern as the noise of the crowd increased and police on duty in front of the municipal headquarters began forming themselves into lines several ranks deep to face them. Nor was he conscious of experiencing any sense of immediate alarm when a few of the men at the front of the crowd started hurling insults at those members of the police nearest to them. It was all part of the ritual, the kind of demonstration

183

expected on these occasions, and nothing to worry about, Munro thought easily, and made a note for later.

Margaret Armstrong nudged his arm and pointed. "I think that young shop steward you know is trying to attract your attention," she said.

Munro saw Willie McGrandle in the crowd and waved.

"He seems a nice lad," Margaret Armstrong remarked, smiling.

Munro was non-committal. "Ambitious, certainly," he replied.

Margaret Armstrong frowned. "What's wrong with that?" she inquired.

Munro shrugged and didn't answer.

"We need more people like him," Margaret Armstrong asserted, "from the working class, with ambition."

"You don't even know him," Munro objected, sharply.

"I was speaking generally," Margaret Armstrong insisted.

Munro sighed. "Of course," he replied.

Margaret Armstrong frowned. "You must agree, surely?"

"In principle, yes, I suppose so," Munro conceded, grudgingly.

Margaret Armstrong stared at him for a moment. "Why do you pretend not to care?" she inquired, finally.

Munro brushed her question aside with an impatient shrug. "That's your interpretation, not mine," he retorted.

Alick Robertson chuckled. "Save your breath, Margaret," he advised.

Margaret Armstrong wasn't finished, however. "Don't you understand what's happening here? These men are making a commitment to a cause!" she cried.

Munro responded sharply. "Don't bother me with causes!" he snapped.

"I'm sorry," Margaret Armstrong responded roughly. "I forgot."

Munro tried to reduce her anger with an apologetic shrug and failed. Alick Robertson laughed.

"Frank hates people to think he's got any kind of conscience. The story is all that interests him, or so he says, although I don't believe a word of it, not for a moment. If you really want to know the truth, Margaret, at heart Frank's an old softie, marshmallow through and through!" Alick Robertson explained.

Munro glared at him. "What got you started?" he demanded.

Alick Robertson grinned and resumed his study of the crowd.

"There's something I want you to try and understand," Margaret Armstrong informed him harshly.

Munro waited.

Margaret Armstrong went on: "These people aren't fools. They know the world is capable of providing more of a life, a better life, a decent life, for themselves and their families than anything they've been allowed to enjoy s far. They know because they can see for themselves how people with money, the employers and the landlords especially, are able to work the system to their own greedy advantage!"

She paused. People were crowding towards them, shouting and singing, spreading out from the central garden area on to the road, and from there to the pavement's edge. The woman carrying the red flag brushed against them and part of the flag's lower folds settled around Margaret Armstrong's shoulders. Mrs Reid smiled happily and nodded encouragement as Margaret Armstrong gripped the rough cloth tightly and raised her fist in triumph to the crowd.

> The people's flag is deepest red
> It shroudest oft our martyr'd dead

"Isn't this simply amazing?" Margaret Armstrong gasped.

Mrs Reid was singing now, swaying in time to the workers' hymn, red flag waving, her face alight with pleasure, as she vanished into the crowd.

> And ere their limbs bgrew stiff and cold
> Their heart's blood dyed its ev'ry fold

Alick Robertson groaned. "For God's sake, Margaret, spare us the words of that damned song," he pleaded.

Margaret Armstrong ignored him. She didn't take her eyes from the crowd. "These people are so damned marvellous," she breathed.

> Then raise the scarlet standard high!
> Within its shade we'll live and die!
> Tho' cowards flinch and traitors sneer,
> We'll keep the red flag flying here!

Her eyes swept the crowd, searching for faint-hearts, Frank Munro thought wickedly. "That's why I rejoice whenever I meet the likes of Willie McGrandle," she added earnestly.

Frank Munro shrugged. Margaret Armstrong turned to look at him and was silent for a moment. Finally, speaking quietly, she told him: "Don't tell me the world can't change. People like Willie McGrandle can make it change."

Frank Munro said nothing.

"All those men and women here today, at no little risk to themselves, don't forget, are just hoping for a new beginning and the start of a better life for themselves and their families," Margaret Armstrong continued. "They are willing themselves to achieve it whatever the government decides."

Munro cleared his throat. "What happens if they are forced to leave here disappointed?" he inquired. "If the government says no, that could be the end of all their dreams."

"No!"

"Surely you must concede the possibility?" Munro insisted.

"Never!"

Munro remained silent. There was no point arguing further.

"Obviously, we need time. But make no mistake, however long it takes, these people will prevail," she said.

They could see Willie McGrandle pushing towards them through the crowd. Munro grinned. "Here he comes, a genuine hero of the working class," joked Munro. "Prepare to rejoice!"

Margaret Armstrong smiled and shrugged. "You'll see," she promised. "I am right, you know."

Munro grunted. "Don't wait for me on the road to Valhalla," he requested. "It's a long way on a hard and stony road."

Margaret Armstrong appeared undismayed. "I never said it would be easy. But we'll get there, one day, you'll see," she replied.

Alick Robertson sounded anxious. "Didn't the Chief Constable say that demonstrators were to keep clear of the pavement in front of the City Chambers?" he asked.

Munro nodded. "Not once but several times," he agreed.

Alick Robertson indicated a small group of men in working-clothes standing on the pavement close to the kerb. "Then I'd say that lot are asking for trouble," he observed.

Margaret Armstrong looked puzzled. "Why?" she demanded.

Alick Robertson shrugged and tried to explain. "When the Chief Constable of Glasgow issues an instruction he expects it to be obeyed," he told her.

"They aren't doing any harm," Margaret Armstrong protested.

"What they are doing isn't the issue," Alick Robertson responded drily. "It's where that matters. What do you think, Frank?"

Munro wanted to support Margaret Armstrong but he was forced to admit that he didn't like the look of things either. All morning hundreds of demonstrators, unable to secure a place in the central garden area, had been spilling on to the road, making it impossible for traffic to enter the square, and milling about in noisy, exuberant groups, constantly narrowing the distance between themselves and police guarding the front of the City Chambers. In some places he could see that police and strikers were close enough to mix and trouble was within easy reach of anyone wanting to start a fight. Frank Munro didn't believe the demonstrators offered any serious threat to the police. What worried him was how the Chief Constable might react to the men's presence on the pavement in front of the municipal headquarters, in direct opposition to his orders. James Verdier Stevenson, having made such a fuss when he issued the decree, was bound to view anything which went against it as an open challenge to his authority.

Now, as he looked everywhere for signs of trouble, Frank Munro could see hundreds of demonstrators, jostling gently, drifting towards the territory proscribed by the Chief Constable. "This looks bad," he muttered, as police and strikers mingled dangerously.

Margaret Armstrong gripped his arm. "Look!" she gasped.

Crossing from the road to the pavement less than thirty yards away they saw Willie McGrandle put a hand on a policeman's shoulder to steady himself as a shift in the crowd appeared to bundle them together. McGrandle grinned and raised both hands in a gesture of apology and surrender. Without speaking, the policeman turned, baton rising, and felled him with a single blow.

"Oh, my God!" cried Margaret Armstrong, her eyes blinding with tears. "What's happening?"

Frank Munro couldn't believe his eyes. Strikers were being harried in all directions at once, pursued without warning, and not many signs of mercy, by at least a hundred uniformed men who had been stirred to action, Munro assumed, by some prearranged signal he, for one, hadn't seen or heard. Wielding their batons with most of their strength, the police appeared intent on teaching anyone who had been foolish enough to venture on to the pavement a lesson he wouldn't forget.

Overcome at first by the unexpectedness of the attack, and unable to defend themselves against the superior organisation on show from the forces of law and order, dozens of demonstrators were chased on to the road and back into the central garden area.

Margaret Armstrong was determined to assist Willie McGrandle.

"Watch out!" Munro cried as she began running towards the injured striker.

A young constable, baton raised, tried to grab her arm. Margaret

Armstrong glared at him. "Don't you dare!" she warned. "Do you know who we are?"

The young constable hesitated. "There's nobody allowed on the pavement, missus," he retorted.

"Do we look like strikers?" Margaret Armstrong insisted.

He looked uncertain. "It's our duty, missus," the young constable said.

Margaret Armstrong glared at him. "We are going to the aid of that injured man," she replied, indicating Willie McGrandle, who was on his knees, blood spurting from a gash behind his ear. "I warn you not to try and stop us."

The young constable shrugged. "We'll see," he replied stubbornly.

Margaret Armstrong frowned. "We are personal friends of the Chief Constable," she warned.

His baton remained raised. "If you know the Chief Constable, what are you doing here" he asked, addressing Munro.

"My friend is a nurse," Munro told him. "I'm a reporter."

"I didn't think you looked like strikers. At least the lady doesn't," he added ambiguously.

Munro tried to sound friendly. "Constable, I think you should listen to the lady. She does know the Chief Constable and she is also a friend of the Lord Provost," he advised.

Baton never lower than chest high the young constable started backing away. "You'd better be careful, missus," he said.

By the time Munro and Margaret Armstrong reached Willie McGrandle he was on his feet with his hair and clothes covered in blood. "The bastards will kill us all!" he cried.

"For God's sake what happened?" Munro demanded.

McGrandle shook his head. "They started hitting us for no reason and without warning," he replied.

"Keep still!" Margaret Armstrong ordered.

She brought a tiny, linen handkerchief, too small for the purpose, from her pocket, hoping to mop blood from his neck and prevent the wound from bleeding. "This won't do," she announced. "You need a doctor."

"Aye," McGrandle acknowledged grimly. "Do you think I'm the only wan?"

She didn't answer.

"Pity aboot the hankie," McGrandle added, grinning. "It looked dinky."

"Don't be silly," she instructed.

His mood changed. "Whoever started this will pay," he promised. "Put that in your paper, won't you, Mr Munro?"

Injured strikers littered the pavement and road or wandered about in a daze. There was no sign of policemen in similar distress, however.

Their remarkable good fortune angered Frank Munro.

From his own close view of events there was nothing to justify James Verdier Stevenson allowing his men to descend on the crowd with such force. His action had been calculated to encourage panic among the demonstrators knowing that the vast majority would flee without a fight.

"Look at Gallacher!"

Impulsive as always, and heading for trouble, they saw Willie Gallacher storming through the crowd. "He's after someone!" McGrandle shouted.

Gallacher was much admired by the men and widely respected as a key member of the Workers' Strike Committee. It was often claimed that certain large groups preferred him to Shinwell and wanted him as leader. Gallacher made no secret of his total dedication to the class war and was a revolutionary at heart. His quick temper made him quarrelsome, even at the best of times, but Munro found him likeable and honest and always enjoyed meeting him personally.

When the police action against the demonstrators started, Gallacher was addressing a section of the crowd in front of the Gladstone monument. He could see across the heads of the demonstrators as far as the front of the City Chambers, where police were forming lines and some people in the crowd were beginning to drift on to the pavement. A mild-mannered workman of his acquaintance, feeling nervous in the midst of the huge crowd which filled George Square, stood with his back against the wall of the municipal headquarters, simply keeping out of the way, Gallacher assumed, and causing no-one any trouble. Suddenly, and for no apparent reason, Gallacher saw the man being grabbed and thrown to the ground by two policemen working together. When the workman, protesting vigorously, tried to rise, Gallacher witnessed one of his assailants, a sergeant, draw his baton and chase him into the crowd. A moment later the area in front of the City Chambers was in turmoil.

In an attempt to control those nearest to him, Gallacher immediately started shouting for order. Then he tried looking for the Chief Constable and spotted him conferring with a group of city officials.

Surrounded by a guard of about a dozen constables, James Verdier Stevenson appeared to be directing the operation himself. It was the temerity of his attack which caught everyone by surprise. All anger focused on one hated figure, fists raised and smashing forward. Gallacher crashed through the ring of guards and hurled himself at the Chief Constable.

The first blow landed with stinging force on James Verdier Stevenson's handsome face. The Chief Constable staggered and almost fell, taking him away from Gallacher, who tried to hit him a second time with equal severity and missed. Next thing Gallacher knew, as he gathered himself to deliver what he hoped would be a bone-splitting punch to the side of an exposed jaw, the Chief Constable's guards were hauling him away with little regard for his general comfort. Gallacher realised vaguely that he was at the mercy of men with a career in the Glasgow constabulary to protect. Discouraging assaults on the Chief Constable would be an important part of their responsibilities, Gallacher figured. Group pride would be hurt because he had been able to burst through their ranks and attack the Chief Constable: an assassin could have killed him given the same opportunity. Whether or not they cared for James Verdier Stevenson personally, or felt any serious concern at the thought of him suffering grievous bodily harm at the hands of a known troublemaker like himself, was purely academic. What interested him most going down in the face of their assault was the realisation that more than a dozen uniformed men were quite clearly committed to the idea of revenge. And he was their number one target.

"They're murdering Gallacher!" someone shouted.

A young man who emerged from the crowd succeeded in throwing himself on top of Gallacher, hoping to protect him, and was immediately knocked flat by a blow from a baton aimed at the strike leader's face. Gallacher winced as the weapon descended on the young man's head with a force which cracked his skull.

"It's me you want!" Gallacher roared. "Leave the boy alone!"

Elsewhere it was evident from their actions that the police wanted the whole area in front of the City Chambers, including the roadway and gardens, cleared of demonstrators. If they could find the means, the entire square would be emptied of more than fifty thousand people in a single sweep, with or without the demonstrators' consent, Frank Munro decided anxiously.

Most of the demonstrators would move along quietly in response to a bullying look or the threat of a few harsh words. However, the moment someone said to watch out when the police said move because today they meant business, there would be men in that crowd who would grin and rub their hands in anticipation of a good fight. Once people on the far side of the square heard about the disturbance outside the City Chambers some of them might take the view that they were required to retaliate for the sake of their own good name, and in support of the city's reputation for toughness. How they might react when news reached them about how the Chief Constable's men treated Willie Gallacher was something else for the authorities to consider. There would be no point anyone arguing that Gallacher struck the Chief Constable first: none of the people Munro had in mind would listen.

Munro didn't discount the idea that the Lord Provost of Glasgow, supported by the Chief Constable, was taking these precautions on behalf of the city, and risking a bloody confrontation with the demonstrators, most of whom were also citizens, because the authorities expected an attack on the City Chambers the moment Shinwell delivered the government's answer to their demands. In which case the mood of optimism which had been prevailing amongst the strikers and their families for most of the week was about to be shattered.

"Are you all right?" Margaret Armstrong inquired anxiously.

Munro nodded. "For the moment," he told her.

"Can you see what's happening to Gallacher?" Margaret Armstrong inquired.

Willie McGrandle interrupted. "He's still surrounded by police. I think they're going to take him away," McGrandle said.

"I'm surprised he's still in one piece," she retorted.

Willie McGrandle grunted. "At least they've stopped hitting him," he said.

"Gallacher must be mad!" Alick Robertson insisted. "Imagine trying to attack the Chief Constable! What a damned stupid thing to do!"

"I wish I'd tried," Margaret Armstrong replied.

"Where is Stevenson, anyway?" Munro inquired.

"Who cares?" McGrandle muttered.

"There's Shinwell!" Margaret Armstrong cried.

Shinwell raced from the City Chambers followed by Davey Kirkwood and Neil McLean, the Member of Parliament for Govan. Noise from the disturbance had been heard inside the City Chambers and brought them rushing to the scene. There was a look of horror on all their faces. "What started this?" Shinwell shouted.

An injured striker left sitting on the ground attracted his attention.

Shinwell ran to the man and knelt beside him. One side of his face was open to the bone. He held his cheek in the crotch of his hand. Blood ran down his arm and into his sleeve. Shinwell looked everywhere for help.

Several policemen with a senior officer in charge appeared to detour slightly to avoid him. Their manner made Shinwell suspicious. The officer was aware of Shinwell looking at them and could be heard ordering his men to hurry.

It was Davey Kirkwood who recognised the silent, unresisting figure of Willie Gallacher propped in their midst. "Are you insane?" he yelled, and ran to the rescue of his old friend.

The officer waved him away. "It will be the worse for you if you interfere," he warned.

Gallacher opened his eyes. "Hullo, Davey," he murmured from the centre of the group. "Did we win?"

The condition of his old friend made Kirkwood cry. "What have they done to you, man?" he sobbed.

"Some of them aren't looking too good either," Gallacher gasped.

The officer tried to push Kirkwood aside. The big man refused to budge. "I warned you once," the officer said.

"Better watch yourself, Davey," Gallacher warned.

Kirkwood was unconscious before his face hit the ground. He never saw the sergeant who had brought him down without warning from behind. "Bring him as well," the officer ordered.

Neil McLean rushed to intervene. Knowing he was a Member of Parliament the officer treated McLean with respect.

"These men are under arrest, Mr McLean. Please don't interfere," he said.

"On what charges?" McLean demanded.

"Incitement to riot," the officer replied.

"That's preposterous!" the Member of Parliament exclaimed.

"That may be your view," the officer told him. "The law will decide. Please stand aside, Mr McLean. You of all people should realise we are in lawful pursuit of our duties."

McLean let them go. "There was nothing I could do," he told Shinwell and the others afterwards.

Shinwell sighed.

"They're both in a bad way," McLean added.

"Of all the people to pick on," Shinwell muttered. "Poor Davey!"

Munro knew what he meant. Everybody said Kirkwood was a gentle soul. Gallacher was a tough.

Shinwell turned to him. "Were you here when it started?" he asked.

Munro nodded.

"How did it start?"

"Nobody knows," Munro told him.

Margaret Armstrong interrupted impatiently. "You can blame the police," she declared. "Nobody else."

Shinwell looked satisfied. "That's what I thought," he remarked.

"Did any of our people retaliate?" Neil MacLean inquired.

"You saw what they did to big Davey. There wasn't time," McGrandle replied.

Neil McLean nodded. "Did you see what happened to Gallacher?"

Margaret Armstrong recalled the moment with enthusiasm. "He threw himself at Stevenson!" she cried.

Shinwell chuckled grimly. "Good for Willie!" he retorted. "That's worth a medal at least!"

Neil McLean was less impressed. "In that state?" he asked.

Shinwell shrugged.

"Has anyone seen Mr Stevenson?" the Member of Parliament continued.

"Only at a distance surrounded by guards. He could look a lot worse," Willie McGrandle admitted.

"Yes," said the Member of Parliament, "I think I know who would come out best from that sort of encounter."

Shinwell sounded impatient. "We'd better find Stevenson," he declared.

"Can you tell me what happened in there?"

The strike leader smiled. "Is that a serious question, Mr Munro?"

"Of course," he replied.

"You mean you don't know?"

"I wasn't there."

Shinwell smiled. "I wasn't here when the trouble started but I'm sure I know what happened," he said.

"I need you to tell me for the record," Munro insisted.

"You could always ask Downing Street."

"Someone else will ask Downing Street," Munro responded patiently. "I'm asking you, Mr Shinwell."

"This is going to be an interesting day, Mr Munro. Take my word for it," Shinwell told him.

Munro nodded.

193

"On the other hand you might care to arrange a visit to Paris, where you could address your question to the Prime Minister himself," Shinwell suggested grandly.

"I'd like to know today," Munro told him.

Shinwell smiled. "I thought I'd told you," he said.

"I understand what you're saying, Mr Shinwell."

"Well?"

"I'd still like you to say it," Munro insisted.

"They said no."

Munro heard Margaret Armstrong gasp and Willie McGrandle trying to stifle an oath. He could imagine Alick Robertson's look of disapproval at Shinwell's method of revealing the news.

"What happens now?" Alick Robertson asked.

Shinwell didn't hesitate. "We fight, that's what."

Willie McGrandle couldn't wait to begin. "When do we start?" he asked.

His impatience amused Shinwell. "Just looking at you I thought you'd started already," he said.

McGrandle shook his head seriously. "That was them," he declared. "I let them have first go. Now it's my turn."

Neil McLean sounded worried. "We must find the Chief Constable and make him see sense."

Shinwell nodded. "I agree. People are expecting a message from the Prime Minister," Shinwell continued. "How does Mr Stevenson propose they hear it now, I wonder?"

"There is bound to be serious crushing if the police keep pushing everyone to the back of the square," Neil McLean went on. "Someone could be killed."

He noticed Margaret Armstrong frowning again and thought it must be nerves. Her question increased his concern, although it wasn't one he could answer with any certainty.

"How many people on the other side of the square know about the disturbances here, or what happened to Gallacher and Kirkwood, do you think?"

Willie McGrandle didn't hesitate. "That kind of word soon spreads," he replied.

"Wait a minute!" Frank Munro objected.

Shinwell didn't bother to hide his irritation. "Is something bothering you, Mr Munro?" he inquired.

Munro nodded vigorously. "So far you've managed to keep all those people under control," he replied. "Now you propose some kind of mass leak in order to tell them the government refuses to support their demands. That on top of what happened to Gallacher and Kirkwood."

Shinwell interrupted. "What about Gallacher and Kirkwood?" he snapped. "How does what happened to them affect anything?"

"You can't be serious!" Alick Robertson protested.

Munro stopped him. "Alick, please, give me a minute. Mr Shinwell, you know exactly what I'm driving at," Munro continued. "Whether you like it or not, whatever you do to prevent it, people are certain to be fed false information the moment word of what's happened begins to spread."

"Meaning?"

"The stirrers and troublemakers who are hell-bent on causing real strife will start work with a vengeance," Munro said. "People won't know the truth of what's going on or how you and the rest of the leadership expect them to respond to the government's decision. The whole city could explode if you aren't careful!"

"Are you blaming us for what happened this morning?" Shinwell demanded.

"That isn't the point. If you conspire to turn George Square into a battlefield you'll be in serious trouble," Munro warned.

"Is that what you want?" Alick Robertson asked.

Shinwell glared at him. "Are you trying to provoke me, Mr Robertson?" he demanded.

Alick Robertson glanced at Neil McLean. "Not at all," he replied. "I'm agreeing with Frank and advising caution, that's all."

Shinwell's fists clenched. "That's all, is it?" he snapped angrily. "Don't you think I know what's best for the men?"

The two journalists exchanged glances.

"You want me to send them home, is that it?" Shinwell continued.

"I want you to do everything possible to avoid trouble," Munro replied.

"Perhaps I could persuade the Chief Constable to adopt more agreeable methods of crowd control," Shinwell countered.

"You could ask Mr Stevenson to withdraw his men from the square while the demonstrators disperse," Alick Robertson suggested.

Willie McGrandle stared at him. "Are you being serious?" he demanded.

Shinwell chuckled. "Do you think he would agree on the grounds they make the place look untidy?" he asked.

195

"It's his job to maintain order," Alick Robertson insisted. "If you offer to send your people home while the Committee considers its next move, I believe he would cooperate in keeping the peace by ordering his men to withdraw."

"You forget one thing," Willie McGrandle retorted. "Stevenson's dying for a fight. He won't want to miss this chance."

Neil McLean looked worried. "He must be made to make his men withdraw before a tragedy occurs," he said.

Shinwell put a hand on Frank Munro's arm. "You said something about what would happen if we let ourselves become involved in a conspiracy, Mr Munro," he began.

Frank Munro waited.

"Don't you know there is already a conspiracy at work here?" Shinwell continued. "It involves the government and the city authorities, including the Chief Constable, of course, together with the employers and the landlords. Right from the start of this dispute they have conspired to defeat the legitimate claims of the working people of Glasgow. Are you surprised that there is a limit to our patience?"

Munro said nothing. The huge crowd occupying George Square was about to be infiltrated by much bad news, he thought.

Shinwell nodded briskly and left him to worry. The chairman of the Workers' Strike Committee was reconciled, it seemed, to the prospect of confrontation involving police and strikers on a dangerous scale.

Immediately in front of the main Post Office an empty tram crawled like some cornered beast along the southern side of George Square. Hundreds of demonstrators marched alongside, chanting their slogans and threatening the driver, a man in his early thirties who wore a ten-year service badge pinned to his tunic.

Margaret Armstrong frowned anxiously. "Don't you think he's taking his responsibilities a bit too seriously under the circumstances?" she inquired.

Willie McGrandle grinned. "Maybe he thinks Dalrymple will gie him a medal for saving his caur," he suggested.

The demonstrators obviously wanted to stop the cumbersome vehicle dead in its tracks. "They should go for the trolley," McGrandle added knowledgably.

Several strikers jumped on board and ran from the rear to the front, pushing and jostling the driver, who resisted with an angry scowl, leaning across the controls, and waving at people to keep clear of the track. Finally, one young striker ran upstairs and pulled on a rope, hanging outside, which controlled the trolley against an overhead cable. The sudden loss of power brought the tram to a halt with a jolt and the driver cracked his brow against the window in front.

"That was clever," McGrandle chuckled.

The driver tried to go upstairs to replace the trolley and found his way blocked by grinning strikers. The driver withdrew, accepting the loss of his tram, and went inside to sit down. Demonstrators cheered and rattled on the windows and came on board to look at him and gloat. The driver said nothing. He reached into his pocket and found the remains of a two-thirds-smoked cigarette, which he turned between his fingers, coaxing the tobacco into shape, before lighting.

"Just a minute, driver."

The driver recognised the young man who had been responsible for disconnecting the trolley.

"There's nae smoking doon here," the young man said. "Didn't ye know? Go upstairs if ye want tae smoke."

The driver smiled pleasantly. "Why don't you just fuck off," he replied.

Everyone laughed.

"Look!"

On the far side of George Square dozens of police could be seen running for their lives pursued by several hundred strikers kicking at their heels. "The boys will have their guts for garters!" Willie McGrandle roared joyously.

Frank Munro grunted and glanced at Margaret Armstrong. It was a safe bet some of them would try, he thought, grim-faced, and without surprise. Harried and bullied by the police all morning, it was always odds-on that some of the harder citizens would respond in a fury eventually. Considering the serious nature of the day's events, and the fate of Gallacher and Kirkwood in particular, the police were lucky, in a crowd that size, that large numbers of demonstrators didn't retaliate earlier.

The sudden change in the behaviour of the crowd probably started with people at the front, finding themselves in danger of being crushed, turning on those at the rear. Faced with the huge mass of demonstrators trapped inside George Square refusing to leave, the police couldn't possibly hold the line against them.

"This is madness!" Munro muttered.

Margaret Armstrong nodded anxiously. "The police are bound to turn on them in earnest," she said.

197

"Naw!" scoffed Willie McGrandle. "Stevenson's men are a' feart!"

"I'm glad you think so," Frank Munro replied.

The demonstrators didn't appear organised in any real sense. Their success in routing the police was due entirely to numbers. Once the police found reinforcements they were certain to try and restore order, using whatever means could be placed at their disposal, and with no regard for the level of damage inflicted on the other side.

"Will the men stand and fight, do you think?"

"Everything depends on the level of Stevenson's response," replied Munro.

Margaret Armstrong nodded. "In that case the men won't stand a chance!" she declared.

Willie McGrandle stared at her. "What do you mean?" he demanded.

"Stevenson's ruthless when it comes to this kind of thing," Margaret Armstrong retorted. "Don't forget, he can't afford to lose, not under any circumstances."

A young constable, with blood all over his face, minus his helmet and looking dazed, walked past them into the City Chambers.

"There's wan o' them at least who isn't looking too good!" McGrandle grinned.

Frank Munro nodded. He expected sections of the crowd to stand and fight regardless of the forces ranged against them. They wouldn't all run, not in a million years, he thought admiringly. However, as the number of policemen entering the City Chambers suffering from injuries inflicted by the demonstrators in the first stages of the battle increased, it occurred to Munro that the police were certain to be up against a large number of hooligans who belonged to a different social category from honourable city hardmen. Neighbours and workmates, the same people who treated the hardmen with respect in the street and at work, openly despised the hooligans on account of their socially irresponsible and often criminal behaviour. Their favourite weapons included chains, knives, iron bars, and knuckledusters made from brass, and the police in full flight provided a handy and attractive target. In fairness to Stevenson and his men, there was never any chance the hooligans wouldn't present themselves in George Square in force on a day like this, fully equipped and looking for trouble.

An ambulance worker appeared and suggested in a quiet voice that it might be an idea if Willie McGrandle went with him into the City Chambers. "That cut needs a doctor," the ambulance worker added.

"You expect me to go in there?" McGrandle inquired.

"There's a first-aid station set up in the yard," the ambulance worker explained.

McGrandle smiled bitterly. "That was quick," he remarked.

"The man's right," Margaret Armstrong told him.

"No," McGrandle insisted, shaking his head. "Anybody who goes in there needing treatment will be arrested first. What do you think happened to Gallacher and Kirkwood? Besides," he added determinedly, "there's going to be real trouble out here, starting any minute now, and I don't want to miss it."

Alick Robertson stared at him. "What do you call this if it isn't real trouble?" he demanded.

McGrandle chuckled harshly. "Listen, boss," he replied. "What you've seen so far will be like a Sunday school picnic compared to what's bound to happen next. Don't tell me you back the bobbies in a real fight?"

The ambulance worker responded morosely. "It sounds like being a busy day for us," he said.

"Have you seen Mr Shinwell or the Chief Constable anywhere?" Frank Munro inquired.

"I saw them over there, less than five minutes ago," the ambulanceman replied, "shouting at one another."

"That figures," Alick Robertson grimaced.

"Shinwell better watch out, or the Chief Constable will put him inside," the ambulanceman added seriously.

"Where did you see him?" Munro asked.

The ambulanceman pointed. "On the corner not far from that caur," he said. "Shinwell finally left. He looked in a foul temper and seemed in an awful hurry. I don't know what happened to the Chief Constable. He could have gone inside, I suppose," the ambulance worker added, indicating the City Chambers.

He looked at Willie McGrandle. "You're sure you won't come with me and have that cut fixed?"

McGrandle shook his head. "I'm all right," he insisted.

"Suit yourself," the ambulance worker replied.

A lorry piled high with wooden crates containing hundreds of empty lemonade bottles tried to enter George Square from the east. Willie McGrandle saw it and roared: "That's what we need!"

McGrandle dashed to the lorry and, yelling at the driver to stop, jumped on the running-board. Dozens of angry strikers surrounded the vehicle, or clung to the sides, grabbing at ropes holding the crates. One man climbed on top of the crates and, swaying dangerously, began lobbing bottles into the crowd for his mates to catch and use against the police. The lorry driver grinned through the open window at McGrandle. "Have you been waiting long?" he asked.

"Turn into North Frederick Street," McGrandle ordered.

"Then what?"

"Stop when I tell you."

"Am I some kind of hostage?" the driver inquired good-humouredly.

Willie McGrandle grinned. "Is that what you want to tell the wife?" he asked.

The other man chuckled. "She'll want tae know what happened," he replied.

McGrandle pointed. "Stop there!" he ordered. "Tell her what you like," McGrandle went on. "Just so long as you don't want to be a hero, I don't mind."

"It isn't ma lorry," the driver informed him. "I just drive the bloody thing."

"You can keep the lorry," McGrandle told him. "In the meantime, you could always help me."

"Naw, thanks, not me," the driver answered, halting in the middle of North Frederick Street, as instructed.

"You're sure?"

"I'm sure," the driver told him. "Good jobs are hard tae find."

"That's true," McGrandle conceded.

The driver laughed. "Anyway, mister, I suggest you go ahead an' help yersel," he said. "There's no' a world shortage o' lemonade bottles so far as I'm aware."

McGrandle ran to the rear of the lorry to organise the rest of the men. "I want all those crates off the lorry and on to the road!" he shouted.

The men understood immediately and, with cries of great excitement, started piling the square wooden boxes on their sides, quickly establishing a solid barricade several feet high between themselves and the main square.

Willie McGrandle encouraged the others with a roar. "This'll give the bastards something to think about!" he shouted, grabbing a bottle and hurling it in the general direction of a young constable standing alone on the edge of the crowd. "They don't stand a chance against us now!"

The bottle fell several yards short of the young constable and McGrandle chuckled, undismayed. "That made the bastard jump!" he cried happily, reaching for another bottle, as the young constable retreated to the other side of the street, just in case.

Frank Munro, together with Margaret Armstrong and Alick Robertson, tried to avoid the worst of the fighting by sheltering for a while in a service doorway at the side of the City Chambers. George Square and the surrounding streets resembled a battlefield by now and it was clear to all of them that they were caught in the middle of a full-scale riot during which anything could happen. In the early stages of the conflict the two sides appeared surprisingly well-matched. The strikers enjoyed an enormous advantage in terms of numbers, and operated with great vigour, charging about the square in all directions, throwing bottles and cobblestones mostly, although on three occasions they saw large groups of men armed with hammers and iron stanchions marauding in packs, and one young man waving a bayonet. The police, who relied on superior organisation and training to defend themselves at first, also employed maximum available force and used their batons without regard for the amount of serious damage they could inflict on the other side.

"Are you all right?" Munro inquired.

"What do you think?" Margaret Armstrong replied.

He could see she was making a great effort to control her fear. "I want to get you out of here," Munro declared.

Margaret Armstrong shook her head stubbornly as they ventured out on to the pavement. "I'm staying," she said.

"Recognise anyone?" Alick Robertson inquired.

There was no mistaking the familiar and uninspiring figure of the Lord Provost, Sir James Watson Stewart, a well-meaning but ineffectual administrator, in Munro's opinion, who chaired meetings of the Town Council and acted as a figurehead in the external affairs of the city. It was perfectly in order, considering the circumstances, for him and the Chief Constable to be seen walking together in George Square. It was the presence of the third man in the group, just leaving the City Chambers, which Munro found intriguing.

A tough-minded, no-nonsense individual, whose responsibilities included interpreting the law, and dispensing justice, across most of the country's industrial heartland the Sheriff of Lanarkshire rarely appeared in public outside his own courtroom. His presence in George Square, in company with the Chief Constable and the Lord Provost, was unexpected and alarming, thought Munro.

The group stopped within hearing distance of him and the others.

Sheriff Mackenzie carried a document which, in a loud, clear voice, he began to read.

"Our Sovereign Lord the King chargeth and commandeth all persons being assembled immediately to disperse themselves and peaceably depart to their habitations or to their lawful business," the Sheriff intoned, "upon the pains contained in the Act made in the first year of King George the First for preventing tumults and riotous assemblies. God Save the King!"

Preceded by the Lord Provost, and followed immediately behind by the Chief Constable, the Sheriff then returned in a hurry to the safety of the City Chambers. Few people had been aware of their presence in George Square and the significance of their mean little ritual would be lost on most of those who saw it. Nevertheless, more than two hundred years after they were first concocted, during a dark period in the nation's brittle history, the obnoxious, simple-sounding words of the Riot Act had been invoked against the people of the second most important city in the empire, Frank Munro thought angrily. He glanced at Margaret Armstrong and saw that she was on the verge of tears. "There's nothing can be done about it now," she said.

The clatter of hooves made them turn. From behind the City Chambers a large force of mounted police appeared, already moving at a gallop and building to a charge, long sticks raised, hunting for heads.

Munro and his companions pressed themselves hard against the door of the service entrance to the municipal building and waited until the last of the horsemen swept into George Square before venturing into the open to witness for themselves what was happening.

One large group of mounted police was busy descending North Frederick Street intent on attacking the barricade of lemonade crates from the rear. The lorry driver saw them coming and sounded a warning. Willie McGrandle turned quickly, threw a bottle at the head of the leading rider, and missed. The mounted policeman charged and swung at him with his stick. McGrandle fled.

Margaret Armstrong pointed to the body of a middle-aged woman lying face down in the street. "We must help her!" she cried.

It was Mrs Reid.

"Wait here!" Munro ordered.

The woman's face was covered in mud but there was no sign of blood or any serious injury.

"Isn't she the one you see marching with the large red flag?" Margaret Armstrong asked.

Munro nodded. "It's probably lost or stolen," he replied.

Mrs Reid offered them a small, brave smile. "No," she told them firmly. "I gave it to some of the lads."

Margaret Armstrong wiped the woman's face and steadied her against the wall of the City Chambers. "I think she's all right," she said.

"It will be safe with them," Mrs Reid continued happily. "They are all good boys."

Alick Robertson shook his head. "I always thought you showed more courage than sense," he told her, "carrying that huge thing about with you all the time."

Mrs Reid smiled weakly. "Don't grudge me my bit of fun, mister," she pleaded.

Alick Robertson shrugged. "You'll be black and blue in the morning," he warned.

Mrs Reid sighed happily. "I don't mind," she replied. "I wouldn't have missed this morning for anything."

Alick Robertson grunted. "I dare say," he agreed.

"This has been the most important day in my life," the woman continued, "considering everything that's happened."

"It's one you won't forget in a hurry," Alick Robertson conceded roughly.

Mrs Reid smiled. "You sound like a good sort," she told him. "Thank you, comrade."

Alick Robertson squirmed. "You've got the wrong idea," he complained.

The huge crowd was beginning to disperse. The woman turned to address Munro. "It was good of you to help me, comrade," she insisted.

Munro nodded. "I'm glad you're all right," he told her.

Mrs Reid smiled happily and said, "I feel much better than all right, comrade."

Munro waited.

"I feel proud," she explained simply.

Margaret Armstrong nodded enthusiastically. "Yes," she agreed. "I know."

The two women embraced. Munro and Alick Robertson exchanged glances. Munro didn't blame the demonstrators for abandoning George Square. It was the sensible thing to do under the circumstances, he thought. Anyone who stayed risked being charged down and trampled, or at best having their skulls cracked open. There was never any chance of the Chief Constable agreeing to an honourable settlement involving both sides. James Verdier Stevenson desired nothing less than total victory.

"In the end what happened this morning doesn't matter. Don't you agree?" the woman asked.

Her mood was infectious, Munro thought. "I feel sorry for the men," he replied.

Mrs Reid shook her head firmly. "There's no need to feel sorry for the men. Don't you see? They were wonderful!" she declared.

# CHAPTER EIGHTEEN

F rank Munro had been on the move from the moment the last of
the demonstrators abandoned George Square pursued, in some
cases, by groups of policemen on foot and on horseback. Except
to make occasional visits to his office in Buchanan Street, to update
copy and learn more about the wider picture, Munro spent what
remained of the day, into the evening, and right through the night,
trying to follow events. There were several early reports of running
battles involving police and strikers which lasted for hours, stories of
widespread vandalism, arson and looting, and even a claim that the
Workers' Strike Committee believed they were in political control of
large sections of the city. On a visit to the office in the middle of the
afternoon he was told by Alick Robertson, who had been talking to the
Lord Provost, that the authorities appeared to believe the present
unrest would continue until the strikers won or were crushed. From
what Alick Robertson told him he was able to conclude that the
authorities were in no mood to underestimate the strength of feeling
which lay behind the day's events; and the strikers' determination to
succeed at whatever cost to themselves. Munro hoped a peaceful
solution, which took account of the workers' legitimate claims, could be
found before the present disorder spread and something truly serious
occurred.

In a public house in Gallowgate, where he stopped for a pie and a pint
shortly after six, a barman told Munro about a running fight which
started somewhere near Saltmarket and ended as a pitched battle on
Glasgow Green. Dozens of police retreated injured and the strikers
were claiming total victory. Someone who admitted with considerable
regret that he didn't see it happen, because he could think of nothing
better he wanted to see in the whole of his life, maintained it was true
that a mountie, complete with horse, had been thrown from the Albert
Bridge into the Clyde. A woman who said she saw it happen confirmed
the story later. "He deserved it," the woman, who refused to give her

name, insisted. "He kept charging in among us, tryin' tae land us wan wi' yon big baton. So a crowd of the lads surrounded the cuddy, grabbed its legs wi' him still oan it, an' threw them baith o'er the parapet intae the river!"

Her eyes gleamed. "It wis a bonny sight, ah can tell ye!"

Munro wanted to question the story. "You say you saw it happen?" he asked.

"Oh, aye," the woman assured him. "Ah wis there, don't forget! Wance ah had tae jump for it or he'd've gi'en me a right good wallop wi' his stick! Ah'm tellin' ye, mister."

And then, as if anxious to emphasise the importance of the incident for the benefit of the following day's newspapers, she added happily: "If there's wan thing that's happened this week ah'm glad no' tae have missed, it wis that! When ah think how hard it's been for us wi' oor men no' at work, an' nae money comin' in, an' yon Stevenson an' his gang siding wi' the bosses against their ain folk, they deserve a' the bad that's comin' tae them!"

"Did anyone bother to throw him a lifebelt?"

"Don't be daft!" the woman cried. "People were mair inclined tae try an' save the cuddy! A dip in the Clyde was the least yon polis deserved. It's just a pity we couldnae dae the same fur Stevenson." She chuckled. "But at least Willie Gallacher managed tae gie him a sore face, they tell me. Wasn't that great? Trust Gallacher! He's no' feart o' anything or anybody."

Later the same evening a telephone call from Willie McGrandle informed Munro that troops were on their way. The strike committee had been alerted by a call from a sympathiser in England. Munro went immediately to Buchanan Street station, where he found a large group of strikers, led by Willie McGrandle, with his head in a bandage, waiting to greet the soldiers and try to persuade them to desert.

From the moment the train arrived in the station, and McGrandle and his men started running alongside, shouting at the soldiers to stay out of Glasgow, mingling with them on the platform while they sorted their kit, giving them their side of the story, pleading with them not to interfere, the officers and NCOs in charge of the troops did their best to keep the two sides apart.

Used to being obeyed, and hoping to intimidate them with their manner and air of total command, the officers prodded at the strikers with their canes and shooed them away; while NCOs ran along the under-lit platform shouting for discipline and speed. The least Willie

McGrandle wanted was an assurance from the soldiers that they would refuse to turn their rifles on the workers if ordered. But these new arrivals, wrestling with their kit, looked like recent recruits, rather than men with experience of the front, who might have been sympathetic to the workers' struggle and easier to persuade. Once assembled in full battle gear, ready to depart Buchanan Street station for whatever quarters had been arranged for them in the city, none of the soldiers seemed to show any interest in the strikers' case. If anything, without anyone telling them what was required, they appeared impatient to begin whatever task they had been sent to accomplish.

Clattering through darkened streets, over cobblestones which rang sharply beneath heavily nailed boots, Willie McGrandle and some of the other strikers continued to run alongside the soldiers, pleading with them to disregard orders; even to lay down their rifles and join the ranks of the strikers. The soldiers, not surprisingly, chose to ignore them. Similarly, the crews of several tanks which arrived in the city shortly afterwards, cumbersome and noisy, their tracks striking sparks from cobblestones and tramwaylines, as they clattered through empty streets, waking the city from its sleep, paid no attention to the blandishments and insults of the strikers. Threatening everything in sight, they trundled along, making good speed, main gun pointing straight ahead, crewmen visible through slits in the sides, an officer standing in the open tower, unfamiliar, dangerous-looking beasts heading towards a depot which had been arranged for them in the cattle market in Duke Street not far from the city centre.

According to rumour the Lord Provost, acting personally, and against the wishes of the Chief Constable, requested the presence of the military. Frank Munro accepted this version of events, at least in part. James Verdier Stevenson was unlikely to welcome the arrival of soldiers and tanks on the streets of Glasgow. He was bound to argue that his men could be relied upon to restore order without outside assistance. The presence of ten thousand men dressed in khaki and armed for combat, effectively undertaking the duties of his own much favoured bluecoats, offered a certain denial, on the part of the city he served, to his own golden opinions of himself and his men.

Following the events of the previous day, any discomfiture suffered by James Verdier Stevenson was almost certain to please and amuse Munro. However, in this respect he was forced to agree with the Chief Constable. James Verdier Stevenson probably lost the argument because the Lord Provost panicked. It was hardly surprising. Sir James

Watson Stewart wasn't the kind of man you could depend upon in a crisis.

The sight of unfriendly soldiers on the streets of Glasgow horrified Munro. No-one involved in the decision to bring in the troops would be affected in any meaningful sense by the consequences of their actions. The only ones it truly scarred were the ordinary working people of Glasgow, the families who lived there and dreamed there, and tried to build their lives there, its citizens, men and women who saw the unthinkable happen, and because of it felt betrayed.

However, their presence failed to frighten Willie McGrandle. "What we need now is the key to Maryhill Barracks," he told Munro. "Let's see them try and intimidate the H.L.I."

Munro didn't doubt he meant it.

By morning the city had been ringed by steel. People going about their business who questioned the meaning and timeliness of the Army's sudden and well-organised appearance decided it was the work of the government acting on special instructions sent from France by the Prime Minister himself; with orders to the High Command to do everything necessary to crush the revolt in Glasgow before it could spread to other parts of the country.

Machine gun crews on top of all the main buildings covered the entrance to the City Chambers and the whole of George Square. Sand-bagged positions had been established at ground level to control the surrounding streets. Troops guarded the docks, the railway stations, power and gas plants, and all the important works where, only a day earlier, the Workers' Strike Committee threatened to take control and disrupt the city.

Lance-corporal Peter Hore, guarding the roof of the main Post Office building, framed the huge unfamiliar head in his sights and speculated privately on the extent and accuracy of his aim. "Who is that up there?" he inquired absently. "Does anybody know?"

Nobody answered.

Lance-corporal Peter Hore kept the head of Sir Walter Scott framed in his sights. "Doesn't anybody know?" he asked.

"Who cares?" another soldier inquired.

"Shoot his balls off, Peter!" one of his mates suggested.

"It looks just like Nelson's column," Lance-corporal Hore went on pensively. "Whoever it is he must have been important, I suppose."

"Nobody cares whether some Scotchman was important or not," the first soldier declared emphatically. "I don't care about them at all."

"Mike's right," someone said.

"Go for his gooleys, Peter!" the soldier called Mike insisted.

"Go on, Peter, I dare you," the other soldier said.

"Wouldn't it be fun?"

From the roof of the main Post Office there was nothing to be seen beyond a radius of half a mile. The soldiers understood there were hills to the north of the city covered with snow. But their view was obscured by an enormous smoke cloud which hovered all morning, grey-black and poisonous, above the tenement tide. Street built upon street, green fields concealed from the weak winter sun, the residue of the city's industrial and domestic heartland obliterated all sense of the wild, unspoiled country so near to its suffocating sandstone sprawl.

"Scotland's strange," a soldier observed curiously.

"My mother's sister married a wandering man who came from the Black Isle," Lance-corporal Hore offered mysteriously.

"Where's that, on the west coast someplace, presumably?" someone inquired.

Lance-corporal Hore shook his head. "It isn't even an island," he informed them, scornfully. "It's somewhere on the mainland, up north, beyond Inverness."

"Is that right?" he was asked.

"I never knew her," Lance-corporal Hore continued. "She was away to London with the Scotchman before I was born. My mother always said she was the wild one of the family."

"Did your mother know your father, by any chance?"

Lance-corporal Hore reached for a dead beer. "Another crack like that," he offered evenly, "and I'll throw you into the street."

"Do you know something?"

"What?"

"The first time the Jerries set eyes on the Jocks they thought we were sending women to the front to fight them. My brother told me," the soldier said. "He was at Ypres. The kilts fooled Jerry completely, he said."

Another soldier chuckled. "Poor Jerry!" he exclaimed.

"Can you imagine how those Krauts must have felt when they found out?" someone inquired.

"How did they find out?"

"What do you think?"

Everyone laughed.

The soldier called Mike grunted. "What daft fucker sent us here, and why, do you think?"

Lance-corporal Hore chuckled grimly. "The same daft fucker who wanted to send you to France most likely. He doesn't need a reason for anything," Lance-corporal Hore added simply.

The other man's surprise sounded genuine enough. "I thought we'd heard the last of him!" he protested.

"In that case," Lance-corporal Hore suggested drily, "you're the one that's daft!"

The young soldier scowled. Lance-corporal Hore, having resisted the temptation to open fire on the statue of the country's foremost man of letters, pointed his gun at the sky.

"In fact," Lance-corporal Hore continued roughly, "you're the kind of chap he wouldn't want to miss. I'd say you have been most fortunate to survive."

He rose from behind the gun and his voice hardened. "What are you doing here, Private?" he barked. "Weren't you at the front? Then why are you alive? You're a great disappointment to King and country, Private, as well as all of us here at the War Office. We thought you were bound for glory. Don't you realise you're old enough to be dead? Why aren't you dead, Private?"

"That's enough, Peter," someone suggested uncomfortably.

Lance-corporal Hore smiled. "Is it?" he inquired quietly. "Why?"

"Forget it," he was told, "that's all."

Lance-corporal Hore thought for a moment. "You mean Ypres and the Somme, for instance? Forget all that?"

"Yes, forget it."

"In other words, forget why we aren't dead?"

Nobody answered.

Finally someone said, "That poof in the kilt who got his arse felt when he arrived from France wanting to be King of England. It was our King's brother, the Duke of Cumberland, who bashed him."

"Three cheers for the Duke of Cumberland!"

"Fuck the Duke of Cumberland!"

"After you with the Duke of Cumberland!"

"I'm next."

"Thanks, mate."

Everyone laughed.

Then someone inquired, chuckling, "Can you imagine what it would be like with a Scotchman as King? They'd make us all wear kilts!"

"That happened once," another soldier said.

"Don't be daft!" he was told. "How could it?"

"I think it did," the solder insisted stubbornly.

"Is that right?"

"I'm sure it did."

"That's amazing."

Lance-corporal Hore yawned and stretched. They had been warned to look out for snipers and expect hand-to-hand fighting in the streets and everyone had been ordered not to take chances. The young lieutenant who commanded Lance-corporal Hore's unit waited until his men were safely housed in tented quarters, in a goods yard less than a mile from George Square, before parading everyone in front of him and telling them why they had been sent to Glasgow in the first place. The security and future of the realm itself was at risk, he informed them gravely. They were dealing with desperate men, Bolsheviks, who wanted to overthrow Mr Lloyd George and the elected government of the country and join forces with the Russians, the young officer continued. All the time he was addressing them, Lance-corporal Hore noticed, training and instinct dictated that he tried to look stern and in command of himself and his troops. He wanted them to know that the Army and the system it represented was in control of its own destiny and whatever terrible events lay ahead. The young lieutenant sounded nervous and ill at ease throughout his address to the troops, however, resulting perhaps from a fear that some of his men might be attracted to the idea and desert to the revolutionaries. It was natural enough, considering the circumstances, Lance-corporal Hore thought evenly, but the young lieutenant needn't have worried, in his opinion. No-one he knew gave a thimbleful of shite who ran Scotland. Nor did they care greatly for the Prime Minister and his so-called elected government sitting in London. Lance-corporal Hore and his mates followed orders because they were soldiers. Doing otherwise simply invited trouble. Besides, they weren't interested in politics.

From the roof of the Post Office building traffic in George Square appeared to be running normally. A long line of trams blocked the north side outside the North British Hotel. Groups of policemen patrolled in pairs, anxious to recapture their lost authority and restore their personal dignity after events of the previous day. Soldiers who had been brought in to assist them loitered beside sand-bagged positions outside the City Chambers and at junctions with other streets. The soldiers didn't need to be told that not everyone appreciated their presence in the city. Most people were unable to hide their feelings. A few cursed and threatened, but not many. Those who were hostile to the troops usually satisfied themselves by treating the soldiers to a sullen look before hurrying past without speaking. Others, nearly all of them elderly women, Frank Munro noted, quite often offered the soldiers a cheery word of welcome, accompanied in a number of cases by gifts of food and drink.

Munro felt sorry for the soldiers. It was a rotten job playing the role of policeman in a strange city, especially in the present circumstances. It was a role the troops themselves would be hard-pressed to understand or accept with any enthusiasm, and the kind of activity they were ill-equipped to handle.

Usually maintained in showpiece condition for the benefit of citizens and visitors alike, the centre of civic pride, George Square itself was a mess. There hadn't been time for workers from the city's general services department to clean up after the riot and broken bottles, wooden crates, pieces of torn clothing, and cobblestones ripped from the roadway during the worst stages of the clash involving strikers and police the previous day lay scattered everywhere. Windows in most of the surrounding buildings, including the City Chambers and the Post Office, had been smashed, railings torn from the ground, and the flower-beds in the central garden area trampled beyond recognition.

It was a sad and sorry sight, thought Frank Munro, surveying the damage from the steps of the North British Hotel, with Margaret Armstrong alongside. Silently, Munro condemned the incompetence of the Chief Constable and the stupidity of the Lord Provost, the people in authority he blamed most for bringing the city to its present dangerous state. James Verdier Stevenson had been wrong from the outset of the struggle to make it appear he wanted confrontation and would be more than happy to oblige those on the other side who thought they could win, and followed Shinwell all the way, employing his own peculiar brand of heavy-handedness to ensure victory. But more than anything, in Munro's opinion, when it finally mattered it was the uncritical support of the Lord Provost which allowed the government to send troops into Glasgow, the second city of the empire, to suppress the free voice of a large number of its citizens. One word in public against the idea from Sir James Watson Stewart and the Prime Minister himself would have been forced to abandon the whole dangerous enterprise. It was the kind of leadership people expected and rarely enjoyed in a city where privilege counted. For generations the landlords and the employers, the business barons especially, sustained by their friends on the Town Council, usually managed to obtain the best for themselves at the expense of everyone else, not least the vast majority of workers whose complaints were seldom heard.

"Isn't that Henry Wason?"

"Where?"

Margaret Armstrong pointed to a group containing police and army personnel standing outside the Post Office on the opposite side of George Square. "It's him, definitely," she said.

Munro sounded surprised. "You're right," he agreed.

"Didn't you say he went back to London?" Margaret Armstrong inquired.

Munro nodded. "That's what he told me on Wednesday. I thought it strange him leaving early."

"It's the coat I recognised," Margaret Armstrong went on.

"It would cost me more than a month's wages, that coat," Frank Munro remarked evenly.

Margaret Armstrong looked at him sharply. "Didn't you tell me you couldn't understand how a young agency reporter could afford to dress like him and live in the Central Hotel?"

Munro grunted. "At first I thought he was a rich young agency reporter. You find them sometimes. A kid with money who can't find a job on a real paper. They always claim to be writing colour pieces for papers or magazines you never see," he added, thoughtfully.

Margaret Armstrong looked puzzled. "I always thought he looked strange, compared to you I mean, and other reporters I've known." she said.

Munro laughed. "You won't find a mould," he told her, chuckling. "We come in all shapes and sizes. And that's only me!"

"Be serious!" Margaret Armstrong ordered.

He nodded.

"What are you thinking?" she asked, the familiar frown clouding her face.

Munro nodded in the direction of the group surrounding Wason. "He's managed to infiltrate some pretty senior company over there, wouldn't you say?"

"Infiltrate?"

"Just an expression," Frank Munro replied softly.

Margaret Armstrong responded sharply. "I know the expression!" she snapped.

"Has it ever occurred to you that the government would want some first-hand reports about what was happening here in Glasgow during the strike?" Munro inquired bleakly. "From one of their own people,

I mean, someone they could trust absolutely," he added.

It wasn't a question. "You think he's a spy," she said.

"It's possible," he replied.

"Based on what evidence?"

"I don't count the coat," Munro chuckled.

Margaret Armstrong frowned. "Can't you be serious?' she asked.

"Just a hunch," he replied.

"Why don't you ask him?" Margaret Armstrong suggested.

"All right," said Munro.

Henry Wason, who was in a marvellous mood, and feeling highly pleased with himself, spotted Frank Munro and Margaret Armstrong walking through the central garden area towards him and waved. The events of the previous three days continued to affect his system. Anyone could see he was in a state of considerable excitement. Wason remembered seeing Frank Munro on Wednesday. Since then his own, highly secret, activities had included a return rail journey to London and a visit to the War Office.

Colonel Naismith wanted him to deliver his report to the War Office in person. He had been disappointed not to obtain an interview with Churchill. Instead he was forced to surrender the envelope containing his report, on which he had written FOR THE EYES OF MR CHURCHILL ONLY, to an official whose highly superior manner suggested he attached very little importance to the document inside; and was annoyed to be troubled by someone evidently junior so close to lunch.

Wason bridled then. "It is a matter of the utmost importance that Mr Churchill sees these papers immediately," he informed the official coldly and with all the authority he could muster.

The rest of the day had been spent waiting and hoping for a personal call from Churchill. It didn't come. He was summoned instead to the office of his chief, who reported the great man's satisfaction with his report on the potentially dangerous circumstances prevailing in Glasgow. Evidently it was pretty much what the Secretary of State for War and Air expected to hear. But from what Churchill said on the phone, Colonel Naismith continued, beaming and hinting at a promotion pending a possible decoration, which he couldn't promise of course, as that was a matter for the King, it was obvious Wason acted in the best traditions of the service while in Glasgow. In fact, said his chief, from the Secretary of State downwards, everyone was so impressed with his work they wanted him to return to Glasgow immediately. Colonel Naismith shook his head admiringly. The speed with which Wason succeeded in establishing contact with revolutionary tendencies in the city was an astonishing piece of work, worthy of Sidney Reilly at his best. Yes, said his chief, rising to shake his hand and lead him to the door, in the event of real trouble his presence in Glasgow would be invaluable to the nation. Wason murmured appreciatively: after the disappointment of not seeing Churchill he was beginning to feel good again.

Alone in the corridor outside the office of his chief he glanced at his watch. He had been back in London less than twenty-four hours. The thought of returning immediately to Glasgow, in the company of one of the main military units being sent to take command of the city, was strangely exhilarating.

"Frank!" he cried warmly, going to meet them, and reaching to take Munro's hand. "I was about to ring you. What a story, eh?"

"I thought you were in London," Munro said, shaking hands, and glancing at Margaret Armstrong.

"I didn't want to miss the fun," Henry Wason replied, smiling.

"You remember Miss Armstrong?"

"Of course!" Wason exclaimed. "Nice to meet you again, Miss Armstrong."

Margaret Armstrong nodded coldly.

"How did you travel?" Munro inquired.

Wason looked puzzled. "By train, of course," he replied.

"What kind of train?" Munro asked.

"I don't understand," Wason told him. "What do you mean?"

"Was it a military train?" Margaret Armstrong interrupted harshly.

Henry Wason looked startled. He stared at Frank Munro, who shrugged apologetically. "It occurred to us, in view of what's been happening here, that you might be a government agent," Munro explained in a matter-of-fact voice.

"He means a spy," Margaret Armstrong added.

"Are you?" inquired Munro.

Henry Wason paled. "Are you being serious?" he asked.

Frank Munro nodded. "Well?"

"Don't be silly!" Wason stammered. "You know what I do."

"All I know is what you told me," Munro replied evenly. "The truth may be something different. I'd like you to tell me."

He nodded towards the group of people they had witnessed Wason talking to at some length outside the main Post Office. It included an

Army captain dressed for combat and a number of senior police officers, also wearing uniform, as well as several other people, dressed in civilian clothes, who looked like officials. Munro didn't recognise any of them. "Anything there for me?" Munro inquired.

Henry Wason smiled ruefully. "They wouldn't talk to me, I'm afraid. I wanted to find out what was happening to Shinwell and the others but they wouldn't tell me," he said.

"Really?" replied Munro. "From the other side of the square you and them looked quite chummy."

"I don't understand," said Wason.

"Did you know most of the leaders have been arrested?"

"Yes, I knew that," Wason answered. "I also heard a story some of them had been caught burning important papers."

Munro looked interested. "Where did you hear that?" he asked.

Wason smiled. "You don't expect me to reveal my sources, surely?" he asked in too quick a voice.

Munro glanced at Margaret Armstrong. She was staring at Wason. "What do you think will happen to Shinwell and the rest of them?" Margaret Armstrong inquired.

Wason looked away for a moment. "I suppose we can expect a trial," he replied finally, turning to stare at her. "When do you expect to learn the full extent of the charges?" he went on, looking at Munro.

"When they appear in court today," Munro replied. "Tell me the truth, Henry, you know no newspaper will dare print it, least of all mine. Are you a spy?"

"Tell us what you do," Margaret Armstrong added coldly.

"You know what I do," Henry Wason replied stubbornly. "I'm a reporter."

Margaret Armstrong's eyes blazed. "Reporting where, and to whom, and what did you tell them about the extent of the trouble here?" she cried savagely. "That's the point, isn't it?"

Henry Wason said nothing.

Munro glanced round George Square with its soldier-guards armed for combat. From their appearance and demeanour the soldiers clearly believed they were about to confront a dangerous enemy. Munro didn't doubt that each man was ready and willing to open fire on whatever target happened to enter his sights the moment someone in command issued the necessary order. That was the Army's way and what the generals expected.

"Nobody gave you the right, Henry," he told the other man sadly. "It was never your fight."

Wason stared at him for a moment. Suddenly he was no longer pretending. "I don't agree. People were frightened," Henry Wason replied.

"What people?"

"Just people," Wason told him.

Munro nodded. "So they organised an armed invasion of the second most important city in the empire in order to protect their own peace of mind," he replied. "I hope none of them sleep better as a result."

Henry Wason turned to walk away but Munro stopped him. "One last thing you might want to report," Munro said.

The other man waited. Munro smiled.

"People here won't forget in a hurry."

Henry Wason nodded. "We'll see," he replied.

# EPILOGUE

The trial took two months to arrange and lasted three weeks. The presence on the bench of the Lord Justice Clerk, dressed in a white satin cape splashed with little red crosses depicting blood, emphasised the importance of the occasion. Seven accused, including Shinwell, Gallacher and Kirkwood, occupied the dock, sitting between white-gloved policemen with batons resting across their knees, guarding them.

Shinwell had been arrested at five in the morning at his home in Linthouse. He was allowed to kiss his sleeping children farewell, took a last defiant swipe at the punchbag hanging in the lobby, and departed his tearful wife to confront whatever fate awaited him at the hands of the authorities. He had been taken to Govan Police Station and then to the Central, where he found Willie Gallacher and Davey Kirkwood already in custody.

While in Duke Street Prison awaiting trial a guard Shinwell didn't like smirked and said, "You'll get ten years for this. Or maybe hanged. Do you fancy being hanged, Mr Shinwell?"

"Don't be daft!" Shinwell answered.

"It isn't daft. I know some people who'd bring their own rope," the guard replied.

The trial had been moved to Edinburgh, forty miles to the east, to reduce the chances of an organised protest similar to the George Square demonstration further disrupting the peace of Glasgow and putting the entire country at risk from the Bolsheviks. A huge crowd filled the streets around Parliament Hall and the public benches of the High Court in Edinburgh were packed for the occasion. When the seven emerged from the cells beneath the court and took their places in the dock on the first day Willie Gallacher, who chose to defend himself for the whole of the trial without the assistance of counsel, bowed to the seated pressmen and grinned.

Witnesses for the Crown included the Sheriff of Lanarkshire and the

Lord Provost of Glasgow. For much of the time, as the trial progressed, the jury also heard evidence from a long procession of policemen, headed by the Chief Constable, offering their version of the events which led to a complete breakdown of law and order in the city of Glasgow throughout the day and most of the night following the George Square riots, the witnesses claimed. There was a gasp from the public benches when the Lord Advocate described why it became necessary to send troops to occupy the city. At the mention of tanks an undetected voice Frank Munro thought belonged to Willie McGrandle, seated at the rear of the balcony, cried "Shame!"

When the time came for the defence to present their case a cantankerous-sounding working man refused to take the oath and then, in a loud voice, informed the judge that he resembled a Punch and Judy man peering down on everyone from his perch. The Lord Justice Clerk was the second most important judge in the country after the Lord President of the Court of Session and could be relied upon to conduct the most difficult trial with scrupulous regard for the rights of both sides. However, notwithstanding his reputation for fair-mindedness, the Lord Justice Clerk was known to believe the authority of his position needed safeguarding at all times, and that judges required to be vigilant against any form of disrespect, both for their own sake and to protect the majesty of the law they were empowered to enforce. He noticed that the insult caused a pained expression to cross the face of the Lord Advocate, who had been the leading prosecutor on behalf of the Crown. In addition several people in the public gallery guffawed and a shocked usher was forced to call for silence. Accordingly, the Lord Justice Clerk was left with no option. "Remove that man to the cells immediately!" he thundered.

Two policemen, grim-faced and determined-looking, descended on the witness box and endeavoured to drag the offending citizen away. "Keep yer hauns aff me or I'll gie ye wan!" the witness warned, raising his fists, and scowling in a threatening manner.

The ambitious nature of this outburst, considering the circumstances, brought another ripple of amused laughter from people on the public benches close enough to hear. Frank Munro, who was sitting on a bench reserved for the press within a few feet of the witness box, chuckled admiringly at the unexpected valour of the man and exchanged hidden smiles with other reporters. He could see that all the accused, with the possible exception of Gallacher, appeared discomfited by the behaviour of the witness, however. Most of them were showing signs of strain as the trial approached its conclusion, and the last thing they wanted was someone from their own side antagonising the court and jeopardising their chances of acquittal, he thought. They either muttered anxiously to one another or whispered to counsel, who were seated at a large table piled with books and papers immediately in front of them.

His moment of defiance was the absolute limit of the working man's triumph, it seemed. In the course of a brief struggle he was wrestled to the floor and his arms pinned in an iron grip against his sides. Last seen, he was kicking out with both feet as the two policemen lifted him through the courtroom door. People on the public benches laughed and applauded while several ushers moved amongst them trying to restore order.

Frank Munro assumed the disruptive witness must have known he didn't stand a chance against two policemen operating in front of the Lord Justice Clerk and a long list of notables and dignitaries who could help make the policemen's life a misery if they failed in their efforts to bring him under control.

Not that any of it affected the final verdict in the main trial, as Frank Munro recorded later. In his own private notes on the trial, not meant for publication, he wrote: "That judge deserves a medal!"

With the exception of Shinwell and Gallacher all the accused had been acquitted by the jury. Shinwell had been sentenced to five months in prison by the Lord Justice Clerk and Gallacher three months. Everyone else, including Kirkwood, was freed and went home.

"It was never much of a revolution, was it?" Margaret Armstrong asked afterwards.

Frank Munro smiled. "Do you remember what Henry Wason said?" he inquired.

Margaret Armstrong frowned.

Munro turned and took her in his arms. "We'll see," he replied.

# ENDSCRIPT

In 1922 Emmanuel Shinwell was elected to the House of Commons as Member of Parliament for Linlithgow. He served as an MP for various constituencies almost continuously for nearly fifty years. Appointments to the Cabinet included a period as Secretary of State for Defence. Shinwell became a Peer in 1970 and died in 1985, aged one hundred and one, the oldest surviving parliamentarian in British history.

Willie Gallacher became a founding member of the Communist Party in Great Britain and was elected to parliament for West Fife in 1935. He served at Westminster for fifteen years and died in 1965, aged eighty-four.

Following the General Election in 1922, Davey Kirkwood joined Shinwell on the Labour benches in the House of Commons, where he served as a Member of Parliament for almost thirty years. He was ennobled as first Baron Kirkwood of Bearsden in 1951 and died four years later, three months short of his eighty-third birthday.